The Elders
Mind Dimensions: Book 4

Dima Zales

♠ Mozaika Publications ♠

Copyright © 2015 *Dima Zales*
www.dimazales.com

Published by Mozaika Publications, an imprint of Mozaika LLC.
www.mozaikallc.com

Edited by Elizabeth from
arrowheadediting.wordpress.com

Cover by Najla Qamber Designs
www.najlaqamberdesigns.com

e-ISBN: 978-1-63142-075-7
Print ISBN: 978-1-63142-076-4

DESCRIPTION

Going to Level 2 gives me unimaginable power. So naturally, now that everyone I care about is in trouble, I can't do it anymore.

The Elders can, but will they teach me, and if so, at what price?

Ultimately, it comes down to a choice.

What am I willing to sacrifice for those I love?

CHAPTER ONE

Funerals are weird. Doubly so when you're the one who killed the person being buried. Triply so when you'd kill him again if you had the chance.

Despite my lack of remorse, I do feel a twinge of *something*.

Hundreds, if not thousands of cops were at the wake that preceded this funeral, honoring Kyle. Their somber faces were everywhere. Maybe it was their respect and loyalty for one of their own or their show of solidarity that was bumming me out. It was touching, though misplaced.

To them and to the media, Kyle died a hero—a detective killed by the Russian mob while in the line of duty. A man taken from the ranks of the brave far too soon.

In other words, they didn't know a thing about the real Kyle Grant.

It's fine, though. I understand that people need a hero from time to time, and I won't take away their delusions. It's just hard being among the few who know the truth.

It wasn't just the mourning cops that got to me. It was the sheer scale of the event: the traffic-blocking motorcade through the city, the solemn flag-draped coffin, the mayor's speech—all culminating in a couple of freaking helicopters doing a fly-by.

What made it even worse was the presence of all the Guides. Considering the New York Guide community is supposedly small, some of them must've come in from out of town just to attend Kyle's funeral. At least, I assume the crowd I saw consisted of Guides. A few of the faces I recognized from the nightclub Liz had taken me to so I could meet other 'Pushers'—like Bill, aka William Pierce, my boss at the fund. We didn't get a chance to speak at the wake; we only exchanged glances. I guess he and the others were there to pay their respects to a fellow Guide. Almost all of them looked genuinely sad, which meant they didn't know the real Kyle either.

The Guide community probably believes the same thing as the media. I wonder whether they're planning to investigate Kyle's murder. I hope not. Some cop will more than likely kill Victor—Kyle's shooter—and judging by what I've seen on the news, they'll do it soon. If the authorities think you're a cop killer, your fate is dubious at best. Once Victor is gone, I'll be in the clear, unless Liz or Thomas rats me out. They don't know for certain that I'm responsible for Kyle's death, but they'd be stupid not to suspect. Besides, I pretty much spelled everything out to Thomas before he asked me to stop talking. And I know if I go to therapy, Liz will want to discuss everything. But I'm not planning to go, mainly because I don't want to hear her say, "I told you you'd need therapy if you killed your uncle."

At least none of the Guides followed us here, to the burial. Things are much simpler at Cypress Hills Cemetery. Only the people considered closest to Kyle are present. They consist mainly of a few dozen cops who worked with Kyle or knew him well, and my moms and me in the role of 'the family.' Mira is here too, as moral support. And last but not least, there's Thomas.

Why is Thomas *really* here? The question, or rather, the possible answers to the question make me uneasy. He certainly has no official reason to be here.

I suppose he could be here for Lucy, since he's her biological son and might be feeling guilty over the critical role he played in what happened.

Alternatively, he might be here to pay his respects to his biological father, Kyle. That's the possibility that worries me. Could he be upset with me for taking Kyle away from him before he got the chance to know the bastard?

No, I'm probably overthinking this. After all, given what Thomas knows about Kyle and Mom and what happened between them, he might be at the funeral in the same capacity as Mira—moral support for myself, or perhaps for Lucy.

I can't fathom what Thomas is thinking, especially with his face as unreadable as always. Is he holding a subconscious grudge? Is that why he's standing off to the side, not really part of the funeral gathering? I hope not. He's my recently discovered adoptive brother of sorts and a good friend. I don't want Kyle to posthumously mess that up.

I look around the greenery of Cypress Hills Cemetery, searching for something positive. With the grass and oak trees all over, the area is tranquil, provided I ignore all the tombstones. In fact, for a cemetery, it's almost soothing.

With effort, I focus on something less morose. Kyle's parents had him when they were rather old, so thankfully, I don't have the added burden of watching a mother or father mourn the loss of their son. No matter how much of a son of a bitch Kyle was, that would've sucked. It's bad enough that my own mom, Lucy, is crying over him. She almost never cries. Of course, she doesn't know that this funeral is a huge blessing in disguise. If she knew everything he'd done to her, she'd probably spit on his grave and celebrate. Unfortunately, it's only been ten days since Kyle died, and Liz hasn't had the chance to work enough of her magic on my mom to get her to the point where she can safely remember what happened.

Okay, my attempt at thinking positively failed. Then again, I'd choose these thoughts over listening to the priest's spiel, especially since they're distracting me from the undertaker lowering the casket into the ground.

As I realize the ceremony is almost over, that weird feeling comes back with a vengeance. Maybe it's because my mom Sara is also crying. After Kyle tried to use a belt on me, Sara liked him about as much as I liked my ballet lessons—which, in case it isn't clear, was not at all.

And what's this? Is my chest actually tightening from reminiscing? Am I thinking fondly of the time Kyle tried to whip me? Can't be. But my eyes feel all watery. Dust must've flown into them, or maybe my allergies are acting up from all the damn ragweed that blooms in the fall.

I don't get a chance to berate myself for feeling whatever it is I'm feeling, because all of a sudden, the world freezes.

The sobs coming from my moms stop, as does the rustle of leaves in the warm autumn breeze.

The resulting silence is the familiar, telltale sign of the Quiet, only it's not my doing.

I look around.

Everyone is frozen in place, except Mira. One version of her is animated and looks worried, which is unusual. Annoyed, sure. Angry, too often for my liking. Sarcastic, always. But worried is not a common expression for her. She's standing next to a calmer-looking, frozen version of herself.

"Split out, get right back in, and pull me in," she says, her voice tense with urgency. "I might not have enough Depth."

"But what—"

"Promise you'll do it," she insists.

"Fine, I'll do it," I say. Now I'm beginning to worry.

Without saying a word, she touches her frozen self, and I'm back in the real world.

I instantly phase in and pull Mira in, as ordered.

"What's up?" I ask as soon as she turns up. "Why did you pull me in before? I don't exactly want to savor—"

"Shut the fuck up for a second," she says, "and look at those cops."

She points at the somber-looking men in uniform. They're standing near Thomas, on our left and about a dozen feet to the side.

"What about them?" I ask, walking toward the men.

"Look at their hands."

Closing the distance, I take a look. It *is* odd. Every officer is reaching for his or her sidearm, and they're all looking at my frozen self.

"I don't like how this looks," I say.

"No shit."

"Maybe there's a good explanation? Maybe they're planning that salute thing they do at military funerals? Don't they do that for cops too?"

"In that case, what are *those* idiots for?" She points at the rifle-bearing dudes who have been standing off to the side for a while. She walks up to the nearest cop and takes his gun. "Also, they only do the salute with blanks."

She shoots the cop in the foot. The hole in her victim's shoe confirms that the gun is most certainly not filled with blanks.

"Crap," I say.

"You can say that again."

"So why are they looking at me like that? Did you Read them?"

"Just some superficial thoughts, but they *are* about to shoot you." She pauses. "They're being Pushed."

Pushed. That's the last thing I expected to hear, yet it's the only explanation for why cops I've never met before would want to shoot me. Only, the man who was behind similar orchestrations, the man who Pushed people to kill me in the past, is being buried as we speak. Unless—

"Are you there?" Mira asks, interrupting my thoughts.

"Yes. I'm just trying to digest this."

"Digest it later. You have to act."

"If someone is Guiding them, I can override the order," I say.

"Provided you're more powerful than whoever is doing this."

She says this without any anger. My acknowledgment of my Guiding abilities has recently stopped receiving strong negative reactions from Mira. In general, I'd say her feelings toward Guides have warmed. I like to think I'm the catalyst for her change in attitude.

"Yes, well, thus far, I've been more powerful than anyone I've met," I say without false modesty. "But shouldn't we pull Thomas in to apprise him of the situation?"

"A Pusher is controlling these cops," she reminds me. "Don't you want to make sure Thomas isn't the one doing the Pushing before you pull him in?"

Okay, maybe I see what I want to see when it comes to Mira's improved outlook on Guides—a term she's still not the biggest fan of. In this case, the problem is compounded by her general mistrust of strangers. She hasn't interacted with Thomas as much as she has with my aunt Hillary, whom she was stuck with at the Miami airport. Mira's attitude toward my favorite miniature relative is what gives me hope. Though I wouldn't go as far as to say that Mira and Hillary became BFFs following their ordeal, Mira does treat my aunt with reserved trust and, more importantly, begrudging respect.

"You can't seriously think Thomas would do this," I say, looking at Mira. Despite my words, liquid nitrogen fills my stomach at the idea of Thomas attempting to kill me. In a flash, I replay the episode of Kyle getting shot in front of him and recall my own emotions when I learned that Kyle killed my biological family. I wanted—no, I *needed*—to kill Kyle afterwards. Is Thomas feeling the same way about me?

No. I don't want to accept this possibility. It's just fear talking. Kyle was guilty of more than the murder of my biological mom and dad. Had he only been guilty of that, I'm not sure I would've killed him for it.

Or maybe I would've.

"You're at his father's funeral." Mira's words echo my dread. "You know how his father died. Do I need to draw you a fucking diagram?"

Instead of responding, I walk up to Thomas, all the while thinking, *This can't be right. Could Thomas do something like this?*

Thomas is frozen in the process of moving toward my frozen self, which is odd. The funeral isn't over, and a sermon isn't exactly a good time for a stroll.

Then I see his face. His glassy eyes are looking intently at something in front of him.

I follow his gaze. He's staring at the immobile me.

"Yeah," Mira says. "I wasn't just talking out of my ass. He's giving you the evil eye."

"There has to be another explanation." I wonder whether she detects the hope in my voice.

"Well, you can tell the 'tone of voice' of the Pushing instructions during a Read. Why don't you check to see if you can recognize your buddy Thomas in there?" She knocks on the head of the cop she shot.

"He's also my adoptive brother," I say. "And why can't *you* do that?"

"I tried, but I couldn't tell if it was him. But I didn't even have to check. Given what we know, he's the most logical choice."

"He's the least logical choice," I say stubbornly, wishing I felt as confident as I sounded. "I'll prove it to you."

Walking up to a large cop, I touch the hand that's reaching for his gun.

* * *

We're watching Kyle Grant's funeral. It's more than a little selfish to be thinking about the upcoming game, but as the priest says his sermon, we get flashbacks to when we used to zone out in Sunday school, and our thoughts wander. We think about the team we've assembled. As the department's designated quarterback, we know every player's strengths and weaknesses. We know that Kyle was one of our best guys. With him dead, the guys from thirty-third will wipe the floor with us . . .

I, Darren, disassociate. I must've jumped in a few seconds ahead of the Guiding.

I let the memory unfold. It consists of more plans and worries about the precinct's football team. Some people never outgrow the 'being the team's quarterback' stage of their lives, a stage I missed out on in high school on account of being younger than everyone else. I still wanted to try out, knowing the Quiet would've helped me dodge people, but the coach laughed me out of his office when I brought it up.

A presence enters the cop's mind, and I forget all about football.

You will mentally count to a hundred and then get your gun out. You will aim and shoot the young man standing between Detective Wang and her lesbian life partner. You will shoot to kill. He's a dangerous suspect from the FBI's most wanted list.

I try to determine whether I recognize this 'voice.' Apart from Kyle, I can only recognize two other people this way: Hillary and Liz. Hillary's voice I learned by entering Bert's head. Liz's voice—by spying on what she did to Lucy's mind during their therapy sessions. This voice doesn't sound like either of them, nor does it sound like Kyle's—not that it could. Voice aside, the phrase 'lesbian life partner' in lieu of 'wife' *is* something Kyle would've said.

Though I don't know who this Pusher is based on the 'voice,' I know one simple fact: this person just made an enemy of me, and not just because he or she wants to kill me. This mystery person is Guiding these cops to shoot me while I'm standing next to my moms and Mira.

This degenerate just put everyone I care about in danger.

I'm livid. I'm not sure whether my anger is so strong because I'm afraid, but whatever the cause, the fury makes it hard to think. Still, I realize I do recognize something about the Pusher's tone, though I can't verbalize what it is. Could it be Thomas after all?

If so, he and I will be exchanging words.

I exit the cop's head.

* * *

"I don't know who it is," I say and look at Thomas. "Something doesn't add up, though. I don't think it's him."

"What makes you so sure?" Mira asks.

"For starters, I'm standing next to Lucy, his biological mother." As I say it, I realize this is a good argument, so I add, "Do I need to draw *you* a diagram?"

Mira looks thoughtful. "I didn't think of that. Can you do to him that thing we agreed you'd never do to me?"

"You mean go to Level 2 and Read him?"

When girls say 'we agreed,' and especially when Mira says it, it's code for 'I commanded.' I never agreed to not Read her if I could. During the last ten days, I've been trying to replicate the feat of going to Level 2 without any luck, so arguing about whether I'd Read her or not is useless.

Just in case, I attempt to enter Level 2 for the millionth time. I do what I usually do in the real world to phase into the Quiet. I try to forget that I'm *already* in the Quiet and will it to happen with all my being, but again, nothing happens—not even that 'hitting a mental block' feeling I sometimes manage to bring on.

"I can't," I tell her. "I still haven't figured out how to make it work. You're right, though; it would be the best way to deal with this."

"Fine. Then our only course of action is to have a little chat—"

"That's a great idea," I say and walk up to Thomas. He'll explain what's what.

I hear Mira say, "Wait," but I'm already touching Thomas's neck.

Immediately, a second version of him shows up in the Quiet.

He looks around without the usual confusion people get when they're suddenly pulled into the Quiet, and when his gaze falls on Mira, he doesn't react at all. That's weird.

Then he glances at me.

His eyes look as though they've zoomed in on their target, all Terminator-like.

Without blinking, he silently walks toward me.

"Thomas, you won't believe what's happening—"

My words are rudely interrupted by Thomas's fist hitting me in the mouth. I taste the metallic tang of blood, and all I can think about is what Mira will say in her most vindictive tone: "I fucking *told* you so."

CHAPTER TWO

"Thomas!" I block his attempt to hit my Adam's apple. "What the hell?"

In answer, Thomas kicks my shin. With all my talking and confusion, I didn't see the kick coming, and damn it, it hurt. The mixture of betrayal, incredulity, and resurfacing anger intensifies the pain.

As Thomas moves to attack me again, I swerve out of the punch, but something else distracts me, something relevant to the fight at hand. A part of me—the part that's been waking up during fights ever since I Joined with Caleb inside the head of the Israeli martial arts guru—registers that Thomas's 'interesting' fighting style is Hapkido-inspired.

As if to confirm my guess, Thomas grabs my arm as I move to hit him in the stomach, and overextends my elbow joint. An eruption of pain instantly follows. Then he throws me over his shoulder. *Two Hapkido classics*, I think as I sail through the air.

As I'm about to hit the ground, the world slows a little, so I have some hope as I try, yet again, to phase into Level 2 of the Quiet. My fight with Thomas has recreated the conditions of my last phasing to a T: if I land on my head, I will break my neck and die.

I hit the ground. Air rushes out of my lungs as I land on my back rather than on my head. Clearly, nothing happened as far as Level 2 phasing is concerned. The only result of my fall is the excruciating pain in my tailbone.

"You will stop, Pusher." Mira's voice is cold and commanding. "Now."

Were she addressing me, I'd strongly consider stopping.

I try to say, "Listen to her," while I begin rolling over onto my stomach, but what comes out is a hiss as Thomas kicks me in my exposed side.

A gunshot rings out.

Thomas's body falls on top of me.

Is he dead? I'm torn between the hope that she did shoot him, which would stop the fight, and not wanting Thomas to get hurt, because, well, it's Thomas. I haven't yet accepted that he's attempting to kill me for real; I could think of another explanation if people would just stop kicking my ass.

When he grabs me in a headlock, I realize I was wrong—wrong about him being dead and wrong about his fighting style. This is more of an Aikido headlock. What I also know about this lock is that once you're in it, you're usually done for.

"Darren, stay still," Mira says.

All I manage is an affirmative grunt. That done, I pretend like I'm choosing not to move in order to comply with her request.

She fires another shot.

Warm liquid sprays all over my body, and Thomas's hold on me slackens.

I try to move, but I'm not ready for that yet.

Mira puts the gun's safety back on and fumbles with Thomas's body, rolling him off me. I immediately feel lighter.

"Are you okay?" She gently touches my face.

"How do I look?" I ask and spit blood. I wiggle a tooth with my tongue. That's not good. Teeth are usually stable, unmovable objects.

"You look . . . disturbing. Let's get you out of here."

Cringing, I half crawl, half turn so I'm next to Thomas, and then I feel for his pulse.

The heartbeat is there, though faint. His breathing is ragged, and I'm not sure how long he has.

"You shouldn't have done that." I frisk Thomas for guns or any clue as to why he attacked me. No luck. "Unless I phase out, Thomas will be Inert."

"You've got to be fucking kidding me," she says. "You'd rather he make you Inert?"

"No, but—" I crawl away from him, toward my frozen self's body.

"He tried to kill you, probably to prevent you from overriding your would-be killers." She nods in the direction of the cops. "Something you should actually do, by the way, and as soon as possible."

She's right. If Thomas made me Inert, those cops would've shot me in the real world, which reminds me that she's also right about this second point.

I need to stop all these cops from shooting me. I only have a few moments to phase out and back in again. A few moments that would buy me the chance to reset my injuries, as well as Thomas's. The cops' hands are far enough from their guns to allow me this luxury.

Deciding that crawling isn't efficient enough, I get up, even though doing so makes me feel as if I've suddenly aged three centuries.

Mira turns toward Thomas, drops to a crouch, and checks his pulse. She looks unhappy with what she finds.

My heart sinks. I didn't make it. He's already dead, which means he's now Inert.

A part of me says, *Oh well. Maybe it's for the best.*

Then Mira stands up and aims her gun at him.

I was wrong. She must've discovered that he still has a pulse and decided she wants it gone. She wants him Inert.

It's not clear to me why I do what I do next.

With my body screaming in agony, I leap for my frozen self.

I fall a foot away from me/him. I'm certain I just broke something else, as the pain is incredible. On the bright side, I feel on the brink of phasing, but I hit that mental wall again. If I could climb over it, I'd reach Level 2. Then again, I've hit this wall before with zero results.

Mira hears me move and her big eyes widen in a 'are you insane' kind of look. Then her eyes narrow in realization.

"Idiot," she says and removes the gun's safety.

No Level 2 this time, I think and extend my shaking right hand, snaking it under my frozen self's pant leg to touch the ankle. I feel the hairy leg under my fingers, and all my pain dissipates.

The sounds of the world return, and in the next moment, after I phase back in, everything is still again.

I'm back in the Quiet and all the injuries Thomas inflicted on me are gone, as are Thomas's shot-up body and Mira.

I let myself reflect on the fact that I didn't hear Mira's gunshot, which means Thomas isn't Inert. Yay?

I debate bringing her in, but decide against it. She's probably pissed at me for thwarting her plan. I don't want to deal with that right now, not until I secure the area.

I walk to where my moms are standing. Even though I'm about to neutralize the cops as a threat, I Guide my moms to get on the ground in case my Guiding doesn't go according to plan, and in case Thomas has a gun hidden where I couldn't find it. I'm certain he doesn't, since he would've used it to shoot me when he was attacking me, but when it comes to my family, I err on the side of caution. For good measure, I make sure they won't notice if any shooting starts. They're to ignore any violence that occurs in the next few minutes. I don't care if my moms experience slight amnesia; safety comes first. With any luck, they'll think they zoned out because of the priest's monotone voice.

Knowing my moms will be safely on the ground, I approach the uniformed officers.

I find two female cops and Guide them to walk toward us, get on the ground, and cover my moms with their bodies. It may be overkill, but better safe than sorry.

I then approach every officer and give the following Guiding instructions: *You will not reach for your weapon. You will not move from this spot for the next twenty minutes. You are absorbed with emotions of loss, and you will not pay attention to anything but the ceremony. You are solemnly observing a few minutes of silence for the fallen hero.*

I give similar 'ignore the world and don't move' instructions to the rest of the civilian-clothed cops, as well as to the priest and the guys with rifles.

When it comes to the Quarterback and a couple of other bigger-looking dudes, I give them a few extra instructions.

Happy with my progress thus far, I walk back to my body and phase out.

As soon as the world comes back to life, I phase in and out of the Quiet every fraction of a second to make sure the cops aren't reaching for their weapons anymore.

To my huge relief, on the fifth check, I find that they aren't.

I phase out of the Quiet again.

"Area secured," I whisper to Mira as soon as the sounds of the world return. "But just in case, be ready for anything."

She doesn't reply. I guess the incident in the Quiet garnered me the silent treatment. Instead of worrying about Mira's mood, I focus on my surroundings. After counting exactly two Mississippis, I spot movement in the direction of the cops.

I also see Thomas taking a step toward me, the beginnings of a run.

I return to the Quiet to make sure my extra Guiding worked. It did. The movement I saw in the corner of my eye was indeed my doing. I phase out and focus on Thomas.

He's running in earnest.

The blur of movement coming from the crowd of cops gets closer.

Thomas is mere feet away from us when the Quarterback smacks into him with all the grace of a horny rhinoceros. I don't know *that* much about football, but this looks like great work to me. Thomas flies into the air—*far* into the air—and lands in the dirt that's destined to go on top of Kyle's casket. I hope the dirt softened his landing and try not to feel too guilty about what I made the Quarterback do to him.

My guilt increases as the Quarterback falls on top of Thomas. He's keeping my friend down until I can figure out what the hell is happening. The other larger officers form a makeshift human pyramid on top of them. As I recall from when this sort of thing happened to me, this doesn't hurt the person on the bottom too much.

Granted, this happened to me back in kindergarten.

Suddenly, my world is filled with pain so visceral that my eyes water. Air escapes my lungs with an audible whoosh.

Trying to comprehend what's happening to me, I realize with a shudder that the pain is coming from my most treasured and intimate of places.

I focus on inhaling air and not falling, and at the same time, I phase into the Quiet.

Oh, the sweet relief. The pain is instantly gone. Its absence highlights just how bad it really was, and I feel as though I've been given a shot of morphine.

From my new vantage, I see what happened and recoil in disbelief.

Mira is frozen in the act of kicking me in the balls.

CHAPTER THREE

Is she *that* pissed at me for stopping her from making Thomas Inert? We need to have a talk, I decide, and pull her in.

"What the fuck, Mira?" I say as soon as she shows up in the Quiet. "If you're upset with me, you can just say so. Do you have any idea how much that hurt?"

Her eyes lock onto me and do that thing that Thomas's eyes did.

Before she takes a step, I remember the theory that had been on the tip of my tongue earlier, before she made me doubt Thomas. That theory would cover all the weird stuff that's been happening.

For good measure, I still ask, "Is this about Thomas being Inert?"

Instead of answering, Mira closes the distance and attempts the exact move her currently frozen self is doing to my real-world body.

Kick me in the nuts once, shame on you. Kick me there twice, shame on me. I put my arms in a crisscross block. The backs of my hands sting where her foot connects with them, but it's nothing compared to what would've happened had I not blocked her kick.

She swings at me with her fist, and I dodge her punch, my certainty about what's going on increasing. All the pieces fit. The cops. The way Thomas looked at me and attacked me. The way he ignored Mira while we were fighting—a bad, irrational move. And the reason Mira is now intensely focused on attacking me.

"You're being Pushed," I say as I step aside, dodging her punch.

She staggers, swinging at me again.

"Snap out of it!"

She doesn't reply and continues her relentless attack.

I know I shouldn't be offended that she hasn't stopped—no one ever said that telling someone they're being Guided will allow them to break out of the compulsion—but it's hard to imagine that I'd ever attack her, even if someone did Push me. I feel as if I'd be able to exercise my free will somehow. Then again, she probably didn't consciously hear me when I told her she was being Pushed. In her mind, she may not be fighting *me* right now, but rather some illusory enemy.

If I can't talk her out of it, I have to stop her some other way. I decide to go for something ungentlemanly that doesn't cross the line into hitting a girl. Before I start, I remind myself that this is the Quiet, and Mira will only suffer for a brief moment—if one can even suffer while in the state of being Guided.

I dodge a few punches, searching for my opening. When she moves to kick me, I see my chance. I catch Mira's leg before she can inflict any damage. It hurts my palms, but hey, no pain, no gain. Firmly holding on to Mira's foot, I unceremoniously raise it in the air.

The result is as I hoped. Mira falls backwards. To my surprise and relief, she manages a soft landing, falling much more gracefully than I would have.

Her landing isn't important, but the freedom from her strikes is, as it gives me the opportunity to run up to my body—and I rush to do so.

Seeing the pained look on my statue-like face reminds me that I'm about to return to something very unpleasant, but I touch my frozen self's arm without hesitation.

The world is back, as is the pain, which actually seems worse than before.

I force another breath into my lungs and, clutching my family jewels, use every ounce of my strength to avoid falling on the ground. If I do, it will not end well for me.

Mira doesn't wait for me to recover. She capitalizes on my inactivity by punching me in the face.

My cheekbone stings, but I ignore it. The pain is nothing compared to the blow my pride will sustain if a girl beats me to death.

She aims her next punch at my stomach, and I manage to catch her wrist with my left hand. Without realizing what my body is doing, I move closer to Mira, the way I've done to initiate our million and one make-out sessions. Only this time, after I'm in her space, I circle around her. I bring her arm for the ride until it's folded at an odd angle along her spine, ensuring that any movement will be extremely uncomfortable. If her kick to my balls didn't preclude such thoughts, I'd find this position mildly erotic.

She continues to struggle.

Crap. I can't rely on pain as a means to restrain her, not in this case. She'll only hurt herself.

I consider my options and do something that isn't inspired by any martial arts training. I give her a tight hug from behind, pinning her arms to her sides. When she tries to twist out of my arms, I lock my fingers across her ribcage and hold on. Standing like this, with my crotch against her butt and the tips of my fingers brushing against her breasts, the situation goes from mildly erotic to full-on hot. Hey, Mira's kick didn't cause any permanent damage—that's good news.

All eroticism instantly vanishes when the back of Mira's head connects with my face. Luckily, thanks to some martial-arts instinct, I leaned back in time. My chin hurts, but at least my nose isn't broken. When Mira swings her head back again, I dodge. This hug maneuver is not sustainable.

Out of the corner of my eye, I catch a blur of movement.

Just what I need, I think and phase into the Quiet.

The lady cops I Guided to protect my moms are moving in. I get inside each of their heads and change their directives, then return to the real world.

I dodge Mira's head-butts a few more times before help arrives.

One butch-looking lady grabs Mira's shoulders from the front and the other pushes me aside. In a fluid motion, the cop locks her handcuff around Mira's right wrist. Before I even register it, both of Mira's hands are securely handcuffed.

"That was smooth," I tell the cop, even though she probably won't remember it later.

They gently lower Mira to the ground, ignoring her thrashing legs and screams.

Handcuffed and disheveled, but still futilely trying to reach me, Mira looks like a hot zombie. It's eerie.

I phase into the Quiet.

In the silence of my safe place, I can finally think about what's happening.

Someone is doing to my friends what I did to Kyle. Someone else can reach Level 2, the psychedelic netherworld that's so unlike our everyday reality.

This someone Pushed my friends.

Did this person attempt to Push me too? I'm guessing not. If he or she had, it's likely I would've been pulled into Level 2 with them. If they could get inside my head, they probably would've Pushed me to commit suicide, making this whole ordeal with my friends and the cops redundant.

So who's doing this?

I recall the telltale signs of Pushing I discovered inside Kyle's mind at the science conference, the signs I wanted to investigate but couldn't because Kyle's head was in the process of blowing up from Victor's shot. Could the 'voice' in the minds of the cops belong to the same Pusher? Damn, I wish I'd Read Kyle far back enough to hear the actual Pushing instructions. Then I'd have some reference to compare this voice to.

In a moment of political correctness, I decide to call this new mystery Pusher a 'she' until I know more details. Also, to distinguish her from all the others, and given what she can do, I decide to call her the Super Pusher. For all I know, I might be right, and it could be some powerful girlfriend that Kyle was dating without my knowledge. If the Super Pusher is actually a guy, well, calling him *her* is like calling him a bitch—which is fitting, since this individual is one.

I walk around the graveyard and closely observe my surroundings. Wherever the Super Pusher is, I assume she wouldn't have bothered walking too far in the Quiet to Push my friends, which means she might be hiding in this very cemetery. My guess is that it's one of the Guides from the wake. She probably followed us to the cemetery and is now hiding like the coward that she is.

I inspect all possible hiding places in about a fifty-foot radius before realizing how futile this endeavor is. There are too many places where one can hide in a cemetery. You have crypts with doors, tall trees, large tombstones, bushes, and many other hidey-holes. Hell, she could even be sitting inside her car in the parking lot.

Wait a second. That's actually a good place to check.

I run toward the parking lot, thinking that if I were this Super Pusher, that is where I'd be.

The parking lot is relatively empty, considering its size. There's a long line of police cars off to the side, which I check first.

Two Honda Odyssey minivans catch my eye, probably because they're parked right next to Lucy's Crown Victoria, so close that unless they move, we can't leave the lot.

I approach the nearest van and experience my third shock of the day.

Inside it, I see the familiar bald-headed, orange-robed figures.

The monks from the Temple of the Enlightened.

I even recognize the Master, the monk whom I fought at the Miami airport.

Shit. I run to look inside the second van. Besides more monks, I find someone much worse.

Caleb.

I'm not sure why I'm so shocked he's here, since I know he works for the Enlightened. I guess I was hoping he would still be occupied with whatever trouble my aunt had gotten him into at that airport.

But no, here he is, riding shotgun with grim determination on his face. Whatever happened to him, he's going to take out that frustration on me if he gets the chance. As Eugene likes to say, trouble doesn't travel by itself.

I try to stay calm. They're most likely here to take me back to the Temple, so that my grandparents and the rest of the Enlightened can continue persuading me to 'do my duty,' which they define as screwing Julia, or whoever else they deem worthy of carrying my baby.

Unless they somehow sniffed out the truth about my new ability. Then they'd want to use *me* for whatever it is they need my future offspring for.

No, this latter possibility is less likely.

Regardless of why they're here, this development changes everything.

I barely escaped this crew in Florida, and that was in a crowded airport without some Super Pusher hunting me.

I debate pulling Caleb in and telling him about this Pusher. If he believes me, he'll probably get out of here. After all, the Super Pusher could take control of him as easily as she took control of Thomas.

The thought chills me. I hate the idea of dealing with Caleb in general, but especially so if an unseen enemy is controlling him. Of course he won't believe me, and the likeliest outcome of me pulling him in would be me becoming Inert, with the tiny chance of me phasing into Level 2 as he brings me close to death. No, thanks. That option just doesn't work for me. I need to have my powers if I'm to have any hope of getting out of this alive.

I evaluate my options as I hurry toward my body. It doesn't take long to realize I have only one: I need to run, thus getting the attention of this Pusher and these monks away from my friends and family. If I'm lucky, the Pusher and the monks might fight over me.

Then again, I can't just leave my moms, Thomas, and Mira here. What if the Super Pusher takes control of Caleb and does something to them?

I return to the burial site and formulate a quick plan.

The men holding Thomas will get off him, cuff him, and drag him to Cypress Hills Street.

The ladies holding Mira will take her to Forest Park Drive.

I Guide my moms to run in the direction of the Jackie Robinson Parkway.

All of them—the cops holding Mira, my moms, and the Quarterback and co.—are instructed to grab a cab and meet me at what I now think of as Eugene's new lair, the lab I funded for him in Bensonhurst, Brooklyn.

I then Guide every single remaining person, including the priest, to stop the monks and anyone else who's not part of the current ceremony. Since the majority of these people are cops, I have to make the important decision of whether to allow them to use lethal force. As annoyed as I am by these orange-clad idiots, they're just tools of the Enlightened, and I'm loath to see them killed. So I Guide the armed officers to empty their guns before the operation starts, but pretend as if they're armed and dangerous. Seems like a good compromise to me.

Preparations complete, I decide to finally leave the Quiet.

I run toward my body, slam into my frozen self, and as the world becomes noisy again, I keep running.

In my peripheral vision, I see everyone take action, on their way to execute my commands. All this mass Guiding would've made my aunt Hillary— the person who usually does it—proud.

I sprint so fast that after a mere minute at this pace, I feel like my lungs might burst. I ignore the pain and run even faster, vowing to add more cardio to my usual workout routine. Finally, when I feel as though I'm about to have a heart attack, I see the welcome sight of the road at the edge of the cemetery's green grass. Knowing that it's the infamous East New York neighborhood beyond those gates doesn't diminish my elation. The six-foot fence in front of me is all that stands in my way. I climb the fence, trying my best to not get impaled by the leaf-shaped spikes, and carefully jump down.

When I land safely on the pavement, I look back through the fence. I'm not being immediately pursued, but that's no reason to relax and do something stupid, such as wait until they catch up with me.

I phase into the Quiet and examine Jamaica Avenue, the street in front of me. To my right, I see the subway in the far distance and a bus stop a block away. No go. I'm not taking public transportation in this part of town. Plus, I'd be moving slower than if I got a ride. I look across the street and see a drab Honda Civic.

Much better.

I cross the road, approach the frozen Honda, and open the driver's door. The rotund woman inside must've just come out of the deli, given the shopping bag she's holding. I touch her on the forehead and focus. Once inside her head, I give her some Guidance:

Look across the street. That strapping young man is your nephew. You decided to lend him your car. You're going to leave the car running with the keys inside and then locate a cab. Your nephew might keep the car for a few days. You will not worry about your vehicle, nor will you report it stolen. In a couple of days, you'll remember that you left your car at a Hertz car rental in Bensonhurst. When you get the car, make sure to look in the glove compartment, where your nephew left you a thousand bucks.

I'm happy with my work and hope that I can use this car to pick up the rest of my crew, which would work out so much better than them looking for cabs.

I phase out and the earlier exhaustion hits me. I ignore it. I have enough strength for one final sprint across the street. Thus determined, I run toward 'my' vehicle.

Something catches my attention.

The lady I just Guided is looking at me with wild eyes. She's gesturing at me and her mouth is moving as though she's shouting, but the car windows muffle whatever it is she's saying. I decide she must be happy to see her 'nephew.' As a jest, I wave back— and at that moment, I hear the screech of tires and feel a world-ending thump.

Shit, I think as I fly through the air.

My head hits something hard, and I black out.

CHAPTER FOUR

I wake up nauseous.

Am I hung over?

I open my eyes.

The light hurts, so I shut them again. I examine myself and realize a lot more hurts than just my eyes. My body feels like one big bruise.

The nausea gets worse, and it's not because I'm drunk. It actually feels like a very bad case of carsickness. Then it hits me: I *am* in a car, and I'm being driven somewhere.

I open my eyes and force them to adjust despite the pain. Shoddy Brooklyn streets pass me by. The car I'm in is moving relatively fast, and the ride is very shaky, which is a big contributing factor to my nausea. I'm grateful I'm riding shotgun; when I get motion sickness, it's usually worse when I ride in the back.

Bits and pieces of what happened come back to me.

I was crossing the street; then something happened.

I decide to phase in to figure things out from the Quiet. Overloaded with adrenaline, I easily enter the Quiet. When the sound of the engine is gone, I notice that the nausea is too.

Without the sick feeling, my situation becomes clearer. For one, I recognize the woman behind the wheel. I recall Guiding her to give me her car, the very one we're in. What the heck is she doing driving me? She was supposed to leave her car for me. And where are we going?

Only one way to tell for sure. I reach out and touch her forehead.

* * *

We're looking across the street. Our nephew is about to cross the road. He looks to his right, but doesn't look to his left.

He's never been a fan of basic safety, our nephew, we think as we see the limo steamrolling his way.

"The car," we scream at him and wave. "Watch out!"

What's the driver thinking? Is he stoned? We feel our blood pressure rising.

Our nephew waves at us and doesn't notice the car that's about to hit him. The limo attempts to stop. We hear that frightening sound of tires screeching against pavement, but it's no good. The car hits our nephew.

He flies into the windshield, shattering the glass.

We exit our car, screaming.

A thin, balding man gets out of the limousine.

"You maniac," we scream at him. "Are you drunk?"

"He c-came out of nowhere," the man stutters. "I swear."

"Shut up and help me get him in my car," we say after examining the boy. Thank goodness he seems intact, with no visible broken bones. "I'll take him to the hospital. He might have a concussion . . ."

I, Darren, disassociate. It's interesting how she saw me, and how she confabulated a whole story about me in order to explain the events she was witnessing. Ironically, I agree with her fictional assessment. I *was* being an idiot. I didn't check the road before crossing, though I usually do. If I were to blame something, I'd blame my prior trip into the Quiet. I'd crossed that road a moment earlier while in the Quiet, so when I phased out, I just kind of repeated the same action, almost on autopilot. I was laser-focused on the Honda and on picking up my friends and family. So in a way, it's the fault of the monks and the Super Pusher.

Speaking of them, how long has it been since I got hit? Did everyone else get out okay?

Determined to find out, I exit my 'aunt's' head.

* * *

As soon as I'm back in the Quiet, I phase out of it.

When the nauseating ride resumes, I say, "Stop the car, Aunty."

"Oh, thank God you're conscious," the woman says. "I feared the worst."

"Yeah, I'm okay," I lie. I may not have broken bones, but I feel more than a little banged-up. "Now stop the car."

"Are you crazy? The hospital is a block away."

"I don't have time to argue. Stop."

Instead of stopping, she pushes the gas pedal. This make-believe aunt of mine is one stubborn lady.

I phase into the Quiet and Guide her to see things my way.

I then exit the car to check my surroundings. I have no clue where I am, but I spot a sign in the distance that says 'Jamaica Hospital.' I suppress the temptation to adjust my plans in order to swing by the hospital for a shot of morphine; I'll just have to tough it out.

Proud of my restraint, I phase out.

The world returns to life and my 'aunt' makes a U-turn so suddenly that my urge to throw up multiplies a hundredfold.

I'm amazed that we didn't get into another accident. I should've used more finesse with my Guiding. I really need to get my shit together. I won't be of help to anyone with broken bones.

"Do you have any painkillers?" I ask while we're stopped at a red light.

"There's Motrin in the glove compartment." She slams on the gas pedal, a stomach-churning maneuver she's done at every light change.

I fish out the pills and dry-swallow a triple dose, hoping my stomach can handle it.

Then I close my eyes and slow my breathing—a 'how not to throw up' trick I learned from Lucy as a kid. After a few blocks, I feel more like myself, which is likely from the breathing exercise or from some placebo effect. I doubt Motrin works *that* quickly. And then the car's brakes screech, and any semblance of normality is over.

"This is where it happened," the woman says when I open my eyes. "Where that monster hit you."

"Thank you, Aunty," I say. "I'll take it from here."

She looks uncomfortable. My directive to 'do as I say' is clearly clashing with my equally convincing directive that we're family. She's rightfully hesitant to let her hurt nephew get behind the wheel. As I'm about to Guide her once more, I see the 'do as I say' instruction win out. She slowly unbuckles her seatbelt.

"Please take this," I say, handing the woman all my cash—around four hundred bucks.

When she refuses to take it, I Guide her again. I know I'm totally abusing my power, but in this case, it's for a good cause.

I then have her program her number in my phone. "I'll call you to tell you when to get the car from Hertz."

"Have a blessed day," she says.

"Later, Aunty." I close the car door.

Okay. What's next?

I look at the dashboard clock and scrap my earlier idea of picking up my folks and friends. It took my 'aunt' fifteen minutes to drive here from the hospital, which means it's been at least half an hour since I got hit by the limo. Everyone is probably long gone and on their way to Eugene's lab.

That's where I decide to head, but first, I want to take one last look at the cemetery.

I phase in and leisurely walk back toward Kyle's grave. In the safety of the Quiet, I allow myself to register my environment, a luxury I couldn't afford when I was running. As far as I can tell, this is a very nice cemetery. Then again, this was my very first funeral, so all cemeteries might look like this.

I'm a hundred feet away from my destination when I notice that something's gone terribly wrong.

I come across the body of a cop.

I break into a run and see another cop on the ground.

Then another.

Then two more.

The closer I get to the burial site, the more cops I find lying about in every direction.

I approach one at random. This officer's wrist is twisted at an unnatural angle. His eyes are closed. Is he dead?

I kneel next to the body and touch the cop's good hand.

* * *

"Raise your hands," we say to the bald man in the orange robe. "Lie down on the ground and put your hands behind your head. Slowly."

Instead of obeying, the man closes the distance in a series of jerky motions and grabs our wrist.

"Let go of the gun," our attacker says calmly, almost soothingly.

"Fuck you," we say and try to punch the man with our left hand.

Our punch doesn't land, and our right arm is on fire. We realize the fucker broke our wrist when he did whatever it was he did; he moved too fast for us to see.

Ignoring the agony, we reach for our handcuffs, ready to employ a desperate maneuver. Before our hand even reaches the cuffs, there's an orange blur in the direction of our right temple and the world goes blank.

* * *

I exit the officer's head and look around.

More cops are in similar unconscious conditions. It takes a quick Read of each one to see the same pattern play out. Though all the men I check are alive, every officer got his ass handed to him by the monks. Most of their memories are a variation of the weapon disarm I saw in the first cop. In a few rare cases, when the cops were above average when it comes to self-defense, what I witness reminds me of a mix between the martial arts training Caleb and I experienced in the Israeli master's mind, and a Hong Kong kung fu movie about Shaolin monks.

The cops who faced Caleb have some broken ribs and are in noticeably worse shape, leading me to believe that the monks were trying to inflict as little damage as possible while pursuing their goals. Caleb, however, almost relished the violence. It was Caleb who knocked out the priest—a dickish and unnecessary move, in my opinion.

Throughout my Reading, I curse myself for being such a shortsighted humanitarian. I made the cops empty their guns. The monks' lack of respect for the authority of the police force, as well as their apparent disregard for guns, created this mess of a situation.

Even with bullets, these cops would still have had it rough, though lots of monks would've died. Still, because of my meddling, what could've been a tough fight became an easy slaughter of these men and women in uniform. Thinking of *women* in uniforms gets my heart beating much faster.

I run in the direction I sent Mira and her handlers in.

It's not long before I find the first lady cop on the ground. Then the second. They're both lying there with various injuries.

I run in the other direction, to where Thomas was led. Twenty feet in, I see someone I recognize: the Quarterback. He's the first person beginning to get up. Must be his resilience as a football player at work. Reading him, I learn that he and his larger friends did marginally better against the monks, who probably had to carry a few of their brethren away, but the cops were outnumbered and the monks were swifter, so the eventual outcome was the same.

I check the direction my moms went in and see nothing at all. I wonder whether that means they escaped. They didn't have a police escort and maybe that saved them. I sure hope so.

I run toward the parking lot, determined to learn more, and end up following a trail of macabre breadcrumbs in the form of beat-up police officers.

I suppress my growing panic.

It's still within the realm of possibility that Thomas and Mira somehow escaped their escorts. Maybe Thomas came to his senses and Guided the cops to let him go?

And what about my moms? I see no evidence that they might be in trouble.

I increase my pace, sprinting toward the parking lot.

The minivans are gone, and I notice tread marks on the asphalt, which tells me they left in a hurry.

I frantically follow the driveway and leave the lot.

I Read the stylist of a nearby hair salon. She has a good view of the cemetery from her shop. Using her brain as one would a surveillance camera, I search for what I need. Yep, she noticed the vans. The screech of their tires drew her attention. She saw them turn right onto Liberty Avenue.

I leave the hair salon and walk down Liberty, Reading people as I go. It takes a dozen more Reads before I find any sign of those damn vans. Inside the mind of a McDonald's cashier, I see two Hondas turn onto Conduit Boulevard.

On a hunch, I follow the signs that lead to Belt Parkway—the big highway in Brooklyn. Reading what feels like a hundred people on the way confirms my suspicions: the two Odysseys are heading toward the highway.

I push a frozen bike messenger off his bicycle so I can take advantage of his ride. Bikes are useful for long-distance travel in the Quiet. Rolling up my suit pants, I get on and start pedaling toward the highway.

Usually, I would be marveling at my surroundings. Though I've ridden bikes in the Quiet before, I've never ridden on a congested highway like this. There's a certain charm to doing things I'd never dare to do in the real world. But I can't enjoy this ride, not when all I can concentrate on is the mantra repeating in my head: *Please don't be in the vans.*

I ride on and on, feeling as though I'm in the Tour de France.

Finally, in the distance, I see two vans with the symbol of a shiny H inside a square.

I ride up to them and jump off the bike, letting it fall with that chains-on-asphalt noise.

Peeking inside van number one with trepidation, I get my first dose of disillusionment.

The monks have Mira and Thomas.

My friends appear to be sleeping. I don't dare touch them, as that would bring them into the Quiet with me, and I'm not sure whether the Super Pusher's instructions are still in effect. The last thing I want is to fight them. Then again, the chances of them still being under the Super Pusher's influence are small, if Eugene's theory on the matter is correct. He thinks that Reading or Guiding someone from Level 2 will expend that person's Depth much quicker than normal. Mimir—the strange being who resulted from my Joining with the Enlightened— suggested the same thing when we spoke in Level 2.

Reading the monks doesn't yield any results, aside from the same useless meditative white noise I got from them at the Temple and at the airport.

I'm so stunned that I can't admit how bad things are, at least not until I get the full picture.

I carefully walk up to the second Honda and open the side door to look inside.

They have Lucy in the front, strapped in with a seatbelt, with Sara set up similarly in the back. Just like Mira and Thomas, my moms look as though they're sleeping.

I give them a quick Read. Sure enough, the last thing they remember is a needle prick. Caleb must've drugged them the way he drugged me when he abducted me from the hotel in Miami.

In frustration, I drag a frozen monk out of the car and give him a couple of kicks to the face.

The exercise only makes me angrier.

I take a breath and try to think rationally, searching for any kind of silver lining. The best I can come up with is that at least they don't have those black bags over their heads.

Nope, that doesn't help at all. I kick the limp monk in the ribs a few more times and then take a few more calming breaths before contemplating my options.

With Caleb here, in Mira and Thomas's van, I'm tempted to pull him in and take out my frustrations on someone more animated than my monk-shaped punching bag.

But no. As therapeutic as it would be, I dismiss the idea. Even if by some miracle I manage to kill Caleb in the Quiet, what would that accomplish? He'd still be here on the highway, and I'd still be miles away in the cemetery. I could Guide the surrounding drivers to stall the progress of the vans, but even that wouldn't help; the resulting traffic would also slow down my pursuit.

Then it hits me. I don't need to follow them because I already know where they're headed; it's as obvious as why they're doing this in the first place. Caleb and his monk posse took everyone as a means to ensure I come to *them*, to the Temple.

They want to force me to comply with my grandparents' crazy demands.

Just thinking about that makes me so angry I almost want to pursue them on my own and do something desperate. Then I take a deep breath and force myself to calm down. I need to act with my brain and not my testosterone.

I jump on the borrowed bike and pedal my way back to my body.

As I do, I can't help but dwell on all the different ways I'll make my grandparents regret this kidnapping. And if something happens to Mira, Thomas, or my moms . . .

Let's just say this very first funeral I've attended won't be my last.

* * *

By the time I find my way back to my frozen body, I'm officially sick of cycling. I *will* add a cycling class to that extra workout regimen I'm planning to implement in the future. I'm sure with practice I'll be able to tolerate doing it for longer periods.

My frozen self looks horrible. I'm dirty, and my black suit is torn in places. I'm pretty sure my skin underneath is scraped and bruised.

Bracing myself, I touch my face and phase out.

As soon as the world comes alive, the physical exertion I felt in the Quiet becomes child's play compared to what I'm feeling in the real world. With all the cycling, I managed to forget I was hit by a car.

Yeah, I'm definitely scraped and bruised.

Despite the futility of it, I'm again tempted to chase after the vans, but the rational part of me tells me not to be impulsive. I need to consult with my non-kidnapped friends. They're a smart bunch, and they'll know what to do. Plus, Eugene deserves to know what happened to his sister.

Back in my 'aunt's' car, I enter Eugene's lair's address into my phone's GPS.

On a whim, as I'm driving, I search for Caleb's number, which is listed as Mr. Personality. Not feeling jovial enough for a voice command, I simply press the touch screen to initiate the call.

I'm shocked when he actually picks up.

"Hello," he says, and I can almost visualize that annoying smirk I'd love to beat off his face.

"Caleb, you fucker, you will let them go, now—"

"Darren," he says. "How convenient that you called."

"I mean it, I'll—"

"Whatever you're planning to do," he says smugly, "save it for when you arrive at the Temple. I want it to be a surprise."

And with that, the asshole hangs up on me.

I'm so angry that I spend the entire drive playing out revenge fantasies in my mind.

CHAPTER FIVE

"Mothershitter," Eugene says after I finish relaying the story of my morning. His accent is stronger than ever, and his usually calm voice is loud, the tension in it reverberating through the lab. "If they harm one hair—"

"Dude, calm down," says Bert. He's been Eugene's computer guy and lab assistant for the last ten days.

"It's clear they won't harm Mira," Hillary echoes.

Though I doubt she visits the lab as often as her boyfriend, she was in the neighborhood when I texted her to come over; she and Bert were planning to do brunch.

"Okay, guys. Now that I've told you everything, I have to ask: What the hell is this monkey"—I point to the animal standing with an iPad in the middle of the room—"doing here?"

I noticed the monkey when I first entered the lab, but I was so wound up that I blurted out the whole story in one breath. Somewhat more relaxed now, I can reflect on the incredulity of an uncaged simian hanging out in the midst of all the brain-monitoring equipment and other gadgets that make up Eugene's mad scientist dwelling.

"She's not a monkey," Eugene says, switching to his pedantic tone. "She's an ape."

"Okay," I say. "Let me rephrase. What's this 'damn dirty ape' doing here?"

"Hey now," Hillary says. "Kiki is actually obsessed with hygiene."

I look Kiki over. She returns my gaze curiously. Of course I know she's an ape. I called her a monkey because I find that word funnier. Kiki is one of the higher apes, either a chimpanzee or a bonobo. She doesn't strike me as a clean freak, given the diaper, but who knows? She's currently wearing one of Eugene's head contraptions—not unlike some he's had me wear. What's really impressive is her exemplary behavior. After glancing at me, she returns her attention to her iPad, no monkey business whatsoever.

"I'm sorry, Kiki," I say, rolling my eyes. "I didn't mean to imply—"

"Oh, stop it, you two," Bert butts in. "She's obviously our lab rat, err, chimp."

"Right," I say and look at my aunt. "And you're okay with this?"

"No," she says. "But Eugene developed this 'super safe' device that includes the TMS machine you bought him, and he was about to test it on Bert. So I figured—"

"That you'd rather he test it on a chimp than your boyfriend." I chuckle despite my worry.

"TMS is FDA approved," Hillary says defensively. "It should indeed be safe. I'm just being extra cautious."

She sounds as though she really does feel guilty that she put Bert's wellbeing above that of Kiki's.

TMS stands for Transcranial Magnetic Stimulation. It's a machine I got for Eugene's lab from FBTI, a company I was researching for work before I met Eugene. According to what I've read, it's as safe as can be, since it uses magnetic force as its modus operandi. Then again, if something is approved to treat depression, it's bound to do *something* to the brain, and Eugene is clearly using it off-label.

"So because you were worried about Bert, you walked to the nearest zoo and nabbed a lab monkey?" I ask, this whole development lifting my mood slightly.

"No," Hillary says. Her small face darkens. "I got Kiki as part of my animal rescue program. She belonged to an idiot in New Jersey."

"Hillary, I can't listen to your Greenpeace crap while my sister is being held hostage," Eugene says irritably.

Bert glares at him. "You never want to hear it." Then he turns to me. "When he saw poor Kiki, the first thing he wanted to do was install an electrode in her brain."

In Eugene's defense, he probably would've installed an electrode in his own brain long ago if Mira hadn't been around to stop him. What's more interesting is that Bert is defending his girlfriend. I feel like a parent who's realized their kid is all grown up, only I wish he'd stand up to my aunt from time to time, just to reassure me that he's not her mind-controlled puppet. It's suspicious how he's been in perfect harmony with my aunt's wishes from the start. There's pussy-whipped, and then there's what Bert's become under a maybe-too-hot-for-him girlfriend who can manipulate his mind to boot. If Bert wasn't deliriously happy throughout all of this, I'd feel bad for having set them up.

"If anyone's in danger, it's Thomas," Hillary retorts. "As far as your Leacher leaders are concerned, he's a Pusher. I can't even imagine what they will—"

"I hope they understand that if they do anything to Thomas, they can forget whatever it is they want from me," I say, my anger returning.

"They would still have enough leverage over you, with your parents and Mira," Hillary reminds me.

I frown as I consider that. "They didn't freak out about me being a hybrid, and I didn't get the sense that they harbor ill will toward Guides. Besides, regardless of the leverage they have over me, I think they know I'd kill them if—"

"Would you really?" Hillary gives me an incredulous look. "These are your grandparents we're talking about."

"So what's your point?" Eugene snaps at her. "Should we give up? Or should Darren sleep with Julia to appease them?"

"While we're at it, we'll get Julia out of there too," I promise, finally realizing why Eugene is acting so uncharacteristically bloodthirsty.

It's because he and Julia have a history.

"Yes," Hillary says. "My point is that I think we need to be rational. To maximize everyone's chances of survival, we need to plan, then act. You seem to want to go into hothead mode, which could be detrimental to—"

"That's not fair," I say. "Why do you think I'm here instead of following them in my car?"

"I was chastising Eugene, not you," she says. "You did good coming here."

"Fine," Eugene says tersely. "Let's hear your master plan."

"I only have a rudimentary idea," Hillary says. "We need Darren to master going into Level 2. If he could do this, he could Guide his grandparents toward the outcome we need. This is the only surefire idea I have, for the moment."

"Would that work on them?" Bert asks. "They're very powerful, and if Guiding the monks doesn't work, wouldn't the same be true of their leaders?"

"If by power you mean Depth, then it wouldn't help them, since they showed no indication that they can reach Level 2 the way Darren can," Hillary says. "That's why they're trying to breed offspring who can. That means, in theory, they can be Guided, but I didn't think about the monks' Guiding resistance. If the Enlightened can also do that, then my idea has a problem. But then, why would they even bother learning that? Unless they know what the Elders can do . . ."

"If I could magically master that skill, it would help greatly, even if it doesn't work on my grandparents," I say, thinking about her idea. "I'd be able to control Caleb, Julia, and her mother."

"Exactly," Hillary says. "Plus, there's the issue of our friends being controlled by the person Darren dubbed as the Super Pusher."

"Okay, I buy it," I say. "Level 2 control would be great. But I want to remind you that I couldn't do it today, even when my life was in real danger."

"I was about to mention possible ways in which you could overcome your issues," Hillary says.

Eugene stares at her. "I think I see where you're leading with that. If only I had more time . . ."

"I wasn't talking about your tech," Hillary says. "I had something much worse in mind. But if you think your stuff would help—"

"Can someone clue me in please?" I ask. "What does his research have to do with anything?"

"Dude, didn't he tell you what he's trying to do?" Bert chimes in.

"He tried, but—"

"Wait," Bert says. "You've spent hundreds of thousands of dollars on all this equipment and you never even asked what it was for?"

"How would you like to make out with Kiki?" I ask him threateningly. When Bert pales, I say, "I do know. Eugene is trying to better understand our powers by researching how it all works in the brain."

"That's the oversimplification of the century," Bert says, giving Hillary what I assume is a 'Hey, hon. You'd save me from kissing an ape, right?' kind of look.

"Enlighten me then," I say. "In layman's terms, so even a dummy with a Harvard graduate degree would understand."

"Sure," Bert says, pretending as though he's taking my sarcasm at face value. "The shortest version is that among many other applications, Eugene's research can let a regular person, someone like me, go into the Mind Dimension."

"What?" I stare at him and then turn to Mira's brother. "Eugene, you never told me *that*."

"I thought it was self-evident," my friend says moodily. "Besides, I think I did tell you. You've just adopted my sister's annoying habit of tuning out anything to do with my research."

He's right, but in my defense, when he gets going, he doesn't shut up for hours, and there's a limit to how many words like 'connectome,' 'microtubules,' and 'oligodendrocytes' I can listen to before I get selective with my hearing.

"Okay," I say. "As cool as that is, how would giving Bert this ability help in my case?"

"Without some redesign and tinkering, it wouldn't," Bert says. "But the mechanism Eugene is working on basically combines two effects: it grants a little bit of Depth, and then it jolts the mind into Splitting into the Mind Dimension. The second part might—"

Eugene shakes his head. "We haven't gotten past the animal testing phase, and I haven't given such application much thought. We can't just apply things to Darren's situation—"

"The monkey is going into the Quiet?" Despite everything, I have to fight the urge to laugh. "Will it be a Reader or a Guide? I shudder to think what will happen to the world's banana supplies if she becomes the latter."

"Neither," Eugene says. "The control of those abilities is spread much wider in the brain—"

"This is amazing," I say. "I can't believe you were planning to have a monkey phase without telling me. In the future, as the angel investor of this operation, I want daily reports, written by Bert. I can't miss out on such cool stuff."

"Dumbed-down reports," Bert says. "Check."

I glare at him. "Seriously, dude. My Reach is probably greater than Hillary's, which means she can't save you from an inter-species erotic encounter with your lovely 'volunteer.'"

Bert looks at Hillary, silently asking, *Can he really override you?*

She shrugs and narrows her eyes at me.

I give her my own look that hopefully says, *Would I rather be loved or feared? In this case, feared.*

"I still don't think we can sit around doing research while Mira is riding drugged in a van," Eugene says.

"I wasn't saying that, though the more I think about it, that might be a good idea," Hillary says.

"That's just unacceptable—"

"Let her finish," Bert says. This is the second time he's defended her, or maybe my aunt is cheating by making Bert say stuff.

"Sorry, Hillary." Eugene gives her an apologetic look. "What is your plan?"

"Darren can learn how to reach Level 2 from the people who know how—the Elders," she says.

"That's it?" I raise my eyebrows. "Instead of saving Mira, all I have to do is find the Guide equivalent of the Enlightened and take a few lessons?"

"Yes, that's it, minus the sarcasm," my aunt says. "And you wouldn't be aimlessly looking for them. You'd ask your grandparents for help."

"I'm confused." Bert looks at his girlfriend. "I thought his grandparents were the very people causing this mess."

"Not the Leachers." She sounds only mildly exasperated. "His *other* grandparents. The ones who also, fortuitously, live in Florida."

"You mean—" Bert says, then cuts himself off. "I thought you hated their guts."

"We're estranged," Hillary corrects. "And I hope this highlights my commitment to this cause."

"I do appreciate it," Eugene says. "But at the same time, I'm not sure this kind of detour—"

"Dude," Bert says. "They have warrior monks who can't be Guided, and from what you've been saying, Caleb is a deadly opponent. Unless you have access to a secret army?"

"I don't," Eugene says. "But Darren and Hillary could maybe—"

"Are you seriously about to suggest that I Guide an actual army to do my bidding?" Hillary asks, her eyebrows drawing together. "The logistics of something like that would be extremely difficult, plus it would get extremely bloody, fast. Since when have you heard of hostage situations being resolved through the army?"

"You could Guide a small band of Navy Seals," Bert says, clearly getting into the spirit of it. "The guys who took out Bin Laden would make short work of—"

"Right," Hillary says. "Let's go to Navy Seals R Us and get some."

"Enough," I say in my most commanding voice. Everyone looks at me in shock. "Here's the breakdown. It will take the vans twenty hours to reach Florida. That's without stops and with favorable traffic. That gives us some wiggle room. Given that my Guide grandparents are also in Florida, I say Hillary and I visit them, since it's practically on the way. If I *can* get to the Elders and they can quickly teach me how to better control my powers, great. If not, we can develop a plan on the fly. Meanwhile, you two can spend a little more time trying to see whether this research leads you anywhere."

"Even if we cracked this an hour after you left, how would that help?" Eugene asks. "My equipment is here, in the lab."

"Can you turn a U-Haul truck, or some other type of vehicle, into a mobile lab?" I ask.

"It won't be easy, but—"

"Money isn't an obstacle," I remind him. "I'll give you my credit card."

"I'll help," Bert says. "I think it's feasible. I'll get us some Adderall and—"

"You're not taking any drugs," Hillary says. "I can make you focus if that's what you want."

"You can do that?" Bert looks excited. "Why didn't you—"

"Because I like you unaltered," she says. "If the current situation wasn't dire enough . . ."

"Okay," I say. "Your destination will be Apalachicola. It's a town near the Temple. Hillary and I will fly out, which will buy us some time."

Eugene turns to my friend. "Bert, can you get them the tickets?"

"On it," Bert says and walks up to the computer. The monkey glances at him suspiciously when she hears the sounds of the keyboard.

"You'll fly to Tallahassee, right? That's the nearest airport to that town," Bert says.

"No," Hillary says. "My parents are too far from there. They're closer to the Jacksonville or Orlando airports."

"Okay, let me see what I can do," he says and starts typing. He's about to repeat that trick where he bumps people off the plane. At least the airline will comp them, which marginally beats Hillary or me Guiding people to give up their seats—my plan B.

"You know," I say once I verify that I got my boarding pass on my phone, "this plan also takes care of something else. If I learn this Level 2 phasing, I'll be able to protect you guys should the Super Pusher show up again."

"Yeah, about that." Hillary looks uncomfortable. "I wasn't sure I wanted to bring this up, but how do we know this whole kidnapping isn't, at the core, this Super Pusher's doing?"

"And if it is, this person will be waiting for us at the Temple," Eugene says, his forehead creasing with worry. "She'll be ready to turn me, and even you, Hillary, against you guys."

"Right." Hillary gives me a steady look. "So you see how we can't ignore the Super Pusher issue?"

"Wait," I say, recalling one key element. "This plan has a fatal flaw."

"What do you mean?" Hillary asks.

"Remember when you first told me about the Level 2 ability and how it was rumored that some of the Elders possessed it?"

"Yeah," Hillary says. "At that pizzeria in Miami."

"Right. You didn't mention this at the time, but can anyone other than the Elders utilize Level 2?"

She bites her lip. "No one that I know of. I was hoping to talk to you about this on the way."

"Wait," Eugene says. "You're walking Darren into a possible enemy hideout?"

"No," Hillary says tersely. "At least not exactly."

"It's sure starting to sound that way," I say. "If the Super Pusher is an Elder, is going to see her friends such a good idea?"

"Yes, it is," Hillary says. "Given all that I know about the Elders, they wouldn't sanction what this person has done. Which means that if this is an Elder, she's working on her own and you might learn who it is once you're there. And then you can figure out a way to neutralize her."

"So besides convincing them to teach him some secret technique, Darren will need to play detective as well?" Eugene says incredulously.

"The detective part might not be as hard as it seems," I say slowly. "We know this person was at, or near, Kyle's funeral."

"Exactly," Hillary says. "And the Elders are also reclusive, so the list of suspects will likely be small. This plan still beats going to the Enlightened Temple unprepared and risking getting everyone's minds fucked with."

"So," Bert chimes in, clearly trying to defuse the tension between Eugene and his girl, "even if Darren doesn't learn the identity of the enemy, if he learns how to do this Level 2 thing, could he undo what was done to Mira and Thomas? What about preventing you two from being Guided?"

"I think Darren was right when he said the effect on Mira and Thomas wouldn't last," Hillary says. "But you're also right that yes, in principle, he could undo things done to us, though not really prevent them."

"I don't know what to say," Eugene says thoughtfully. "There are too many variables in this equation. Something is bound to go wrong."

"Darren's life wouldn't be in danger," Hillary says. "The Elders, as a group, don't want him harmed."

"What makes you so sure?" I ask. When it comes to people wanting to kill me, my curiosity works overtime.

"If the Elders wanted you dead, you'd be dead," Hillary says. "Trust me."

"Knowing Darren's luck, they might want him dead once they meet him," Eugene says. "No offense, Darren."

"I make my own luck," I say., waving my hand to show I'm not offended. "Given what Hillary just said, I'll be super charming to these Elders. You just wait and see."

"Oh, they'll love him," Hillary says. "My vote is to stick with this plan, with your research as a possible backup."

"Since Darren is the one who's walking into the potential hornet's nest, I say he makes the final call," Bert says. "It's only fair."

Everyone goes quiet and looks at me expectantly.

I look at each of them.

Hillary looks worried, Eugene is tense, and Bert looks very serious.

I can't bear the idea of my friends turning on me again. If for no other reason than that, I decide to go with this plan.

"Come on, Aunty," I say. "We have a plane to catch."

Tension dissipates, except Bert's face changes from serious to sad.

"So this is goodbye," he says, looking at Hillary like a puppy that lost its favorite chew toy. "I'll see you in a bit?"

Instead of replying, Hillary walks over and kisses him.

I look at Eugene and see a hint of laughter in his eyes, but then he's serious again. I phase into the Quiet to say a few words to him in private.

The world around me stops. As though they have a mind of their own, my legs bring me to Kiki instead of Eugene. Despite the important task ahead, I can't resist this temptation.

I want to Read the chimp.

I walk up to her and put my hand on her face (or is it a snout?). Her fur (or is it hair?) feels softer than it looks. I concentrate, wondering whether this will work at all, and then I'm in.

* * *

We warm. We happy. We not bored. We full.

I, Darren, disassociate from Kiki's thoughts. It's incredible. She actually has thoughts in the same sense as people do. But there's more to it than that. The way she perceives the world is eerily human, and yet different. There's a childlike wonder about her surroundings. A strange contentment seems to be suppressing a number of her basic urges, and it takes me a second to figure out that Kiki is being Guided. It must be Hillary's work, and it explains the chimp's good behavior.

Disappointed that I'm not getting a true experience of an ape being her animal self, I exit Kiki's head while mentally adding 'Read a regular ape' to my to-do list. It goes somewhere between 'Read a dolphin' and 'Read the Pope.'

* * *

Done with Kiki, I walk up to Eugene and pull him in.

"Darren," my friend says. "I was about to pull you in myself."

I pause, searching for the best words, then blurt out, "I wanted to say that if it comes to it, I'll do whatever's necessary to get Mira out. I won't let Hillary's pacifism get in the way."

"Thank you." Eugene's eyes gleam. "I mean it. Thanks."

"Don't even mention it. What did *you* want to tell me?"

"You read my mind." He chuckles. "I wanted to see if I could count on you should—"

"You can."

"Good. There's something else I wanted to tell you. You've been very good for Mira."

"I've been good for her?" He took me completely by surprise.

"You've been a positive influence in her life," Eugene explains. "Transformative, even."

"Me?" I stare at him. "All right, if you say so."

"I mean it," Eugene says seriously. "Did she tell you she's been studying for her GED?"

"No." I blink, taken aback. "She didn't mention it."

"Well, she is, and that's just one thing. She's been happier lately. Warmer. She's more and more like she was before—" He swallows, clearly thinking about their parents' deaths.

"Oh, okay," I say uncomfortably.

If by 'warmer' he means less homicidal, then yes, I've noticed that. If by 'happier' he means she doesn't deliver those treatises about the pointlessness of life, then yeah, that's improved too. I thought these things were due to Mira finally getting her revenge and had little to do with me. Well, my shooting Jacob helped her get her revenge, and killing Kyle—again my doing—completely closed that revenge chapter of her life. But I'm sure that's not what Eugene means when he credits me with Mira's improvements.

I don't voice my doubts, though, and with as much bravado as I can muster, I say, "Let's do this."

"Yeah," he says and shakes my hand.

I phase out of the Quiet, and as soon as Bert and Hillary become animated, I say, "So you're controlling the monkey."

"Just until she gets to the reserve," Hillary says.

"Uh-huh." I know it's not appropriate, but I can't resist. "And if you hadn't Guided it, and it was being bad, do you think Bert would spank it?"

CHAPTER SIX

The ride to the airport, the flight, and the trip from Jacksonville pass uneventfully. My injuries aren't bothering me too much, likely due to the painkillers, but I'm not very talkative and thus get an earful of Hillary's unfiltered propaganda. I now know how Bert became a pescatarian, or ovo-lacto vegetarian, or whatever my former meat-and-potatoes friend is nowadays. Hillary gives me a laundry list of problems that allegedly stem from eating meat, things that range from heart disease to cancer. If I give up red meat anytime soon, I'll know whom to blame.

She also uses the opportunity to tell me about exotic pets—a topic she was about to launch into at the lab when Eugene interrupted her.

Apparently, there are people who are uneducated enough about wildlife and lack self-preservation to the point where they're willing to take on a chimpanzee as a pet. Worse, some try to keep lions, or other creatures that actually want to eat them, as pets. Half the time these people end up really messing up these animals. For instance, some people declaw their lions, which is a polite way of saying that the tips of the lions' fingers are amputated. When that's done to a cat, according to Hillary, they develop all sorts of walking problems. All that maiming doesn't even cover the psychological harm of living in unnaturally cramped conditions. My aunt has apparently been working on putting an end to this practice and owns a rescue in upstate New York.

I have to give her credit for style. The whole rescue runs on large monetary donations contributed by the pets' former owners (Guided by Hillary), who also comprise the workforce. I appreciate the irony of these people cleaning up the dung of the very animals they abused. Even if I don't feel as strongly about it as my aunt does, the idea that these abused creatures finally get to roam in spacious habitats is comforting. Also, not that I was ever going to get a cat, but if I did, I wouldn't declaw it, not if it's the equivalent of cutting a human finger at the knuckle.

Realizing that Hillary's gotten to me, I reflect on how my aunt is good at influencing people, even without needing to resort to Guiding.

Hillary becomes more subdued the closer we get to our destination. As we wait to be let into the Palm Haven private community, she's completely silent. I understand why. She's never forgiven her parents for disowning Margret, her older sister and my biological mom. I think part of her may even blame them for Margret's murder, even though we know Kyle was really at fault. I have mixed feelings about meeting my grandparents, so I can't even imagine what it's like for Hillary.

"You don't have to join me," I say as the security guard Hillary must've Guided lets us through. "You can wait in the car."

"That's insane," she says, turning right at the first intersection. "You can't just walk in and say, 'Hi, I'm your grandson.'"

"Why not?" I glance at her. "That's exactly what I'd do."

"I know." She parks the rental car next to a faded pink house with a large, dry palm tree next to it. "That's why I'm doing all the talking."

"Okay." I slam the car door closed a little too strongly.

She walks up to the house and rings the doorbell.

No one answers for a while, so Hillary knocks on the door with her tiny fist.

The door opens.

A man stands there. He has a look of utter shock, but quickly hides it. Hillary must be the last person he expected to see on his doorstep.

Who is he? He looks too young to be Hillary's father, let alone Margret's, who would've been older than this dude. He looks to be in his mid-thirties, at most. The only thing that makes me think this guy is older is his eyes. They look weary from life, like the eyes of some elderly people.

"George," Hillary says, her voice like dry ice. "What are you doing here?"

"The same as you, I imagine," the man—George—says.

"I doubt we're here for the same reason," my aunt says.

"Wait." George frowns at her. "You mean you didn't hear?"

"About you being one of the Ambassadors? I did. Congratulations."

He sighs. "No, about Ronald."

"What about him?"

"You better come inside," George says and opens the door wider.

As we enter, I get a sense of déjà vu. It's as though I've walked into Gamma and PopPop's house. My mom Sara's parents also live in Florida, and their house has the same dated furniture, is similarly dusty and unkempt, and has the same musty smell. There's also a faint hint of garlic, not unlike Nana and Granpop's house—Lucy's parents. I'm glad those two live in Queens, as it would be beyond odd to have four sets of grandparents living in Florida.

Having three is strange enough.

George leads us into the kitchen, where an old woman is standing with a cup of tea. When she sees Hillary, her eyes widen, and she shakily puts her cup down on the counter.

When she speaks, her voice sounds bitter. "Is this what it takes to get you to visit? One of us needs to suffer?"

"Nice to see you too, Anne," Hillary says coolly. "Can you tell me what you and George are talking about? What's wrong with Ronald?"

"You won't call him Dad, even now?" Anne picks up her tea again, her withered hands cradling the cup as if deriving comfort from it.

"*Mom,* what's wrong with *Dad?*" Hillary asks, managing to make those usually warm words sound empty.

"Come, I'll show you," Anne says. "But leave your Unencumbered plaything in the kitchen. Seeing him will upset your father too much."

Is she talking about me? "I am not—"

"He's not Unencumbered," Hillary says. "He's actually a powerful Guide that *Daddy* would approve of."

Shaking her head in disbelief, my newfound grandmother walks out of the kitchen.

As we go deeper into the house, a new smell permeates the air, that of some kind of medicine. We enter a large master bedroom. In the middle is something that looks like a hospital bed, with an old man lying in it, his expression that of a scowl.

"You're too early," he says to Hillary, his voice raspy. "I'm not dead yet."

"Hello to you too, Dad," Hillary says. "Can you tell me what happened to you?"

"You really don't know?" Anne furrows her brow at her daughter. "You didn't come here to gloat at your father's pain?"

Hillary looks as if her mother slapped her.

"We came here because I need to meet with the Elders," I say, getting aggravated.

Hillary puts a hand on my arm and says, "We think his Reach is high enough to be considered—"

"He's a potential?" Her father's expression visibly softens. "Are you telling me you married someone who suits your station?"

"We're not—"

"—going to discuss anything until I learn what happened to you," Hillary says, this time squeezing my arm.

"What's there to tell?" Ronald says bitterly. "I fell."

"And broke his hip," Anne adds. "Don't forget that part."

"I see," Hillary says, her small face unreadable. "How bad is it?"

"He had surgery," George says, stepping closer to the bed. "After some physical therapy, he might be able to walk again."

"Did you want to tell us anything else?" her father asks. "Besides this lad"—he glances at me—"being a potential?"

Hillary's jaw tightens. "What do you want to hear, Dad? That I found someone better than George?"

She casts a derisive look at the man in question. "Yes, I have. I have a man, and I'm happy."

She squeezes my arm again, but at this point, I know to keep my mouth shut.

"That's good," Ronald says, his eyes watering. "We always wanted—"

"—to make sure that I didn't embarrass you," Hillary says. "That I did my duty."

"You say it like it's a bad thing," my grandmother says.

"I think we should let Ronald rest," George says. "Let's go back to the kitchen."

"I'll stay here with my husband," Anne says, approaching the bed. "I'm sure George can help with this Elders business better than I can, since I would've had to call him for you anyway."

"It was nice to see you," Ronald says to Hillary. "I hoped I'd get the chance to before . . ." He swallows.

"I'm sorry you're hurt," Hillary says, her usually expressive face showing almost no emotion. Before they can say anything else, she follows George into the other room.

When we're back in the kitchen, I phase into the Quiet. Then I make my way back to the bedroom and take a closer look at my new set of biological grandparents. I see the familial resemblance. I share

Ronald's blue eyes, and Hillary and I have the shape of his nose in common. And Anne's cheekbones are very much like those of my aunt's.

I don't know how to feel about these people. They disowned my mother and, being Traditionalists, they'd probably find my hybrid self to be some kind of an abomination. I should be angry with them, but for some reason, I'm not. I feel a sense of regret, mixed with sadness. These people managed to alienate their only remaining daughter with their stupid prejudices. Still, in a weird way, I owe my existence to them. Had they not been such assholes to my biological mom, she wouldn't have rebelled and married a Reader to possibly spite these very people.

If I ever see my shrink Liz again, she'll want to talk about this.

Having had enough of staring at my grandparents, I decide to snoop around and find a family album in the second drawer of the ancient oak dresser.

Jackpot.

Leafing through it, I see pictures of Margret. She was a beautiful young woman, though she looks sad in many of these photos. Younger pictures of George, the guy who opened the door, show up throughout the album as well. Is he a relative? But there was a hint that he had been Hillary's suitor or something. Weird.

Time to learn more about that, I decide, and return to the kitchen.

I approach my frozen aunt, who looks as emotionless as before. We need to have a private conversation, so I touch her forehead.

"Darren," Hillary's animated double says. "I was wondering how long it would take for you to pull me in."

"And how did I do, compared to your expectations?"

"You exceeded them all with your patience."

"Right, okay. Can you tell me who the hell he is?" I point at George, making sure I don't accidentally touch the man.

"He's your great-grandmother's cousin's grandson." As she talks, Hillary walks to the stairs in the middle of the house.

"Wait a minute." I follow her up the stairs. "If he's a relative, why did your parents want you to marry him?"

"He's a distant enough relative where it wasn't his blood that I had a problem with. I just didn't care for him one iota." She stops on the second floor and looks around.

I think about George. Height is the only trait we share. He's a bit taller than me, probably six-one. With his brown eyes and hawkish nose, he could just as easily have been Bert's relative. This reminds me of what Hillary said earlier about finding a man, and I smile. Her parents probably thought she was talking about me.

"Would you like to see my old room?" Hillary asks, nodding her head toward the door on the right.

"Of course," I say. "I'd love to."

She gingerly opens the door and walks in, waiting for me to catch up.

"I didn't peg you for a metal head," I say, examining the Metallica posters plastered all over the walls.

"It was a phase," she says, looking around. Her eyes suddenly well up. "I'm sorry. This was a mistake. I think we should go back," she says, but doesn't move. I guess the dingy bed, the stuffed toys, and those posters are bringing back some unpleasant memories.

I feel like an intruder, so to lessen the discomfort, I ask, "What's an Ambassador? And while you're at it, what's an Unencumbered? Also, why did you lie about me?"

Hillary walks up to a desk and sits down in the rotating chair. Then she picks up an old hairbrush and absentmindedly says, "*Unencumbered* is a condescending term Guides came up with when referring to regular people. My circle of friends doesn't use it. The insinuation is that people without powers are not encumbered by the weight of the decisions we, the mighty and chosen ones, have to make. Baloney, if you ask me. The only good thing I can say about the term is that it's better than something like 'Powerless.'"

"Okay, and what does it mean for George to be an Ambassador?" I watch as she runs the brush through her hair.

"An Ambassador is a fancy term for people who do business for the Elders. There aren't many of them, which is why you've never heard of them." She opens the desk drawer and takes out a photo album.

"How many are there?" I ask, watching her.

"I'm not sure. I doubt there's very many, though I don't know much about it. I only recently found out that George became one. I thought he'd grow up to be an Elder, not one of their lackeys, but given his temperament, it figures." She leafs through the pages of the photo album, almost tentatively.

"His temperament?" I walk deeper into the room and almost trip over a dusty teddy bear.

"The Elders are a very solipsistic bunch, and George always held strong opinions about the outside world and its people. The fact that he's here visiting a sick older relative is very typical of him, but no Elder would deign to leave their secret hideout for anyone outside their little circle." She stops on one page and her expression hardens.

"Would they bother helping me then, if they're so self-absorbed?" I inch closer to see the image she's looking at.

"If they think there's something in it for them, sure, but there's only one way to find out what they'll do." She flips the page, preventing me from seeing whatever it was that upset her. "Let's get George to arrange the meeting."

"And we're still pretending to be a couple? I'm not sure how comfortable—"

"No. That lie was for my parents. If they learn the truth about you, they might each get an aneurism." She keeps her finger inside the photo album to save her spot, lifts her eyes from it, and gives me a wink.

"And George is more open-minded?"

"I have no idea, but it doesn't matter. It's pointless to lie to him, and even more so to the Elders. More than that, it can be dangerous. A lie is not a good way to start a relationship." She reopens the album and moves to another page.

"But what if the truth is worse than the lie?"

She stops her leafing. "They have the resources to learn the truth anyway. I wouldn't be surprised if somehow they, or one of their Ambassadors, already know about you. And besides, saying, 'I'm a Guide who doesn't know his heritage,' will simply pique their curiosity."

"So I tell them everything?"

"You can omit a bunch of things—that's not lying—but you should tell them who your mother is and about the Enlightened taking your friends and family, especially since that will likely motivate them to help you. Just don't talk about your Reader father unless you absolutely have to, and don't mention it to George. If they don't know about that, so much the better, but even if they do, why raise a sour topic voluntarily?"

"What about the Super Pusher? Do I tell them about her?"

"I don't know," Hillary says. "Do whatever allows you to best investigate who might be behind this. You can withhold the information at first, like an ace up your sleeve, but if the situation calls for it . . ."

She turns another page, and a pained look overtakes her.

"What is it?" I ask, unable to resist.

"It's a picture of *her*," Hillary says. "Come over here. It's not fair for me to hide it from you."

Ah. She's looking at pictures of her dead sister—my mom.

I approach her and look over her shoulder. Like before, I don't feel anything more than curiosity when I look at pictures of Margret, who, in most of these, looks very young. I can't even begin to understand what Hillary must be feeling as she looks down at these smiling faces.

"She was very pretty," I say uncomfortably.

"I was jealous of her," Hillary says. "She was so beautiful."

I put my hand on her shoulder and just stand there as she slowly turns the rest of the pages.

With an audible sniffle, Hillary jackknifes to her feet. "Okay, let's get back to business." Her voice is overly chipper.

She makes her way back to the kitchen, and I follow, trying not to trip on the carpeted stairs.

"Why don't we bring George in, so your parents can't overhear us?" I suggest when we're back in the kitchen.

"Good idea." She walks over to him.

"Wait. Are you still doing the talking?"

"No, you can do it," she says. "If there's one family trait we share, it's our ability to skirt around the truth."

"Don't forget awesome looks." I'm glad she seems to be back to her normal self, at least outwardly.

"Right, and our supreme modesty."

I chuckle and watch her bring George in. When he materializes, George crosses his arms and looks at us expectantly.

"Darren needs your help," Hillary says. "Darren, please explain your situation to him."

I proceed to tell George the story in the way Hillary and I discussed. I don't mention irrelevant things, such as dating a Reader girl, or things that could get me in trouble, like killing Kyle. I stress the things I suspect Guides would care about, focusing mostly on the fact that Thomas, another Guide, was kidnapped by the Enlightened.

At the mention of the Enlightened, I can tell I have George's undivided attention.

"The Elders will want to hear about this," he says, his eyes gleaming. "The Enlightened fascinate them, and if they took Thomas, of all people—"

"Wait," Hillary says. "How would the Elders even know who Thomas is? He's not exactly powerful."

"We like to keep tabs on Guides who have, or could have in the future, access to powerful Unencumbered individuals."

Hillary looks confused, but I know what George is insinuating. "This is about Thomas being in the Secret Service, isn't it?" I ask.

"Your nephew shares your wit," George says approvingly. "Yes, indeed. The Unencumbered do not get any more powerful than the so-called Leader of the Free World."

"So the rumors are true," Hillary says. "Ambassadors do control human affairs at the Elders' bidding. That's why you're keeping an eye on any potential competition."

"I will not dignify rumors with a response."

"Knowing you, that means yes," Hillary says, frowning.

"All I can say is, if we Guided the Unencumbered, the world would be a better place for it." George smiles at my aunt. I wonder if he still has some kind of feelings for her—assuming he ever had them, that is. He might've also been getting pressure from his family for this alliance.

Hillary snorts. "In that case, I guess you're *not* Guiding them, since the world is turning to shit."

"We're only speaking hypothetically. But you're wrong. The world is getting more peaceful as of late, a happenstance that would imply someone is looking out for everyone's interests."

"Really?" Hillary gives him a disbelieving look. "With all the violence happening everywhere?"

George's smile fades. "Human society is an extremely complex system that would be very difficult, if not close to impossible, to Guide perfectly, especially for a tiny group such as ours. Still, again hypothetically, you are being unfair. Violence has diminished compared to other times in history."

"Violence is down?" Hillary lifts her eyebrows. "Maybe in the Elders' secret hideout, but not in the world I live in."

"That's a common misconception," George says. "The media makes things seem much worse than they really are. Trust me, compared to humanity's turbulent past—a past where no one, hypothetically, Guided the direction of world events—things have steadily improved."

My aunt is wearing a scornful expression. "Oh, please. You consider the Holocaust a decrease in violence?"

"No." George's face tightens. "That horrible event and the nuclear proliferation that soon followed are times when someone, hypothetically, decided to step in to ensure similar events would not repeat themselves."

"But we had those atrocities in Uganda," Hillary argues as I listen in fascination. "And all the acts of terrorism and the wars in the Middle East."

"Extremely complex system, remember?" George leans against a wall and crosses his arms. "If you look at statistics, wars don't happen as often and are resolved with less bloodshed. We haven't had nuclear war. Despots lose their power much faster than ever before, and people don't get tortured by their states as much. Even the murder rate is down."

"How can you say this about torture when the truth about enhanced interrogation just came out?" Hillary glares at him.

"Again, read your history," George says. "Rectal feeding is nothing compared to, say, the rack, which was extremely common in the Middle Ages. Not to mention that until recently, torture was done legally and openly, and now it's a condemned practice that only the fringe—"

"I'm sorry to interrupt," I say, getting tired of this, "but I really think we should get going soon."

"Right," George says, straightening away from the wall. "I tend to get carried away when the subject of history comes up. Hillary, perhaps we can discuss this further once we get to our destination?"

"I'm not going with you," Hillary says.

"You're not?" George and I say in unison.

"I'm staying here, at least until Darren is done."

George looks vaguely disappointed, but says, "I understand and respect your decision, even if I would've liked to talk some more. Also, Mary would've loved to see you."

"Mary is still alive?" Hillary asks. When she sees my questioning look, she adds, "Mary is my grandmother—your great-grandmother."

"She has Alzheimer's, I'm afraid," George says. "But they arrange for her to be brought into the Mind Dimension when she's lucid. This way, her lucidity can last for many, many years."

"That's incredible," I say, impressed both by the strategy and the fact that I have a living great-grandmother. Hillary never talked about her before.

"Family is extremely important to me," George says. "Hillary knows this."

"You better go," my aunt says.

In the uncomfortable silence that follows, I phase out.

Hillary goes into the master bedroom and comes back with Anne.

"You're leaving so soon?" Anne looks at George. "I didn't even get a chance to feed you."

"I'm sorry," George says. "For what it's worth, Hillary will stay here."

Anne's eyes widen.

"It was nice to meet you," I say to Anne.

"He really *is* going to see the Elders," Anne whispers to Hillary. "I thought you—"

"Bye," I say gently and exit the house. I don't envy Hillary this reunion.

George exits after me and walks across the street. I follow him. He gets inside a BMW in the neighbor's driveway and starts the car, then opens the passenger door for me.

"Where to now?" I ask, getting into the passenger's seat.

"The airport," he says.

"Oh, back to Jacksonville?"

"No, my plane is parked at the local airport."

As he drives, I check my phone for updates from Bert. According to Bert's email, in the hours it took Hillary and me to reach Florida, he and Eugene managed to set up the mobile lab.

"This is Pandora," George says when the car stops next to an airfield.

Pandora is a Challenger 600. If a Ferrari had a sister that was a plane, she would be Pandora. Compared to commercial airliners, the plane's small, but for a private jet, it's huge.

A woman is standing next to the plane. She's wearing military-looking boots and a tight leather outfit that makes her look like either Catwoman or a dominatrix. Something odd is sticking out from behind her shoulder, a black handle of some kind. I notice all of this peripherally, because what stands out most is her overly symmetrical face, with piercing gray eyes that seem as weirdly old as George's.

"Kate, this is Darren," George says to her. "He's going to the Island."

"Are you carrying any weapons, Darren?" Kate asks, looking amused.

"Please cooperate with Kate," George says to me. "She's part of our security force."

With that, he waltzes onto the plane.

"No, I'm unarmed," I answer.

Suddenly, the world goes silent, and a second Kate is standing in front of me. She pulled me into the Quiet for some reason.

"Why did—"

Before I can finish my question, she reaches behind her head for that black handle and pulls out an honest-to-God sword. She throws it on the ground, where I get a better look at it. It appears to be one of those katana swords, though I'm no expert when it comes to weapons.

Entranced, I watch Kate bow to me.

As she leaps toward me, my body reacts before my mind can catch up. I move to block the attack, unsuccessfully.

Kate's slender fist goes right into my stomach.

CHAPTER SEVEN

It takes all my willpower not to cry out. I've been hit a lot lately, too much in fact and by a variety of people, but this has to be one of the most debilitating punches yet. Considering Kate's lean build, the hit seems disproportionally painful. If Mike Tyson had hit me, this would make more sense. Pain aside, the place where her hand made contact with my body becomes the focal point of an excruciating, yet numbing sensation. Did she damage an internal organ?

I block her next hit, or at least I try to. When she sees my elbow rising for the block, she taps it with the knuckle of her right index finger, a sly smile touching her eyes.

The result is as familiar as it is unbearable. She hit my funny bone. For the record, there's nothing funny about hitting your funny bone, nor is it a bone. I believe it's actually a nerve that's close to the surface of the elbow region.

The pain reminds me of what she did to my stomach. Did she go for this effect on purpose?

I retreat and she follows me. The way she moves is really strange. Every large movement consists of smaller sub-movements that are pieced together unnaturally. Every little twitch of her body is like a piece in a strange mosaic, all erratic and hard to respond to. For the first time in a while, I have no clue what this style of fighting is, or even whether it's a type of martial arts or a weird, avant-garde dance. Her movements are fractal—which is a mathematical concept that, according to Bert, is responsible for the way most music players' visualizations work, as well as clouds and tree leaves. How does a person learn to move this way?

I move to dodge her right-handed strike to my neck, so she hits me with her left hand instead.

I fall to the ground, my body completely numb.

I wonder whether I'm lucky enough to have already met the Super Pusher. Could Kate be the one? Could she have been Guiding Kyle? That would mean she's about to make me Inert, and afterwards, she'll likely kill me. Given how good she is, I don't understand why she would bother making me Inert first.

Out of the corner of my eye, I see her walking toward her body.

In the next instant, the strange paralysis is gone and I'm back on my feet, the sounds of the world around us again.

She phased us out.

"What was that about?" I ask Kate carefully. I'm cognizant of that sword, which, in the real world, is still sheathed behind her back.

"Weapons can be of different kinds," she says.

"I told you I'm unarmed."

"One's body can be used as a weapon, so I had to test you."

Though it goes against my best interests, I say, "Actually, I can hold my own in a fight, so I'm not sure if you should dismiss me as—"

"My only concern is your potential as a threat to the Elders. Given their capabilities, you do not pose a threat. Now follow me," she says and starts walking toward the plane.

As I follow her, I don't argue about my fighting skills, since winning this argument might result in me not being allowed to see the Elders. Instead, I ask, "Did you have to make that test hurt so much?"

"Inflicting pain was necessary to ensure you weren't pretending to be uncoordinated. Your suffering was an unfortunate side effect." She runs up the small staircase and ducks to enter through Pandora's small, round door.

I follow her inside, making sure I don't accidentally bang my head on the door and thus confirm what she said. Even Caleb, the rudest person I know, never called me uncoordinated.

Once inside, I mumble, "A pretty significant side effect."

"If it makes you feel any better, you weren't actually *that* bad—for a layman," she says, her eyes looking younger for a moment. "There are some Ambassadors whose asses you could kick, though that's not saying much."

Yeah, okay. "Where do I sit?" I look around the Spartan, military-looking fuselage, which, at a glance, has about a dozen seats.

"First, I need you to take this." She pulls something out of her pocket.

I gingerly approach and look at her upturned palm. She's holding a pill bottle.

"What is that? Why should I take it?"

She opens the bottle and fishes out a pill. "It's zolpidem."

"Oh," I say. "Good old zol-cyanide. Why didn't you say so before?"

"It's also known as Ambien." She walks over and grabs a water bottle off the seat near the entrance before returning to me. "It's a sleeping pill," she explains, "and it's harmless."

"You don't want me to know where the Elders live," I guess, remembering the shot Caleb gave me when he kidnapped me to bring me to the Enlightened. "Thanks for making this voluntary."

"Go ahead," Kate says. "Please."

I reach for the pill and the water bottle and proceed to take my medicine.

"Say *aahh*," she says.

Feeling as if I'm five again, I open my mouth. She expertly checks my mouth to make sure I swallowed the pill.

"Now I suggest you sit there." She points at the seat nearest the cockpit, on the right side.

"All set?" George peeks out of the cockpit. He has a serious-looking headset on, so I'm guessing he's piloting this thing.

"I'm ready." I plop down into the chair, which turns out to be very comfy.

George nods and disappears into the cockpit.

I'm determined to fight the effects of the pill. Just because I took the pill doesn't mean I agreed not to uncover this super-secret location. I heard that if you fight Ambien, you might get a high instead, which would be a bonus.

It takes us about ten minutes to get into the air. With every passing minute, keeping my eyes open becomes harder. I yawn and decide I can still fight the effects of the drug with my eyes closed; it'll just make the hallucinations that much richer.

I close my eyes and focus on staying as alert as possible.

My consciousness goes out like a snuffed flame.

* * *

When I wake up, we're no longer in the air.

Great. There goes my plan of trying to figure out where I am.

I reach for my phone, but it's missing.

And there goes my idea of using my phone's GPS to pin this location.

I unbuckle my seatbelt and check the plane. It's empty, but the door is open.

I exit the plane and find myself in a giant forest meadow that seems to have been repurposed as an airport. Several planes are here, including George's. There's a single-piston Malibu Mirage a few dozen feet away, and a twin-engine Super 700 Aerostar a little farther. I'm planning to buy myself a private jet one day, so I did a little research, in case that wasn't clear. Still, even I don't recognize some of the other makes, except for one—Northrop Grumman B-2 Spirit, also known as the Stealth Bomber. It belongs here, among these private jets, about as much as a lion would on a rabbit farm.

George is standing barefoot in the grass, doing some kind of stretching exercise. He's changed into a gray, homemade-looking poncho. It's drab, but has the feel of a traditional outfit, if the tradition was to take a potato sack, put holes in it, and wear it. The effect is that George now strongly resembles a hippie.

Noticing me, he says, "I'm glad you're up. That Ambien really knocked you out. Kate and I couldn't wake you up after we landed. Just as well you got some sleep, though, since nothing happens on the Island at night. We should get pulled into the Elders' Mind Dimension soon."

"What time is it?" I ask, my throat dry.

"Early in the morning," George answers. "Last I checked, it was six-thirty."

"Good morning then," I say. "They'll just pull us in? No hello?"

"Someone might greet us, but not the Elders. You will never see them outside the Mind Dimension. They do everything they consider stressful—and thus unhealthy—exclusively there," he says with a hint of disapproval in his tone.

"When will this Mind Dimension conversation take place?" I ask.

"Soon. Could be in a minute, could be in an hour. It depends on when they all wake up, and they don't use alarm clocks."

"Where's Kate?"

"She went to stretch her legs."

I lick my dry lips. "Do you have anything to eat or drink?"

George points downward, at a basket sitting on a piece of cloth. "There's some breakfast."

I examine the cloth. It looks like it's made of the same potato sack material as his outfit. If he were to lie on it, he'd blend in like a ninja. "You were planning a picnic?"

The basket, which is just a plastic crate, is filled with cheese, bread, cold cuts, and those little single-use condiments they have at fast-food places. Drink-wise, there's some sparkling water and a couple bottles of beer. Beer in the morning?

"I knew there was a chance we'd have to wait, so I came prepared," George explains at my look.

I sit down on the cloth and make myself a sandwich. George joins me on the ground and mimics my legs-akimbo pose.

"I wanted to apologize," he says, "about Kate attacking you, and about the secrecy."

I shrug. "She wanted to make sure I couldn't use my body as a weapon against the Elders, and I'm not too surprised that this place is a secret."

"I'm glad you understand. I think it's always bad to start a new relationship in the spirit of distrust."

"Well, for what it's worth, I don't trust you either, and I trust the Elders, people I haven't met, even less."

"This is precisely why I wanted to take this chance to talk to you," he says. "If there's anything I can do to repair this—"

"Ever the Ambassador, huh?" I give him a sardonic look.

"Actually, that title is probably misleading, as my actual role doesn't require me to be diplomatic in the way that the Unencumbered ambassadors are. I just want to foster goodwill because you're a relative and I feel like you're a good person."

Huh. Well, this is my chance.

"You know," I say carefully, "I was curious about something. Hillary told me of a rumor. She said the Elders can Split into the Mind Dimension while already in the Mind Dimension, thus reaching a different version—"

"I know about those rumors," George says, his eyes looking even older than before. "I really wish you hadn't chosen this topic as a means to forge trust, because I'm afraid I can't substantiate those rumors."

"I don't think they're just rumors." My sandwich tastes dry, so I add a tiny packet of mayo to it.

"What you described is a subject that we, the Ambassadors, do not discuss. That's all I'm allowed to say on the issue." He looks genuinely regretful.

"Great." Mira-like sarcasm creeps into my voice. "I feel a strong urge to trust you coming on already."

George twists off the cap of one of the beers and takes a sip. "I know how this will sound, but ask me *anything* else, and this time, I'm sure I'll be of more help."

"Okay. This one is another rumored ability." I add extra cheese to my sandwich and take a hungry bite.

"Good." He offers me his Guinness. "There aren't any more abilities I'm restricted from discussing."

I fight my instinct to refuse the beer, and instead accept the bottle, taking a sip. Even though Guinness, with its soup-like texture, is probably my least favorite beer, a welcome wave of relaxation spreads through my body. I hope this little bonding activity will cause George to rethink his stance on not telling me about Level 2.

Sharing beer like this reminds me of when Bert and I shared a forty of Crazy Horse, which I later learned wasn't beer, but malt liquor. That day became known as the time Bert and I woke up at the Kappa Alpha Theta sorority house without knowing how we'd gotten there or why we'd gone. If either of us got lucky that day, no girl came forward to admit it. Then again, us being teenagers, we assumed they didn't step forward because they didn't want it known that they had broken the law by sleeping with underage boys. And yes, in case it wasn't clear, Bert and I had a strange college experience.

"I heard it's possible to control where you appear when you Split into the Mind Dimension," I say and pass the bottle back. "Are you allowed to discuss *that*?"

George takes the bottle, finishes it, and gives me an evaluating look. "Under normal circumstances, I wouldn't tell you about it, but I'll break the rules this one time."

I give him an encouraging nod, doing my best to look grateful, and take another bite of my sandwich.

"The skill is indeed real," he says. "It's something only the Elders, the Ambassadors, and those in our inner circle know about."

"Is it an innate skill only a few possess, or is it something that can be taught?"

"I see where you're going with this," he says. "Yes, I can teach you—I wouldn't have told you of its existence if I weren't willing to do that—but be warned: it's a skill that requires much practice."

"Gentlemen," Kate's teasing voice intrudes. She sounds as if she left unsaid, *And I use that term loosely.*

"I'm glad you're here," George says, looking up at her. "I was just about to teach Darren how to Teleport."

Kate's eyes widen for the briefest moment, but if she has a problem with this development, she doesn't voice it.

"Do you want to partake in his first practice?" George asks. "Or are you hungry?"

"I already ate." She crosses her arms in front of her chest. "I'll help."

I swallow the last of my sandwich and look at George. He appears either thoughtful or constipated; it's hard to tell the two apart.

Then everything goes silent. Instead of sitting on the ground, I'm now standing off to the side. The warm tropical breeze is gone, and I realize I'm in the Quiet. So that's what that look was about; he was Splitting.

George is looking at my feet calculatingly. "Okay. I'd say about a meter. Do you agree?"

"I don't understand the metric system," I say, "but even if I did, a meter from where to where?"

"I'm sorry," he says. "I've been told I'm a terrible teacher. From your body, of course."

I look at my frozen self. He/I am still sitting on the blanket. We're about three feet apart, plus or minus a couple of inches.

"Why does it matter?" I ask.

"You'll see," he says and walks up to his frozen self. Before I can ask any more questions, he phases out.

"Kate, be a dear and bring out a few crates from the plane," George says.

I hear the sound of a cricket coming from the grass. As Kate walks toward the plane, she purposefully steps on where the sound is coming from. The little guy is silenced. Is that her way of hinting at her disapproval? I sure hope it's George, and not me, whom she symbolically crushed.

"Don't move," George says when I try to get up.

Complying, I ask, "Why not?"

"All will be revealed in a moment."

Kate returns with a couple of plastic boxes, exactly like the one that housed our breakfast.

"Over here, right?" George asks, pointing to a spot three feet away from me.

"You mean where I was standing in the Quiet? That is, the Mind Dimension?" I ask.

"No, he means the place where you had a gynecological exam," Kate says, earning a stern look from George that stops her from chuckling.

"Just an inch to the right, I think," I say to George, directing him to where I materialized.

George places the crate in that spot and looks as though he's concentrating. In the next instant, I'm in the Quiet again, only this time it's different.

I'm not standing where the crate is; I'm standing a foot away from it.

"Let's make a note of that," George says and phases us out again.

The next crate goes to the new place my body 'chose' to phase into.

After he pulls me in, I show up three feet away from the last place.

"So I show up in different places," I say on the fourth crate. "How does this teach me Teleportation? Cool term, by the way."

"You're already Teleporting on a subconscious level," George explains. "What else could be preventing you from showing up with your legs inside these crates? Let's keep doing this and see what happens."

I have noticed that showing up in the Quiet always had a convenient quality to it. In a crowded room, I always showed up in an empty spot rather than inside someone's immobile body. I never gave it much thought, though. Maybe I should have.

I let George continue with the lesson, if that's what this is. With each crate, I show up elsewhere. Ten crates later, I'm ending up around fifteen feet away from my frozen body. It's a record of sorts, but it by no means gets me closer to controlling the skill.

"Let's move on to the next phase," George says. "Kate, would you be so kind as to help?"

Kate looks me over, then reaches for her sword. Weapon unsheathed, she walks around the crates in a random pattern. She stays within a tight six-or-seven-foot radius.

"I'm about to pull her in," George says. "She'll continue walking aimlessly with her sword in the Mind Dimension. If you show up in its range, you'll be made Inert. Good luck."

"Wait," I say, but the world goes silent again.

I look around. Kate is in the distance. She stops waving her sword when she sees me. My frozen self and the pairs of Georges and Kates are a good twenty feet away from me. The animated version of George smiles at me as I cross the distance.

"Your range is increasing," he says when I reach him.

"But I just randomly showed up there. I didn't control it."

"This is how it starts," he says. "If you do this sort of thing for a while, you'll learn to control it."

"About how long before I can actually do something useful with it?" I ask.

"The distance you can travel and how fast you can master this skill all depend on your Reach." At the mention of Reach, George looks as uncomfortable as I do when I say hello to someone at work and that person just keeps walking past me. I guess even among Ambassadors, the topic of Reach is outside polite conversation.

"Look over there," Kate says, pointing at something in the distance.

A group of about a dozen people are approaching us, though they're currently frozen in the Quiet.

"Some kind of welcoming committee?" George asks.

"That's strange." Kate frowns in their direction. "Why not just pull us in?"

"Let's find out," George says and walks over to his frozen self.

The sounds come back, and the three of us wait for the approaching people to reach us. They're wearing the same grayish potato-sack garments as George. They all appear to be mostly in their mid-thirties, except for one older guy who might be fifty or so. Even with that guy, they all seem too young to be dubbed the Elders. Considering they're walking barefoot, their pace is brisk.

"Martin," George says when the people are within earshot, "to what do we owe this warm welcome?"

The balding, white-haired big man takes out a gun and unceremoniously aims it at me. A woman to his right also takes out a weapon and points it at me, and then another does the same and another, until finally, the entire crew is aiming weapons at me.

"I am sorry to interrupt your breakfast," the guy—Martin—says. "We are here on the behest of the Elders."

CHAPTER EIGHT

"Before you get any ideas," Martin says calmly, looking at me, "there are snipers hidden in the trees. You will be shot if you show us any hostility. Trying to Split to make anyone here Inert will be interpreted as hostile."

Ignoring the hammering of my heart, I stay quiet while Kate just stands there, tapping her foot on the grass as though she's bored.

George says, "Martin, this is overkill. With Kate beside him, our unarmed guest poses no threat."

"You think I have nothing better to do than to be here?" Martin says. "I have my orders."

What the hell is going on? George seems to understand what these people want, and their presence doesn't seem to concern him, which is reassuring. So why am I being treated as though I'm dangerous?

Before I can analyze this further, I find myself about ten feet away from our belligerent hosts, who are now frozen in place. Someone pulled me into the Quiet, and I guess due to my recent training, I showed up at a random location farther away than normal.

I look at where my frozen body is. Kate and George are standing near their frozen selves. I must have been pulled in last.

I look at the new person on the scene as I close the distance.

The guy is only slightly older than me. Instead of the hippie outfit, he's shirtless and dressed in a pair of swim trunks. He's wearing a pair of those 'barefoot' shoes in lieu of actually walking barefoot, as everyone else seems to be doing. I've seen this specific brand of shoes, Vibram's Five Fingers, on Bert's feet the one and only time we ever went to the gym together during lunch.

It's not the guy's clothes or his lean muscular frame that catch my attention, though. It's his eyes.

As I approach him, I hold his gaze for a moment. His eyes make George's seem like those of an infant's.

"You must be Darren," the strange guy says, his voice too melodious for his buff body.

"Hi," I say unimaginatively.

"I noticed you Teleported when I pulled you in. That was unexpected."

"I'm sure it was a knee-jerk reaction," George says, giving me a look that says, *Don't worry, I'll cover for you.*

"I desperately hope what George says is true," the guy says, "and that you're not considering violence. They *will* shoot you if something happens to me. That wasn't a bluff."

"Darren," Kate says, "this is Frederick, and I assure you he isn't bluffing."

"Great," I say. "Nice to meet you, Fred. I wasn't thinking of doing anything violent just yet. But keep threatening me, and we'll see about the future."

Kate cringes at my words. Maybe I could've been more diplomatic. I think Mira's rubbed off on me. There goes my promise to be all charming.

To my surprise, Frederick doesn't look mad. If anything, a subtle smile touches his weird eyes. After a pause, he says, "If I insist you call me Frederick, it will just make you want to call me Fred that much more. So please, call me Fred."

"What are you, a shrink?" I ask.

My shrink, Liz, has never tried anything like this to deal with my love of pushing buttons. Grudgingly, I notice my desire to call him Fred has lessened. Then I decide to do it anyway; I bet he's double-bluffing me.

"I wonder whether I was like you once," Frederick says to no one in particular. "So carefree, almost a blank slate."

"Are you high?" I look him over. "Is smoking grass part of the shtick? It sure would match these outfits."

"Frederick is one of the Elders," George says. "He really means it when he says he can't remember the time when he was your age."

"I know I look as though I'm your peer, but looks can be deceiving," Frederick says. "For each day of Unencumbered existence, I receive at least a century of experience in the Mind Dimension."

I'm not sure why, but I believe him. My head spins when I try to imagine it. A hundred years in a single day? I know it's theoretically possible. I could, at any given moment, phase into the Quiet and, in theory, spend a long time there. By my last estimate, that time is at least twice my age, so forty-two years.

Of course, I never reached the true limit of my Reach, so that time estimate could be anywhere from two to ten times greater. But let's just go with forty years. I've been alive for twenty-one years, and it feels like a long time to have existed. What would I be like in forty years? I have no clue. What would someone be like after a hundred years? I have no idea either. But here's the kicker: a century is a single day for this guy.

"Surely that's a lot to take in," Frederick says. "I sincerely hope you understand why we have to be so watchful when it comes to our safety."

"No," I say. "Not really."

"Because we have millennia of life experiences to lose," he explains. "Does that answer satisfy you?"

"I guess." I frown at him.

"Good," he says. "We best go. Leave your weapons here."

Kate takes out her sword and drops it. George pulls out a knife and a gun and places them next to her sword. I don't have anything, so I just look at them and shrug.

Satisfied, Frederick says, "Follow me," and walks toward the trees in the distance.

For about five minutes, we walk through the woods in complete silence, but when I spot white marble statues standing between the trees, I have to ask, "What are those?"

"Ah, that," Frederick says. "That's something my brother, Louis, made a long time ago."

They are so well made and so detailed that they remind me of people frozen in the Quiet. They look as though they might come to life. Maybe that's the effect they're supposed to have.

"Wait, that's you," I say, pointing to a statue on my right.

"That's actually my brother. I am over there." Frederick points to a statue off to the side.

"Are you two twins?" I ask, unable to tell the statues apart.

"Indeed," Frederick says. "The only identical twins among the Elders."

"And these are the rest of the Elders?" I ask, looking the statues over. They're all interesting-looking people, varying in age. What really stands out is the fact that only a few of them could be considered elderly. Frederick's youthful exterior is not the exception, but the rule.

"Indeed they are," Frederick says. "My brother wanted to immortalize us in marble. I think he was subtly trying to taunt me."

"Are these real?" I ask. "I mean, do they only exist here in the Mind Dimension? Did he create them—"

"No," Frederick says. "Louis had one of the Ambassadors convince a dozen sculptors to relocate here, to the Island. He then worked on these statues for decades in the Mind Dimension, which of course was less than a second for the sculptors and the rest of the world. When Louis was happy with his Mind Dimension creations, he Guided each sculptor to recreate one of them. When our Mind Dimension session was over, the sculptors got to work in the real world. I'm part of the minority who think the originals in the Mind Dimension were much better."

I let my imagination run wild as we walk farther.

After about ten minutes, the tree line abruptly ends. We're at the top of a hill. I look down to take in the sight.

"Breathtaking, isn't it?" Frederick says. He probably noticed my eyes widen at the view.

I nod. 'Breathtaking' doesn't do it justice.

To our right is a beach that stretches for miles, but that's not what caught my attention. The white sand and the clear blue water—all these things are amazing in a 'perfect vacation postcard' sort of way, especially frozen as they are in the Mind Dimension. But I've seen the surf and the white clouds frozen like this during my visit to the Cayman Islands.

The large village to the right is also not it, though under different circumstances, the strange and colorful homes would be fascinating. Again, you can witness something like this in some European countryside, as I have.

It's not even the variety of plant life—the palm trees by the beach, the giant pine trees that make up the forest east of the village, or the tropical flora to the west. Though I've never seen this combo in one place before, I have seen these things in isolation.

No, what Frederick's talking about is the castle. Except it's not really a castle.

'Castle' is just the first word to come to mind.

This *thing* looks as though someone asked a fancy modern architect to build a medieval castle. Think about those cool buildings all over New York, like the place I plan to move into on 8 Spruce Street. Now imagine a Disney castle built in that style. The towers are done using some warped geometry. Some of the walls are glass, while others are made of some sort of futuristic-looking bricks. Other parts are made of different-sized metal plates that fit together like an eccentric jigsaw puzzle. The more I stare at it, the more mesmerized I become.

Realizing Frederick is waiting for me to comment, I say, "I'm rarely at a loss for words."

"This place is sacred. That's all there is to it," Kate says, her often-teasing tone reverent.

"It's meant to impress," George says, "and that it does."

"Make sure you all tell Gustav how impressed you are," Frederick says, that sneaky smile touching his eyes again. "It will give him pleasure."

"An Elder built this?" I ask.

"Yes. In the same sense as the pharaohs built the pyramids." Without further explanation, he hurries down the dirt path that leads to the castle.

"Does this thing have a name?" I ask, fighting my awe.

"Outside the Island, we call it the Elders' Keep," George says. "But here, it's just the Castle."

Kate follows Frederick, and George gestures for me to follow her.

I take a mental snapshot of the place as I hurry down to the valley below.

As I get closer, the sheer size of the structure hits me. The Castle dwarfs some of the skyscrapers we have in Tribeca.

"George," I say over my shoulder, "how can this place be secret?"

"The Elders have their ways," he says, sounding almost mischievous.

I'm not sure what impresses me more: the architectural achievement or the Elders' ability to keep such a thing secret.

Standing right under the Castle, I feel small and insignificant, and I wonder whether that's the intended effect. The gates are wide open, so I follow everyone inside.

The fountain in the center of the courtyard is frozen in the middle of a majestic water display. In general, splashing water looks very cool when stopped mid-air. In this fountain, the effect is emphasized, making the droplets look like multifaceted diamonds.

Surrounding the fountain are over a dozen familiar-looking people. Some are sitting on the edges of the marble fountain border, while others are just standing around. I recognize them from the statues I saw earlier.

They must be the Elders.

Every one of their ancient eyes is on me, staring so intently that I fleetingly wonder whether they have powers I haven't yet dreamed of, like X-ray vision. After what I've seen, I'd be only mildly surprised.

"George, Kate, feel free to pull in any friends you've missed since your last visit," Frederick says, clearly dismissing them.

Silently, my companions leave.

The stares continue long after George and Kate are out of earshot. They seem to be allowing each other the honor of speaking first, a condition I usually call a 'politeness deadlock.'

"So, Elderly ladies and gentlemen," I say, deciding to break the silence. "What's up with all those guns your people are pointing at me outside the Mind Dimension?"

CHAPTER NINE

"It's a rather unfortunate situation, for sure, but our safety demands it," says an older-looking Elder. He appears to be in his mid-fifties, but his bushy salt-and-pepper beard might be adding a few years.

"Gustav is ever diplomatic, whilst I am not," says a woman with a face whiter than the marble of her statue. She's stunning, despite being at least ten years older than me in biological years. Just like with all of them, her eyes betray a much longer lifespan. "We know what you are."

My heart sinks. I can guess what she's talking about, but I still ask, "What do you mean, what I am?"

"Victoria, dear, please refrain from any xenophobic remarks," Gustav says. "What he is has nothing to do with our precautions."

"If I may," says Louis, Frederick's identical twin. "Victoria is not entirely wrong. There's a correlation between his nature and our concerns."

"I see a correlation between life experience and verboseness," I put in.

Frederick's subtle smile returns, and his brother actually chuckles.

"You're right, lad," says Gustav. "Let me get to the point. We know that your father was a Leacher. That, in and of itself, is not why we took precautions. If anything, it's why we have taken the risk to see you at all. We took precautions because we know you visited the Leacher compound in Brooklyn, New York, on several occasions."

"Twice," Frederick corrects. "That's not exactly 'several.'"

"Right, but the compound was, until recently, run by a man named Jacob—a man who hated Guides with a passion," Victoria adds and gives me a sensuous smile.

Everyone goes silent for a moment. They also avoid eye contact with me, creating a pretty uncomfortable situation.

I can't believe how well informed they are, especially for people who live on an island that's who knows how far from New York. I'm tempted to tell them that far from being in league with Jacob, I was instrumental in his downfall, but I don't. That information is intimately linked with Kyle's death, and the person who used Kyle as her puppet might well be in front of me now.

"The others are being polite, but I will come out and say it: we need those guns in the likely case that you work for the Leachers," says the one Elder who doesn't look much like his statue. His statue made him look as though he were in his late twenties, but in person, I'd guess him to be a decade older. He's also much thinner than the statue, and without the hat the statue had on, his bald head is on full display, with small tufts of long, mousy hair tucked behind his ears.

"You have to forgive Alfred," Frederick says. "He's almost neurotically blunt."

"I know my history, so I am best qualified to speak on these matters," Alfred says pedantically. "Leachers want us dead. Someone who's been to their compound would have been exposed to their propaganda."

I wonder whether I can exploit their animosity for the Readers. They might want to help me when they find out that 'Leachers' kidnapped people I care about, including Thomas, a Guide in the Secret Service.

"He seems like a young man with a brain," Frederick says. "I am sure a little propaganda couldn't have done much damage."

"Propaganda requires respect for authority," I say. "I prefer arguments based on reason."

A few more faces warm up, but Alfred doesn't look amused.

"We don't all share Alfred's paranoia," Louis says. "If we all thought you were working for the Leachers, you wouldn't have gotten off that plane."

"My brother is right," Frederick says. "As I mentioned before, we know of your mixed bloodline. We also know that your aunt, Hillary Taylor, trusts you."

"I didn't come here wishing you any harm," I say. "And that's the truth."

"I concede that your heritage mitigates the risk," Alfred says, "but it's still too great."

"Allow me to play devil's advocate, dear Alfred," Louis says. "Let's say he *is* a Leacher agent."

"Which I'm not," I interject.

"But assuming you are," Louis says calmly, "our overall objectives when it comes to Leachers can still be served."

"And those objectives are?" I ask, trying to hide my excitement. If they ask me to turn on the Readers, it could be a great segue into asking for help against the Enlightened.

"We want to make peace with them, of course," Frederick says. "So, even if you are working for them, you can still be persuaded to bring them our offer of goodwill."

I blink. "You want to be friends with them?" I hope I don't sound as disappointed as I feel.

"Maybe being friends is too much to hope for, but we need to establish an amicable relationship with them. We don't want to repeat any of our not-so-ancient history that so worries Alfred," says another older-looking Elder.

"We want to coexist," says yet another man. "We want them to know that our groups existing is not a zero-sum game."

"It sounds like a pretty old problem," I say, frowning. "What makes you think I can help solve it?"

"Ah, but don't you see that in a very real way, you were born for such an endeavor?" Gustav asks.

"Indeed, no one is better suited to bridge this unfortunate divide," says Frederick.

I consider this. It's great that they think I could be helpful—it means they're unlikely to actually shoot me—but this peace with Readers isn't compatible with what I wanted to ask them.

"You know, if you want to be friends with them, you might consider calling them Readers rather than Leachers," I say. "It's a lot less insulting."

"That's it," Frederick says. "You're getting in the spirit of it already. I shall call them Readers from now on and encourage the others to do so as well."

"I concur," Alfred says. "Though I must ask, if you are not here on the behest of the *Readers*, then why did you come?"

"Umm," I mumble, trying to figure out how much I can share with them.

How would they react to me blurting out all the business with the Super Pusher? If the Super Pusher *is* in this crowd, how would she respond? I also don't know how to best introduce the whole 'the Enlightened kidnapped my peeps' situation. I get a sneaking feeling they might not want to help me if I broach the subject, since they want peace with the Readers and helping me storm the inner sanctum of the most powerful of Readers isn't exactly friendly. But what pretext should I give them for being here?

I decide to try a basic approach and say, "I want to learn from you."

Some of the warmth disappears from most of their faces.

"Darren, Darren," says Gustav, shaking his head. "You must know we've had millennia to get very good at reading people's expressions, so I am sure it is as obvious to the others as it is to me that you are hiding something."

"I—"

Before I can finish my sentence, the world goes away.

* * *

The bright colors are gone. Everything is gone. I feel as though I'm falling into an abyss. Actually, that's not correct. I feel as though I've ceased to exist.

I recognize this lack of feeling.

This is Level 2.

But how did I just reach it after so many failed attempts?

Struggling to not freak out about not feeling my body, not even something as little as my left earlobe, I concentrate on the neural network patterns I was able to perceive the last time I was here—the patterns that make up other minds.

There is one quite 'close' to me, though distance is a misnomer here. A dozen patterns are also slightly 'farther away.' I have to assume those are the Elders. The nearest pattern is alive, with its synapses, for lack of a better term, firing, while the farther ones are static.

Suddenly, the active pattern appears nearer to the frozen ones.

The dynamic pattern begins enveloping one of the frozen ones.

A familiar voice in my head states, "Darren, don't trust—"

Before I can receive the rest of that sentence, the enveloping is complete, and my senses return.

* * *

"You what?" asks Gustav.

"Nothing," I say, my head spinning.

I think I understand part of what just happened. I showed up in Level 2 because one of the Elders accidentally pulled me in. Perhaps he or she wanted to Guide me to make me do their bidding but ended up pulling me in instead. I figured that would happen when one Level-2-capable person tried to Guide another Level-2 initiate. If I'm right, then who just tried Guiding me? And what did they want to make me do?

I look over every Elder. Their faces reveal nothing. Whoever did it is very good at controlling his or her expression. Then again, given how experienced these people are, I'm not surprised.

I assumed that the Super Pusher knew about, or suspected, my Level 2 capabilities. Otherwise, why bother using my friends to try to kill me at Kyle's funeral? She could've leveraged Level 2 against me and had me kill myself—a much cleaner solution. So this implies that whoever just pulled me into Level 2 is *not* the Super Pusher.

It would be great to talk to this person, if only I knew who it was.

Now the part that I don't get—that voice in my head. It was Mimir; I'm pretty sure of *that*. He was warning me, again—that part is obvious. But whom was he warning me against? Why? Dread spreads through my body as I recall what almost happened the last time Mimir warned me about something. Did he want to say, "Don't trust the Elders," or "Gustav," or "anybody?"

"Are you all right, lad?" Gustav asks. "You look distraught."

"I'm overwhelmed," I say, happy he gave me an out. "You kind of ganged up on me with all this."

"Say no more," Gustav says. "I hope I speak for everyone when I say that this conversation can continue at another time."

"I agree. It would be very helpful for Darren to see the Celebration before we continue," Frederick says.

"Indeed," Gustav says. "Surely he will be more amicable once he sees our way of life."

"Just please promise to think on it," Alfred says. "Think about becoming a special Ambassador—our liaison with the Readers."

I nod and try to look more out of it so they'll leave me alone. Under the circumstances, looking confused comes easily.

"If we want to impress the young gentleman, why don't I show him around?" Victoria offers. "I know all the good spots."

"Remember, we have the Celebration preparations to attend to," one of the older Elders says with slight disapproval.

"Of course," she says. "Please, follow me, Darren."

"Nice meeting you all," I say and follow Victoria as she leads me away from the fountain.

I feel slightly relieved. If I assume that Mimir was telling me not to trust a specific person, rather than, say, raw fish, then statistically speaking, the person he wanted to warn me against is one of the Elders. Leaving them puts me in relative safety, assuming Victoria is not the Super Pusher. But she, of course, could be. I did randomly decide to call the Super Pusher a *she*, and Victoria does embody femininity.

People claim that some women can walk seductively. I always thought that was just a figure of speech. I mean it's true some girls' butts look good in certain clothes, and when they walk, it looks hot. Some women sway their hips as they strut, which also looks appealing. But 'seductive' implies a certain premeditation, as though a girl is moving in a specific manner to provoke a specific reaction. I never noticed that before, but I think this is exactly what Victoria is doing. And I must say, the effect her walk is having on me is very similar to when I watch Mira undress, especially when Victoria leads me up a wide staircase.

Thinking of Mira forces me to do the right thing. I unglue my eyes from Victoria's legs and focus on the other wonders of the Castle.

"What are your interests?" she asks over her shoulder.

"What do you mean?" I force my eyes to stay above her neckline.

"We have a great library I can show you if you like to read. We have a glass-blowing studio, a couple of rooms with different sculptures and gardens, rooms full of portraits in different styles, mechanical inventions—"

"This place sounds like the Metropolitan Museum of Art." My concerns momentarily give way to wonder.

"The good people at the Met would sell their souls to have even a fraction of our masterpieces, as would any science museum. Aside from things done outside the Island, we have our own achievements on display, creations that chronicle the span of—"

"Some of the works of art you're offering to show me were done by the Elders?" I look at a gorgeous suit of armor standing in a corner by a majestic floor-to-ceiling window.

"Yes, most, in fact. Also books, music, and—"

"How can you bring a book you wrote inside the Mind Dimension into the real world?" I fleetingly wonder if this is her strategy, to distract me from being wary. If so, it's kind of working.

"We don't always," she says. "Sometimes the books just exist so that we can read them once. Come, let me show you how it works."

She leads me down a corridor and into a huge room filled with manual typewriters.

"This is one of the rooms where I like to write sometimes." She takes me into an adjacent room, which appears to be a humongous computer room with around two hundred frozen people sitting at their workstations.

"You Guide them to type out your books?" I guess. "And you use the manual typewriters for yourselves since you can't use computers?"

"Indeed. We find it easier to Guide a single person to write a single page from the manuscript. Once all the pages are typed out, a special computer program combines the pages into one book. This way we can have a book ready and in the library by the next day's Session." As she talks, she walks through the rows of workstations, topping her earlier sexy walk with a worse, or better, one, depending on how you look at it.

To stop her temptingly swaying hips from distracting me, I focus on my awe at the image of books being written so fast. Then, not for the first time, I feel a strong pang of guilt. Mira, Thomas, and my moms are still in those vans, unconscious, and being taken to the Temple against their will. I shouldn't find room in my heart for wonderment, and I definitely shouldn't be checking out another woman's ass.

Realizing I've been silent too long, I ask, "So the paintings are done the same way? You draw them and then a painter is Guided to recreate them?"

"When we bother doing so, yes. Though sometimes it takes a couple of painters, and sadly, sometimes the results are not the same as the original." She waves for me to follow her and briskly walks out.

"I find the idea of works of art that exist only fleetingly in the Mind Dimension sad." I quicken my pace to stay within earshot of her.

"If you became our Ambassador, you'd get to be in on our Sessions from time to time. That means you'd get to enjoy some of these creations for decades before they disappear." Her smile makes sexual promises. "Sometimes you appreciate something more when you know it will be gone shortly after its creation. For years, I created sand paintings inspired by Tibetan monks. Not a single one appeared outside the Mind Dimension."

"A shame," I say as we practically run through the next room—the one with the manual typing machines.

"Despite what Frederick and some of the others hope, life itself is like art. We exist and our minds develop, becoming beautiful patterns over time—the ultimate works of art in a way. After life is over, they are gone. The ultimate shame." She waits for me next to the door that leads back into the corridor.

"That's pretty depressing." In a bout of chivalry, I open and hold the door for her. "What is this hope of Frederick's you mentioned? It sounds intriguing."

"Despite the extreme longevity we, the Elders, get to enjoy, Frederick is afraid of dying one day." As she walks through, she brushes her manicured fingers over my hand.

I don't know why, but my whole body gets covered in gooseflesh at the light touch of her nails. Unwilling to show her my discomfort, I continue talking evenly. "That's reasonable. Who wants to die? If there was a way not to, I'd take it in a heartbeat."

"Then you're going to be one of *them.*" She waits for me to exit and walks down the corridor at a slightly slower pace. "The ones I call the dreamers."

"The dreamers?" I try not to get distracted by what looks like a painting by Rembrandt on the corridor wall.

"Yes. They believe that immortality can be achieved in our lifespan, or at least biological longevity that goes beyond the current hundred-if-you're-lucky years." She stops next to a large door.

"This is something my friend Bert likes to talk about," I say, nodding. "And from what I understand, it could happen. There's a bunch of biotech research that—"

"Please don't go on. I do hate those boring details. You risk sounding like Frederick and the others." Victoria places her hand on a door handle. "I think that the search for biological immortality is as foolish as the one for the immortality of the mind, be that with uploading human minds to computers or something more exotic. Having an end to life gives context and meaning to it."

"I won't argue with you," I say, "except to ask that if you feel this way, why do you join the Elders in living a hundred years in a day?"

"Ah, that. Would you like to see my latest project?" She twists the door handle. "It might answer your question. It's the result of the better part of a century of painstaking research."

"Sure, I'd love to."

With a flourish, she swings the door open and steps inside, the movement as seductive as her walk.

I follow her in and stop, my breath catching. My eyes drift from one corner of the room to the other. Fear for my life is completely gone, replaced with another emotion, one just as primordial.

When I can speak, I say, "What the—"

"I quite proudly call this *Victoria Sutra.*" She sweeps her hand out in an arc.

I do my best not to blush. Grown men don't blush, or do they? This room is not something I'd expect to find in a museum, unless it was the museum of sex. The 'art pieces' are a mixed bag. There are statues—some of the Elders, some of the people who are holding me at gunpoint outside the Mind Dimension, and some of strangers. The sculptor has captured them in varying, mid-coitus positions. Almost all of them feature Victoria in some tantalizing way. I have to peel my curious eyes from one particularly interesting piece that features a naked, masculine-looking woman, doing something with Victoria that reminds me of a cross between wrestling and sixty-nine.

There are also paintings following the same motif. Some are abstract, and some are so realistic they could've come from the pages of Penthouse.

"I assume that bookshelf is filled with erotica?" I ask with a chuckle that comes out sounding more nervous than I meant it to be.

"Of course," she says, giving me a sly smile. "Let me show you some of my more special creations."

Before I can reply, she walks over to a large dresser and picks up a flute. It seems innocuous enough, especially given that it's not penis-shaped, which would've fit the feel of this room better. It's just a simple instrument made of polished red wood, no pun intended.

"Close your eyes," she says. "Something will happen when I begin playing, and when it does, I want it to be clear that it's the music causing it. I don't want you to think the cause is somehow related to my lips moving in a certain way, or from my body movements as I hold the instrument."

Cryptic, but hell, I'm curious. I close my eyes, even though this feels like a childhood 'open your mouth and close your eyes' prank.

Silence follows and my earlier excitement dissipates as worry creeps back in. I peek through my eyelashes. If she's about to attack me, I want to know about it, but no. In the moment I was sightless, she merely raised the instrument to her mouth. I stop peeking and stand there, waiting for whatever will happen next.

When she starts playing the flute, it just sounds like a beautiful melody, but then I feel myself reacting in the strangest way. At first, I think it might be a coincidence, but it's not.

The music is giving me an erection. No, that's an oversimplification. The song is making me super horny. No, still too crude. I get progressively more and more aroused as the music goes on. Yes, that's it. The whole thing is reminiscent of sex with Mira.

Thinking of Mira instantly reminds me that I should stop whatever this is, so I say, "I get the idea."

I open my eyes and clear my throat. Trusting my voice again, I try to turn this from an intimate situation to an inquisitive opportunity by asking, "How does something like that even work?"

"Music can make us feel all sorts of things." Victoria puts the flute down and walks up to me. "This is not the finished project, but only the start. My inspiration is the male birds that can evoke an orgasm in the minds of the female birds through their songs."

I take a nervous step backward. "It's truly impressive."

"Yes." She takes a predatory step forward, so the distance between us remains the same. "I see how impressed you are."

Her eyes fall to my crotch.

"If you're trying to seduce me—"

Her gaze returns to my face. "I don't try," she says softly. "I succeed."

"That's just an involuntary—"

"Hush." She moves closer and puts a finger on my lips. "Just think. If I can do *that* with mere music, can you even imagine what I can do with my—"

"Seriously, we can't. I can't." I take five panicky steps back. My back is almost through the doorway.

"You most certainly can." She gives me a carnivorous smile.

"I have someone," I say, again trying to fight off her seduction. "It wouldn't be right."

"Come now. We're in the Mind Dimension. It's all within the mind. This experience would be no different than having a fantasy. You know you'll have fantasies about me anyway."

She's right. I will have fantasies about this later, or nightmares—time will tell. Though not all of my blood is in my brain, I begin piecing together clues as to her agenda. She must've decided to help the Elders' cause by seducing me. She must think that sex with her will be so amazing, so addictive, that I'll say yes to anything to do it again.

It's disturbing, but it does seem to remove her from my list of Super Pusher suspects. I don't think that person would want to fuck me so literally.

"How about I show you a dance I've developed?" she says and takes off her shawl.

"Victoria," I say, trying to keep my voice firm. "Thank you for the tour, but I'd like to see the rest of the Castle on my own."

"Are you sure?" She moves her body in a way that makes her flute-playing, and every porn I've ever seen, look G-rated in comparison.

I don't trust myself to stick around for a conversation. I rotate on the ball of my foot, and once I'm facing the door, I rush out, no longer worried about doing it with dignity.

Once outside, I take deep breaths, conjuring up thoughts of cold showers and baseball.

As I struggle to calm myself, I walk aimlessly through the Castle.

When I'm sure I'm not being followed, I enter a room.

It looks like a library—a huge library. The shelves seem to span for miles.

"Darren," says a familiar voice. "What the hell are you doing here?"

It takes me a moment to fully understand whom I'm seeing.

It's Bill, but everyone calls him William Pierce.

He's also known as my boss.

CHAPTER TEN

Once the gift of speech comes back to me, I say, "I think a better question is, what are *you* doing here?"

"I'm being vetted for an Ambassadorship." Bill closes the book he was leafing through. "What about you?"

"I guess I am too. Only it's complicated."

He looks at me the way he always does at meetings when I reveal information slowly for drama. His body language is telling me, *Get on with it already.*

I look at him, wondering if this man I've known and respected for so long could be the Super Pusher. Could he be the person Mimir tried to warn me about? I find this very hard to believe. Firstly, if I am that bad at judging someone's character, I might as well suspect every Guide close to me. Secondly, how could Mimir know Bill is here, which he would've had to know if Bill is the one he was warning me about? That logic points more toward the Elders— the only people rumored to be able to reach Level 2.

In the end, as much as I trust Bill, I decide to err on the side of caution and tell him only what the Super Pusher would already know, plus information that everyone on the Island will soon learn anyway. It should be relatively safe; if there's one person who can keep a secret, it's Bill.

So I proceed to tell him that the Elders want me to be the harbinger of peace between two groups whose blood I share. As I tell him all these things, his eyes get wider and wider, especially when I reveal my mixed heritage.

"You're part Reader?" He stares at me. "But the rumors say it's not possible."

"Clearly the rumors are wrong."

"I never gave it much thought. I mean, who would try to have a mixed-blood child? Not to mention how unlikely it is, statistically, for a Reader and a Guide to meet and fall in love. I haven't met a single Reader in my life, so what's the likelihood that the one I do meet turns out to be a woman and one I'd want to have a kid with, even if it wasn't taboo, which it is?" With his one free hand, Bill rubs his temple as he often does during meetings at the fund.

"Yeah." I walk up to the bookshelf and brush it with my fingers. It's free of dust and impeccably polished, which makes it feel nice and smooth to the touch. "My story is a hard one for people to digest, that's for sure. All things considered, you're taking it surprisingly well."

"I told you I thought you were one of the other guys, so this sort of confirms my initial gut feeling." Done with his temple, Bill moves the large book he was holding from his left hand to his right.

"I still can't believe you'd hire a Reader." I eye the book he's holding. I can only make out something about Statistical Analysis—classic Bill topic. "By the way, I usually just snoop around in the Mind Dimension to get you useful data for the fund. I only learned to Read recently, and I haven't been back to work since."

"Well, that's about to change, I hope," he says with a rare-for-Bill smile.

"Is it?" I try not to sound sly.

"Come now, Darren. That's an amazingly useful skill. You know that when all of this blows over, I'll want you to Read a few CEOs."

"Sure." I give him a wink. "If I make it into the office, we'll discuss it."

"At some point, we *will* discuss your absenteeism." His eyes narrow. "And that of Bert's."

"I'm still amazed you haven't fired me, or him."

"He still does what I need remotely. With you, I think of it as a long-term investment. When you two do show up at the fund, my biggest concern is office morale. People's feathers get ruffled when they see coworkers play hooky the way the two of you always do, but I solved that problem when I announced that you and Bert now work out of the newly established Brooklyn office."

"We don't have a Brooklyn office," I say. "At least, we didn't."

"Exactly." He places the book back on the shelf. "But your colleagues now think there is one. More importantly, they now think of that office as the 'exile location'—the place where employees are sent when they constantly slack off."

"Devious. Now stop changing the subject. Tell me why the Elders want *you* as an Ambassador." I watch for his reaction to this question. In the unlikely event that he's my suspect, he might give something away.

"It has to do with my connections. They're taking the idea of 'money makes the world go round' a little too literally," he says casually.

His answer isn't suspicious. In fact, it makes a lot of sense. Even though I'm fuzzy about Ambassadors' duties, the Elders can't go wrong with choosing someone of Bill's caliber. "Are you going to accept the position?" I ask.

"I'd rather not," he says. "You know how busy I am."

Bill is famous for arriving at the fund before the earliest bird gets in, and staying well after the last person leaves.

"I do, but will they take no for an answer?"

"They will when I tell them that I have a much better candidate than myself."

"You do?"

"Liz Johnson. You know her well."

"My shrink as an Ambassador?" I ask, stunned. "Why?"

"Many powerful people visit her couch," Bill explains. "Not to mention the simple fact that she's the personification of the social butterfly and knows every single Guide in at least a fifty-mile radius from Manhattan."

"I wonder what she'll think of this development." I also fleetingly wonder if *she* could be the Super Pusher? That's the most frightening thought. If she were, my enemy would know me better than even my friends and family. As soon as the thought comes to me, I dismiss it. I know her Guiding 'tone of voice,' and it's not the same as that of the Super Pusher in the cops' heads at the funeral.

"She'll be thrilled, I'm sure." His lips quirk wryly.

"What do Ambassadors actually do?" I ask. "I wasn't clear on this."

"I haven't been officially told as of yet, but given who the previous New York Ambassador was, I can guess. Ambassadors look out for Guides' interests. They influence regular people, the Unencumbered, to follow the general direction decided on at this island. Politics, economy, science—I suspect they have a hand in everything that matters in the world."

"And there's one in every city?"

He shakes his head. "There's usually one in strategic locations. New York has had one for a while. After he died, George looked after things from New Jersey, but with the Washington Ambassador retiring, I think George will be sent there, so someone will need to handle affairs in New York."

"You're very well informed for someone who doesn't yet have an official job offer," I say, not surprised. Bill always had a way of knowing things; Bert and I are just one of his many means of acquiring information.

"So why are you here?" Bill asks. As usual, he doesn't take the bait to reveal how he knows things he shouldn't. "You only told me what the Elders want from you, not the reverse."

"If I tell you, will you be obligated to tell the Elders?" I shift my weight from foot to foot.

"Certainly not."

"Would you be offended if I don't tell you why I came? It's not that I don't trust you . . ."

He shrugs. "Do what you want. I was only trying to help."

I make a quick decision to tell him at least one part of what I need. After all, the Super Pusher is aware of my Level 2 capabilities, so that topic is safe to broach. "I want to learn how to Split once I'm already in the Mind Dimension."

"You want to learn what?" he asks, frowning.

I proceed to explain the concept of Level 2, and a look of recognition soon replaces the confusion on his face.

"Why that of all things?" he asks. "I'm not sure it can even be learned. In fact, sometimes I wonder if the whole idea isn't just a convenient rumor to make everyone respect the Elders that much more."

"It's not a rumor. It's a fact." I try not to feel smug; I'm rarely better informed than Bill. "How else would you explain someone pulling me into this 'rumored' realm right before I came here?"

Bill looks stunned but recovers quickly. "So you're telling me all this mumbo jumbo about Nirvana is true?"

I must be looking at him as if he has two heads, because he explains, "Nirvana is what the rumors call that place, if it can even be called a place."

"Nirvana," I repeat. "It didn't feel all that heavenly, but it sure beats saying, 'The realm you go to when you Split while in the Mind Dimension.' Hell, it's better than my term, Level 2."

Bill stares at me. "If those rumors are true, then only extraordinarily powerful Guides can reach it. From what I understand, the Reach required is—"

"Yep," I say, this time unable to fight my smugness. "I have some very good genes, you see."

Bill's eyebrows draw together again. "This is very worrying. Tell me, is it true what the rumors say? That you can't reach Nirvana while you're in someone else's Mind Dimension?"

"No Level 2—I mean, Nirvana—access from someone else's Mind Dimension?" I repeat slowly, giving myself a chance to think. "No, I never heard of that. Why do you ask?"

"No reason," he says, looking relieved.

"I know you, Bill. You never utter a word without a reason."

"I just had a scary thought, that's all." He gives me a nervous smile. "In hindsight, it was silly."

"Oh, don't be like that," I say, more teasingly than I've ever allowed myself to act around my boss.

"I was wondering whether the reason I'm not ready to fire you yet has nothing to do with my wishes, you see." As he says this, he looks atypically insecure.

I try not to chuckle, finally understanding his earlier discomfort. "You think I might've gone to Nirvana and Guided you?"

"If we were in *your* Mind Dimension, it would've been a real concern," he says. "Come, we both know you're precisely the type of person who would do something like that if you could."

His words don't insult me, partly because he's right. If I wanted to keep my job and if I had to Guide him to do so, I'd do it. The whole 'No level 2 from someone's Mind Dimension' makes a strange kind of sense. Eugene told me that you use up the other person's Depth when they pull you into the Quiet. Going into Level 2 when you're using up someone else's Reach sounds like an activity that can deplete that someone's Reach very quickly, and perhaps our minds protect against it.

"Penny for your thoughts," Bill says, peering at me. He still looks uncomfortable, as confirmed by him saying, "Maybe I *should* fire you, and also stay as far away from you as possible in light of all this."

I can tell that he misunderstood my silence, and that he's only half kidding.

"Doesn't the fact that you can even consider firing me prove that I haven't Guided you?" I ask.

"I don't know," Bill says. "Maybe I'm able to consider it because you can't get to Nirvana right now. Maybe once you can, I'll feel like you're indispensable."

"You'll know for sure when you decide to give me a two-hundred-percent raise." I give my voice a mockingly ominous tone.

Bill chuckles and then says, "Seriously, though, I've treated you well over the years. Promise me you wouldn't use that shit on me, even if you could."

"Of course, William," I say, calling him by his full name to show that I truly do respect him.

He nods, looking satisfied. "And another thing. If this Nirvana stuff is true, that means the Elders might *make* me become an Ambassador. If that happens—"

"Say no more. If it turns out you've become one, I'll look into it."

"Thanks. You might get that raise after all." He winks and then, with mock horror, says, "Wait a minute."

We both laugh, but his laughter sounds strained. I haven't seen Bill this stressed out since the last big oil-price plummet; the man loathes it when anything in the world is beyond his control.

"I think I'll take a walk, if you don't mind," he says. "My advice to you is to have a heart-to-heart with whoever took you into Nirvana."

"Do you know whose Mind Dimension this is?" I ask. "If the rumors you mentioned are true, it would be the same person."

"No, I don't, but I'll let you know if I figure it out."

"Okay, I'll see you later," I say.

After Bill leaves the room, I look over the books.

Sadly, I don't locate a book titled *How to Master Nirvana*, at least not at a glance. Of course, if they kept stuff like that around, the Nirvana stuff wouldn't be a rumor. Some of the topics the Elders do write about are fascinating, though. I flip through a book filled with proofs and other pure mathematics written by Frederick. Next, I scan Alfred's *Detailed Analysis of the Second Iraq War*. After that, I find that Gustav created a catalogue of every species of creatures that run, fly, swim, or crawl on this Island, complete with hand-drawn illustrations.

Locating a genealogy book, I leaf through it, searching for 'Taylor,' my mom's family line. I'm absorbed in this task when I'm interrupted by a faint sound.

One moment I hear the rustling of clothing, and the next I'm having difficulty breathing.

The book falls from my hand to the floor.

I try to say, "What the hell," but only a hoarse grunt comes out.

Someone grabbed me from behind, I realize, and they have my neck in a tight elbow lock. Their other hand is on the back of my head. Unbidden, a thought comes: I'm in a rear naked choke, which is a pretty deadly way of taking out an opponent. I probably have five seconds to react before I suffocate.

Given the circumstances, I don't have to worry about dying, but I do have to worry about becoming Inert.

I suppress the fear and the pain, though it's extremely difficult. My body doesn't realize that the result of this attack won't be truly fatal; it's running through the motions of the fight-or-flight response. I try to calm myself and focus on the fight, and not the flight, part of what my body is so ready for. I have to react before I lose consciousness.

I grab at the arm around my neck.

My head might as well be in a steel vise.

I'm beginning to see a white haze.

My next move isn't a conscious one. I'm only aware of what I'm doing as I begin doing it.

I grab the arm again, but this time, I suddenly squat.

My brain catches up with my body, and I swing the back of my hand to where I hope my attacker's groin is. My hand hits something disgustingly soft, and a satisfying grunt sounds from behind me.

My attacker is definitely male.

The hold on my neck slackens enough for me to grab the hand holding me. I move a few inches to the right, bringing the arm along with me.

I succeed in overextending my attacker's shoulder and use that moment to throw him off balance.

As he falls, I catch a quick glimpse of him, which confirms his gender. This person is far too big to be a woman, at least an average-sized one. He's wearing a strange mask, which prevents me from recognizing who he is. Aside from that, he's wearing a plain black kimono and no shoes.

I pay the price for examining my attacker. He does what looks like a breakdancing move, his legs sweeping mine.

When I trained with Caleb at the Temple, the thing I learned best was how to fall, so I don't flop down like a sack of potatoes. Instead, I make sure I land on my attacker with my elbow out, wrestling-style.

My elbow plunges into his chest area, and his breath rushes out of him like air from a punctured balloon. I use my advantage to reach for the mask; I need to find out who this is since he's likely the Super Pusher. If he is, by the way, then punching him in his privates already proved I was wrong in calling him a she.

I move to complete the identification, but his hands catch mine before I can unfasten the mask. He rolls to his side, and I fight not to roll off him.

We wrestle in the style of the ancient Greeks, each trying to catch the other in a submission lock. Only the Greeks didn't allow dirty moves. Since this isn't the Olympics, I bite his arm when he shoves it in my face. He retaliates by grasping for my genitals. I back away just in time.

Unfortunately, he uses that moment to grab the tail end of the nearest bookshelf and tries to tip it over. Though the shelf doesn't fall, it does lean. I snap to alertness when books rain down, slipping off the polished shelf. As I protect my head from the heavy tomes, he crawls away.

I move to follow and notice he's trying to topple the shelf from the other side. Again it leans, and before I get out of its path, a book hits me in the temple, blurring my vision and sending a wave of nausea through me.

The masked attacker jumps up and makes a run for it.

Ignoring the pain, I scramble to my feet and follow.

He slams the door shut when I'm a foot away.

I hear a click, and rage blazes through me.

The bastard must've had a key to the library door.

In my crazed state, it takes me only a few kicks to break the flimsy lock, which is clearly meant to be decorative. When the door swings open, my attacker is nowhere to be found.

Damn it.

At random, I choose a direction and run, checking rooms as I go. He's not in what looks like a chemistry lab. Nor is he in a room filled with gorgeous rugs or the one filled with murals.

A few more doors down, I find myself near a relatively small room that looks like a painter's studio.

There, without a care in the world and with his back to the door, a man is standing in a black kimono.

What's more, I see the strings from the mask that's tied around his head.

I enter the room silently, filled with grim anticipation. My heart is pounding from the fight and the chase.

Maybe I'll grab his head in a lock the way he did to me, or maybe I'll do a karate-style neck chop first; the pain might disorient the fucker.

Halfway to my target, I marvel at how quiet I am, despite my faster-than-usual breathing. Stealth isn't something I ever thought myself capable of.

"Darren," a voice says from behind me, "what the hell are you doing?"

CHAPTER ELEVEN

Amazingly, the voice doesn't startle my attacker. He's still standing with his back to me. There's something very ballsy about his lack of concern; he's either really self-confident or deaf.

Ignoring the voice, I continue on toward my strangely behaving target.

He still doesn't move.

"Seriously, Darren, what in the world—"

I think I recognize the voice. It sounds like Gustav. I don't dwell on it or turn around to verify I'm right.

Gustav, if that's him, doesn't get the chance to finish his monologue, because I grab the masked man in a deadly lock.

Oddly, the masked man doesn't react in any way. Something is weird about him—a stillness that is kind of familiar.

Another masked figure materializes on our left.

"Who are you?" the figure asks. I don't recognize his voice. "Is it Celebration time already?"

"It is," Gustav says as I turn toward him, battling my confusion as I hold on to my unresisting victim. "Jamie, this is Darren, our visitor."

"Why did you pull me in in such a strange manner?" Jamie asks. "And why are you choking my frozen body?"

"I would also very much like to know the answer to that question," Gustav says, staring at me the way one might look at a rabid kangaroo.

I release my hold on Jamie's body and step back, more than a little baffled. "He just attacked me, in the library."

"I did not," Jamie says, sounding outraged.

"That's impossible," Gustav says. "You just pulled him in."

I ignore my attacker's denial. "He must've been in this Mind Dimension before running back to his body and Splitting."

It's the only explanation that makes sense to me.

"I would have seen him enter this room," Gustav says. "I came here right after we spoke, and I've been here reading. I was planning to pull him in in a few minutes."

"He must've done it somehow," I persist. "How can you defend someone who's clearly up to something shady? Just look at him."

Gustav looks the guy over, appearing more confused than before. "What about him?"

"Do people often wear masks around the Castle?" My hands tighten at my sides. "It's not exactly a—"

"Wait," Gustav says. "Jamie, please leave."

"He's not leaving until—"

"He is leaving right now," Gustav says. What shocks me isn't his words, but where he is when he says them.

A moment ago, Gustav was sitting in his chair, but now he's suddenly standing next to me.

For someone of his late age, or for someone of *any* age, he moved very fast. He must've leapt so quickly and quietly that I didn't even notice.

Placing himself between Jamie and me, he says, "Please don't do anything rash, Darren."

He says it calmly, yet there's enough command and threat in his voice that I unclench my fists for the moment.

I look at the guy he's protecting and belatedly realize his mask may actually be slightly different from the one my attacker was wearing. He might also be a bit smaller in the shoulders. Still, I'm hesitant to let go of my only suspect so quickly.

Taking my stunned expression as his cue, Jamie rushes out of the room.

"Now," Gustav says, "please tell me about this attack."

"Not before you tell me why you let my number-one suspect get away," I say, my voice clipped.

"I explained why he can't be your attacker."

"But the mask—"

"The mask and the black outfit are common during the Celebration, as are white and gray robes."

He walks over to the desk and picks up an object. It's a blue Zorro-style mask, one that only covers the eyes.

I realize he's changed out of his plain hippie clothing and into a blue kimono-type outfit.

The truth begins to dawn on me. "You guys are having a masquerade? In the morning?"

That would explain the two men in masks—three, if I count Gustav.

"We find that the Celebration is a good way for everyone on the Island to start their day, and for us to catch up with friends and family before we start the century without them."

"But masks?" I point at the frozen Jamie's head.

"They can spruce up any festivity, don't you find?" Gustav says, putting on his own.

"So I guess he didn't attack me," I say stupidly, looking at the frozen version of the guy. My heart is still pumping from the adrenaline rush I just experienced.

"No," Gustav says and gestures for me to follow him. "Now tell me everything."

One thing is clear: if my attacker is the Super Pusher, Gustav is unlikely to be him. There's little chance he changed his clothing *this* quickly. So, as we walk out of the room, I proceed to tell him what happened after I left the fountain get-together. Gustav doesn't bat an eye at the story of how Victoria tried to seduce me and looks unreadable as I tell him about the fight.

"That is most unfortunate," he says thoughtfully after I'm done. "But as you now understand, it could've been any one of the people already pulled in for the Celebration."

"Or more likely, one of the Elders."

"No, it wasn't one of us," Gustav says and starts taking the stairs down. Over his shoulder, he adds, "What would give you such a preposterous idea?"

I debate telling him about the Super Pusher, but decide against it. "I only know a handful of people here and most of them are the Elders."

"That is true, but the fact remains that if one of us wished to make you Inert, you would now be Inert." He navigates the slippery stairs expertly, as only someone who's done so a million times could.

"You sound very confident." I place my hand on the rail; unlike him, I could easily trip over the polished marble.

"I do, but believe me, this confidence is not rooted in hubris. It's merely a pragmatic way of looking at reality. Whoever attacked you must have been one of the Ambassadors, or someone who already lives on the Island, which includes the staff, our relatives, and many other people." He reaches the end of the stairs and waits for me.

"But I still think—"

"Darren, why don't you take my word for it for the moment? You will see the truth shortly, during the Celebration's Challenge Game. In the meantime, having me around should prevent any more unfortunate attempts."

"I guess," I say, following him down a corridor.

I don't say more because I'm distracted by masked figures—two men and one woman—walking toward us. My heart skips a beat when I look at the leftmost man. He looks identical to my attacker. I sure hope Gustav will have my back if push comes to shove.

Then I look closer and notice that some of the details in this dude's mask are a bit different from that of my attacker's. For one thing, his mask has small nose holes, whereas my attacker's mask was missing that detail. Seeing these masked people is reassuring in a way; it's not that I didn't believe Gustav, but as Eugene likes to say, "Trust, but verify." On second thought, it's also pretty frightening. This masked event will allow my attacker to walk around like nothing happened. He might even try to go at me again if the opportunity presents itself, and there isn't much I can do about it.

"That settles it," Gustav says as we reach the end of the corridor. He opens the door, allowing me to go in first. "In this room, you should find a suitable mask for yourself."

The room we enter is every hardcore Halloweener's wet dream. There are historical costumes, military uniforms, medical scrubs, and everything in-between.

He points to a rack of robes. "Those are for the Celebration."

Rows upon rows of kimonos of all different colors, styles, and sizes are lined up against the wall. Each robe comes with a mask. The masks, for all their simplicity, differ in subtle ways. Black, white, and gray ones dominate over other colors, like Gustav mentioned, but the whole spectrum of the rainbow is represented.

I settle on a green getup, just to be different.

"Great choice," Gustav says, admiring my new garb. "Let's go."

He exits the room, and I follow him, ignoring the chafing of my over-starched kimono. We walk through the Castle, and I can't help complimenting the intricate wall rugs that look like avant-garde paintings. Gustav seems pleased by my reaction, so I decide to ambush him while his guard is down.

"Can you tell me about Nirvana?" I ask as we round the corner.

He stops dead in his tracks, his eyes like ambers behind his mask. He recovers swiftly, however, and says, "This is something we should discuss when the others are around, though I'd love to know how you came across that term."

Since he doesn't give me an answer, I decide to be vindictive and, in my best imitation of his voice, say, "It sounds like something we'll discuss with the others. I'm a big fan of quid pro quo, you see."

He doesn't say anything back, but I catch him rolling his eyes in annoyance. Good. We walk in an uncomfortable silence for a couple of minutes.

"Is the Celebration taking place outside the Castle?" I ask, noticing that we're walking toward the intricately designed entrance doors.

"It takes place all over, but most of the merriment is happening at the fair."

As we walk farther, he tells me more about this tradition. As he alluded to earlier, this gathering is a way to motivate the Island residents to go about their day. It's also a nice start to the century, which the Elders plan to spend by themselves. I strongly suspect the latter is more of a reason than the former. During the Celebration, the Island's citizens are told the highlights of what the Elders achieved during the prior day's Session—what he calls the hundred or so years spent in the Quiet. Apparently, the Elders don't really talk to anyone after they do this Session. They have this whole set of rules of how they live outside the Quiet, some of which George hinted at. One of the biggest rules, it seems, is to not stress their physical bodies with unpleasant conversations. This rule, he assured me, is to make sure their bodies age as slowly as possible.

"Seems antisocial," I comment as Gustav and I walk into town.

"But don't you see how wasteful it would be to expend our mental resources outside the Mind Dimension?" Gustav retorts. "It's far more rational to conserve our body's energy and conduct our business when real-world time is at a standstill."

"But don't you end up with the most boring lives imaginable while outside the Mind Dimension?"

"Simple lives, yes, but I wouldn't go as far as to call them boring. Even if those lives are perhaps uneventful, we more than make up for it when we Split the next day."

He proceeds to describe what their day outside the Quiet is actually like. It all revolves around a bunch of research they've been doing on the subject of longevity. He explains that when the Elders maximize their lifespans, they don't just add a year here or a few days there as normal people do. It's multitudes of centuries and millenniums of time in the Quiet that they gain. So they try to mingle with close friends and family, with no stressful topics allowed, in order to satisfy their basic needs for human companionship. For nourishment (his term), they eat mostly unprocessed, plant-based foods, emphasizing greens, beans, onions, mushrooms, and berries, with the very occasional wild fish mixed in. They do numerous relaxation techniques, drink a glass of red wine, work out in a special gym, nurture physical relationships with their loved ones (Gustav speak for daily hookups), walk barefoot through nature during most of the day, and make sure to get adequate amounts of sleep.

"So, in other words, when you're not doing your Sessions, you're living in a health nut's paradise," I conclude, casting a suspicious glance at one of my attacker's lookalikes as we pass him by.

Gustav laughs. "You sound just like Victoria. She resents that lifestyle. If we didn't enforce it for all the Elders, she'd probably smoke, curse, and—"

"Why did she join you then?" I ask. "She strikes me as someone who likes her freedom."

"Because she enjoys her Sessions. We all do."

"Arts and crafts for a hundred years? Sign me up."

"That's just one aspect of it," Gustav says. "We do the things that make human beings unique. We do them all, and we take great pleasure in them. Victoria is very much one of us in that."

I nod absentmindedly as I look around.

The houses in this town are more decorated than a suburban neighborhood at Christmas, only the actual motif of this celebration is more reminiscent of Thanksgiving, what with the harvest-oriented decorations. A dirigible so big and colorful it would give the floats of Macy's Thanksgiving Day Parade a run for their money drifts across the sky.

"I heard you pass judgment when it comes to certain Guide-on-Guide crimes," I say when I've heard enough about their lifestyle. "Does that happen during the Celebration?"

"Not exactly," Gustav says. "It's something we only discuss with the Ambassadors. They give us new cases to review during the Session, and when it's done, we hand over our decisions on the prior day's cases."

"Are they all murder cases?" I ask, recalling how Thomas and Liz mentioned something along those lines.

"They concern a variety of complex issues, things that require wisdom to judge."

It's clear he's not comfortable discussing this, and I don't push the issue, since it's not really that important to me.

Throughout our conversation, I noticed more and more masked, cheerful people pulling their friends into the Quiet. My mental tally of near-duplicates of my attacker has reached double digits.

"Can we stop to listen?" I ask as we near a group of masked musicians, one of whom also looks like my attacker. The music they're performing is incredible.

"Sure," Gustav says, lowering his voice.

"What's that song they're playing?" I ask in a reverent whisper after a couple of minutes. "I think it's the most hauntingly beautiful melody I've ever heard."

"Thank you," he whispers back. "I wrote that score myself."

When the song is over, we resume walking, and I wonder whether I'll become desensitized to all this breathtaking art surrounding the Island. I've been meaning to take Mira out to do something 'normal,' and after this, that something might not be a museum, at least not for a while.

We approach a heavily decorated square, and I suspect that my attacker-lookalike count will soon reach triple digits. I surreptitiously move closer to Gustav.

This square seems to be the epicenter of the Celebration. Crowds of people surround stalls filled with games and displays.

Gustav stops in the middle of the square. "I see that the rest of my peers are here already. That means the meeting will be on time."

I look around. He's right. Though masked, the Elders are easy to spot, and though Gustav didn't explicitly say so, it appears the Elders don't prefer the boring black, gray, and white colors. Instead, I see a whole spectrum of colors, from Victoria in pink to Alfred in orangutan orange.

On the left side of the Square is a big black-and-white table. Gustav walks toward it, and as we approach, I see the twin Elders, Frederick and Louis, sitting opposite each other. Despite their masks, they're easily recognizable. They're each dressed in purple, with masks that are just strips covering their eyes, like Gustav's. Their table has one of those checkerboard patterns on it, similar to tables in New York City parks. Fittingly, they're playing speed chess on it. Given the number of spectators, their game must be an interesting one. It's impossible to tell which brother is Fred and which is Lou (as I've decided to nickname him).

"Transformative technologies are a double-edged sword," one of them says after making his move.

"Nanotech could lead to the deadly Gray Goo scenario, with nano-replicators gobbling up the whole world. Robotics and AI could lead to our extinction by a different route, with our own intelligent creations getting rid of us."

"Every technology has risks and rewards, brother," says the other, countering a move, then hitting the clock. "The rewards have prevailed thus far. Nanotech can cure cancer and feed the world. AI can—"

"Check," the first brother says instead of arguing, and moves his bishop to B6 at the same time.

The brothers continue the game. Their banter seems meant more for the crowd than for their own amusement.

"They once played chess for two days," Gustav whispers into my ear with something resembling pride. "Two Sessions that is."

"No way," I whisper back. "Two centuries of chess?"

"Indeed," he whispers back. "They didn't just play it; they also read thousands of books the Unencumbered wrote about the game. By the end of the second Session, they'd written their own books filled with new, revolutionary plays and unbeatable strategies. Of course, as you can imagine, it's impossible for anyone to beat them. Unless one of the other Elders decides to also dedicate some time to chess, they have to play each other. The world's best grandmasters and computers are no match."

"Checkmate," the crowd around us murmurs.

"Looks like Frederick will be our sacrificial lamb tonight," the grinning brother says, finally allowing me to recognize him as Lou. "Gustav, what say you?"

The old man nods gravely and walks to the middle of the square.

"Ladies and Gentlemen," Gustav says in a sports-announcer voice. "Today's challenger will face Frederick."

People clear the middle of the square and go quiet. Everyone's eyes are shining with fascination, but no one seems to want to volunteer for whatever it is Gustav is talking about.

"Is anyone here brave enough?" Gustav urges, giving me a meaningful wink.

The crowd thickens, but no one volunteers.

"Oh, come on," Frederick, the 'sacrificial lamb,' says. "I'll up the usual prize to twenty years."

The crowd murmurs, but still, no one steps up.

"Just think of it: twenty years in the Mind Dimension on the day of your choosing," Fred taunts.

At this point, I can hear people shuffling. The crowd parts as a lithe figure walks through.

Though masked, I can tell the figure is female. No man has curves like that.

She stalks across the space and confidently stands opposite Frederick. Something about her manner is familiar.

When she moves into a fighting pose, I realize it's Kate. I cringe as I remember what happened after she stood opposite me that way.

Unlike me, Frederick doesn't look at all concerned.

"You may begin," Gustav says.

Frederick demonstratively examines his nails, a gesture that's obviously meant to taunt Kate.

Without saying a word, Kate approaches in that strange pattern I observed the other day and tries to strike Frederick.

Only, Frederick isn't standing there anymore.

CHAPTER TWELVE

I don't know how Frederick dodged Kate's strike, but he did—so fast that my eyes didn't fully register it.

The crowd cheers; they seem just as impressed as I am.

What's really odd is that Frederick doesn't counterattack. Kate clearly doesn't care about that and goes in for another round.

She's moving more frantically. What she's doing reminds me of how a martial artist would look in a sped-up and slightly pixelated video. All I see are limbs and legs, all aimed at Frederick, but none of the effort is doing Kate any good.

She strikes at his head, and he dodges in that same lightning-fast manner.

She tries to kick his leg, and he does something that, again, is too fast for my eyes to see. All I witness is the end result: Frederick is not there for Kate's leg to kick.

How does he do that?

Throughout the fight, I don't really understand his strategy or technique. My suspicion that he's toying with her gets stronger. He seems to be giving the crowd a good show.

Kate executes a barrage of attacks, her limbs reminding me of a jackhammer that's been carefully programmed to follow some strange, mathematical pattern.

Frederick dodges the lion's share of the attacks, but Kate lands a few kicks.

A grimace flits across his face.

Emboldened, Kate walks back a few steps, then, in a blur, charges Frederick. This time, she, like Frederick, is so fast she's nearly impossible to see.

Before she can land a punch, something happens that my brain refuses to process at first.

Frederick doesn't do his super-quick dodging maneuver this time. Instead, he vanishes. Instantly and without traversing the intermediary distance,

Frederick is behind Kate. And I mean, one second he was in one place, then instantly, he's in another. There's no mistaking it.

Did he Teleport? I was under the impression it was only possible when you got pulled into the Quiet, but maybe that's not the case. Alternatively, maybe the twins are working together, like in a stage trick. One of the brothers could've dropped into a hidden hole beneath the square, and the other could've jumped out of a similar hole quickly to achieve this disappearing / reappearing effect.

Looking around, I spot Louis in the crowd, which destroys my 'stage trick' theory. I also don't see any hidden doors in the square's ground.

The crowd cheers louder. I guess this makes more sense to them, since here I am standing in stunned silence instead of cheering alongside them.

Kate's back is to Frederick, and he moves as quickly as he did when he was dodging her attacks. He pulls the straps of Kate's mask. Before she realizes what happened, the mask falls to the square's floor. Shock momentarily shows on her now-bare face.

I have to hand it to Kate; she still has some fight in her.

She grabs his wrist and tries to use it as a fulcrum point to throw him to the ground.

Then Frederick does that illusion-like maneuver again. He disappears from where he was standing and shows up behind her again.

Kate's hand is empty. If this were a trick, she would've had to be in on it and a good actress to boot.

This time, Frederick does some kind of sweeping maneuver with his leg, and Kate falls to the ground, landing on her back. Having fallen that way myself, I know it must hurt like a sonofabitch, but she doesn't show it.

In a gentlemanly gesture, he reaches his hand out to help her up, saying, "That was a truly valiant effort, Lady Kate."

She mumbles something, and everyone claps.

Frederick winks at Gustav, grabs his brother, and walks in the direction of the large gazebo on the eastern side of the square.

"Let's follow them," Gustav says. "With the festivities almost over, we should be able to get some privacy to talk with the others."

As we follow the brothers, I notice a few Elders heading in the same direction as us. I'm too perplexed to make small talk, though, still digesting the fight I just saw.

"How did he do that?" I ask Gustav after a few moments. "I mean, I know from personal experience just how quick and deadly Kate is."

Gustav smiles. "Are you convinced now? Do you believe that if one of us wanted to make you Inert, you would be?"

I nod. "If all of you can whoosh the way he did, then yes."

"Teleport," Gustav corrects. "We can do that and more."

So my first guess was right. "People can Teleport once they're already in the Mind Dimension?"

"Only a few can."

"You mean just the Elders, right?"

He smiles again. "Let's save this for the chat we're about to have. We're almost there anyway."

"So this is how you crossed the room so fast back at the Castle," I say, remembering how confused I was by the old man's speed. "You Teleported?"

Gustav takes off his mask. "I did. Now, let's see how everyone is getting on."

With that, he enters the gazebo—our destination.

My heart rate increases. Despite Gustav's reassurances, the Super Pusher might be in this very gazebo. Furthermore, I now know I wouldn't stand a chance against one of the Elders in a fight; that's just transitive logic. Frederick did to Kate what Kate did to me. It's not a comforting picture. The only thing that gives me a modicum of calm is the hope that the Super Pusher would not strike in front of the others.

Unless Mimir's message to me was, 'Don't trust a single Elder. They will gang up on you and make you Inert together.' But no, that's not likely. Given the distribution of power as it stands, them ganging up on me makes no sense, not when one of them would suffice for that task.

With this not-so-encouraging logic, I gingerly follow Gustav.

"Where are the twins?" asks Alfred, who enters with us. "I saw them headed this way."

Since he and the others have taken off their masks, I follow suit.

"We're here," says either Louis or Frederick, and a few Elders move aside so Alfred can see them.

"Victoria is the one who's missing," the other twin says.

Everyone appears to be talking about the Celebration. Half of the Elders are sitting on comfortable benches around the gazebo, while the other half are mingling. As I look them over, I take comfort in the fact that not a single person here is wearing black, which further confirms what Gustav said: my attacker was not an Elder. Of course, if my attacker were an Elder, he could've changed his clothing, and maybe he hadn't bothered using Teleportation when trying to kill me. On second thought, who says he didn't? He showed up behind me without me noticing. Maybe it was Teleportation and not stealth? But then why run away from me instead of going poof?

When Victoria walks in, flashbacks of our earlier encounter interrupt my thoughts. She winks at me as though she knows how I feel. I try to avoid looking down, so as not to draw attention to what's happening there.

"Yes, I know. I'm fashionably late as always," Victoria says in a parody of Gustav's voice. "Sorry about that."

"It's not a problem." Gustav ignores her jibe. "But now that we're here, let's talk."

Everyone goes quiet and looks at me expectantly.

"What?" I ask no one in particular.

"You've had time to think," Alfred says. "What say you?"

"I didn't really—"

"If I may," Gustav interrupts. "You seem like a very curious young man. You've asked me about Nirvana, and you were impressed with Frederick's ability to Teleport."

"Yes," I say cautiously.

"And I'm sure you'd like to learn about these things, as well as other things you haven't even dreamed of?"

I nod. "Yes, of course."

"Well then." He folds his arms in front of his chest. "There's only one way we can tell you these secrets."

"I think I see where you're going with this and I have to say, I did have time to think about this whole business of peace between Readers and Guides." I stop myself from squinting nervously.

"And?" Gustav asks.

"I think it's a great idea, and I'd love to help."

"That's wonderful," Gustav says.

My face clearly didn't betray me this time, in large part because I meant what I said. It would be great to put a stop to the whole Pusher versus Leacher nonsense, and I would be happy to help . . . after I save my friends and family. That's the part I leave unsaid.

"I hope you don't take us for fools." Alfred rubs the top of his hairless head. "You will not learn any secrets until and unless you've proven yourself."

"That goes without saying," Gustav says and looks at me expectantly.

"Sure," I say, my eagerness genuine. "How can I prove myself to you guys?"

"To start, we would need to get to know you better, as we do with all Ambassadors," Alfred says.

"Okay," I say "That sounds easy enough. What would you like to know?"

"What he means is that you would live with us for some time," Victoria says, her pearly canines flashing. "Given that four Sessions is what's customary for a regular Ambassador, I propose we make it five in your case."

"I was going to recommend six, actually," Gustav says.

I look them over, not comprehending. Then it dawns on me. "You want me to spend six days—as in, six hundred years in the Mind Dimension?"

"We know many people who'd give their right arm for such an opportunity," says an Elder whose name I have yet to learn.

"Right, of course." I try to keep my tone even. "And I'm honored, but I kind of have something to do off-Island, something that can't wait even one day. Any chance you can teach me a few things now, and I'll prove my worth when I get back?"

"Impossible," Gustav says, his gaze darkening. "Part of the reason we need this time with you is so that you can understand which secrets are worth knowing and which are not. For instance, you'll learn that Nirvana is an unfortunate waste of Reach—a resource that is much better spent on extending our Sessions."

Crap. I can tell by Gustav's expression that he won't budge on this. Still, I feel like I should at least try. "How about one Session?" I suggest. "Wouldn't a hundred years give you enough time to get to know me?" If they go for this, I'd have to hang out with a bunch of strangers for an entire lifetime, but I'd bear it if the end result was learning how to enter Level 2.

Gustav gives an adamant shake of his head. "Six Sessions, that's the best we can do."

I conceal my intense disappointment and say, "I'm afraid I can't do that. I really do need to get back. With or without you teaching me, I have to leave the Island as soon as possible. I'd be happy to return and prove myself later."

"In that case, you'll spend this one Session with us, and then we can discuss the possibility of you returning," Gustav says, his features tightening. "One Session won't take any real-world time away from your life."

It's true, but the idea of spending a century of subjective time in here while Mira and the others are being held captive feels wrong. Abhorrent, even. Not to mention, this would give the Super Pusher all the time in the world to make me Inert.

I take a calming breath, remembering how good they are at reading hesitation. I remind myself that Kate just went through public humiliation over spending twenty years in the Mind Dimension. Indeed, people would give a limb for such a chance. If the Super Pusher doesn't kill me, I could use this time to figure out who he is. Focusing on this, I try to sound as enthusiastic as I can when I say, "That sounds like a reasonable request. I'll do that much."

Gustav looks at me like a hypnotist. He probably noted my hesitation, but I hope he realizes that people hesitate before making big decisions all the time.

Finally, he nods, almost as if to himself. "So it's settled," he says. "Why don't you go enjoy the rest of the Celebration while we talk amongst ourselves?"

Translation: they want to talk behind my back. And since I couldn't be happier to leave them, I just say, "Thanks. I'm looking forward to getting to know you all."

It's only after I leave that I realize I'm now without an Elder chaperone. If Gustav was right and my attacker was not an Elder, then I just became exposed. But hey, if the Super Pusher attacks me and

I survive, I'll be one-hundred-percent sure my enemy is not an Elder.

As I walk, I notice there are fewer people around. The few who are here have taken their masks off, but most still wear their black kimonos.

One such figure turns out to have a familiar face, so I shout, "George."

A few of the people look at me in confusion. George waves and walks over, and I notice he looks tense, his features tired.

"Darren, what a funny coincidence. I was just looking for you."

"You missed some cool stuff," I tell him. "Did you see Kate fighting Frederick? It was insane."

"I'm sure it was spectacular," he says, not sounding particularly impressed. "Listen, I spoke to Alfred during the Celebration, and he requested that I introduce you to someone."

I feel worry coming on. If an Elder were the Super Pusher, Alfred, with his interest in history, would be at the top of my list of suspects. I dismissed him thus far because he's a bit too thin to have been my attacker, but what if he asked someone else to carry out his will? Could George be taking me to see that same attacker now?

"Is everything okay, Darren?" George looks genuinely concerned.

"Yes," I lie. "I was just, err, wondering why he didn't mention it. I just saw him."

George waves his hand. "He wouldn't have bothered other Elders with this. Besides, I know he thinks I'd be the better person to introduce you to her, even if I disagree."

At the mention of the female gender, my worry is lessened and my curiosity is piqued. "Who is it? And why are you questioning Alfred's idea?"

"Let's just say it's someone who might have a huge problem with the fact that you're part Leacher. So if we're to do this, perhaps don't tell her?"

"I guess . . ." My worry returns; the Super Pusher would have the same problem.

"That also means not telling her who you are, as that would also tell her about your nature," George says, clearly not noticing my discomfort.

"Fine, but can you explain whom we're meeting?" I'm not too eager to meet this Reader-phobic mystery girl.

"You'll see," he says, his tone mockingly conspiratorial. "Her room is near the entrance of the Castle."

He walks toward the looming structure and I follow, albeit reluctantly. Besides this person being slightly suspicious, we're returning to the very place where I was last attacked.

"George, this Teleportation thing you taught me," I say as we make a sharp right turn. "What Frederick did with it—"

"About that," George says. "I would greatly appreciate it if you didn't tell the Elders that I taught you how to Teleport."

"Did you break the rules?" I ask, looking at him. "Kate saw you do it, and she didn't object."

"Kate knows to mind her own business. The Elders would only have a problem with it in your case. I think they want to monopolize their secrets as leverage."

"So you know what they want from me?" I ask.

"No." He rubs the stubble on his chin. "I just know they want something from everybody, and I know what you wanted from this trip, so it doesn't take a rocket scientist to figure out what leverage they'd use on you."

"I'll keep it between us then," I say. "And I appreciate you teaching me, by the way. The Elders should follow your example."

He shrugs. "Like many people with too much power, they've lost their skill at diplomacy. I can't afford to. Besides, to me, you're family."

"So can you also Teleport like they do?" I ask. "Like some kind of comic-book hero?"

"No," George says, entering through the large Castle doors. "Nor would they teach you, unless you became one of them."

"Oh . . ." My shoulders stoop a little. "That would've been cool."

"It's not like the comic books anyway," George says, probably in an attempt to cheer me up. "It's limited to the Mind Dimension, and even for the Elders, there are limits to how far they can Teleport."

I sigh wistfully. "Still, I'd love to be able to do that."

"You can at least master doing it when you first get pulled in," George says and stops in front of a large door. "We're here," he explains. "Let's see if we'll get lucky today."

I wait, unsure what luck has to do with meeting this mysterious stranger.

The door opens a sliver, and smoke comes pouring out. Before I can think 'fire,' a raspy voice asks, "Who is it?"

"It's George."

The door opens all the way. Behind it stands the tiniest old lady. No, not old—ancient. She's holding a silver cigarette holder with a lit stogie in it, which explains the nauseating fumes.

"How are you, Mary? Do you recognize me?" George asks.

"Georgie," she says, her voice quivering. "When I can't recognize *you*, I will ask them to put me down like a dog."

"Please don't. I couldn't bear that."

"You have always been a sweet talker, like your uncle." She exhales another cloud of white smoke. "It's wonderful of you to visit again. This must be what, your twentieth visit this year?"

George walks up to her, gives her a chaste kiss on the cheek, and says, "I'm so glad you're lucid today."

She looks me over with her rheumy, but intelligent eyes. "I am not so lucid as to recall who this young man is, even if he does look strangely familiar."

She steps back into the room.

"The disease is not the reason you don't know him. You haven't met him before." George gestures for me to follow him inside.

"Then why did you bring him?" she asks, shooting me a glance. "He looks too young to be a doctor."

"His name is Darren, and he's under evaluation to become a special Ambassador. Alfred thought it would be courteous for you to meet him."

"Still such a polite lad, that Alfred," she says and takes a deep drag of her cigarette. "It's nice to meet you, Darren."

"Darren, I want you to meet Mary," George says. "She's my aunt, and Hillary's grandmother."

I look at the lady as though she might sprout an extra head—a fire-breathing head, given the current one's propensity of exhaling smoke—and I finally understand.

George just introduced me to my great-grandmother.

CHAPTER THIRTEEN

"Hold on a minute. You wouldn't also happen to be the young man Frederick was just telling me about?" Mary sits down in a rocking chair that looks as old as she is. "The one they want to send on that folly of a quest to make peace with the damn Leachers?"

George raises an eyebrow at this, and I recall how he told me he didn't know what the Elders want with me. I guess he does now.

The place looks like a room from a ritzy nursing home, but with homier décor. I look around to find a place to sit. George notices and gestures toward the small bed next to the chair.

I sit down and George joins me.

In a moment of silence, I look over the old lady. Her eyes have a layer of cataracts, or something else that makes them seem glassy. Where George's eyes look very old, hers look like I'm staring into infinity. And at the same time, there's confusion there, perhaps a sign of the Alzheimer's disease George mentioned back in Florida.

"I didn't agree to it," I say, realizing that besides staring, I owe her an answer. "But given your tone, it sounds like you're against it?"

Her face twists. "Of course I'm against it. Even if the Leachers hadn't taken everything from me, even if I supported the cowardly madness of trying to talk to them, it would all be for naught. Those people aren't capable of not hating us. They are brutes, the lot of them."

"All of them?" I ask cautiously. This whole exchange reminds me of my and Sara's attempts to get Gamma and PopPop to be less judgmental of the welfare system. You need a level of finesse when you play devil's advocate in these situations.

"You clearly haven't met one of those monsters," she says, unfazed. "You talk with the innocence of one who's been sheltered from them, like Frederick and the other kids. That must be why the others think you'd take on such a task. They want to use you so cruelly. Take my advice, my boy, and say no to that lunacy."

"Oh, okay, thanks." I look at George for support, but he looks deadpan serious. I turn my attention back to her. "You've given me something to think about, that's for sure."

She gives me a smile. She has a dimple in one cheek, which gives her a strange, cherub-like appearance—an impression enhanced by her curly white hair and small stature.

She gives her chair a gentle rocking, then looks confused. "What was I talking about?"

"I said, 'This is Hillary's grandmother, and this is Darren,'" George says.

"Oh, I remember the introductions, you sneaky trickster." She cackles, peering at George. "I lost track of something else. But since you mentioned the wild child, tell me, how is she?"

I smile at the idea of Hillary as the 'wild child.' My great-grandmother narrows her eyes at me and looks as if she had an epiphany. "You're sweet on her, aren't you?" she asks me. Before I can reply, she says, "I can't tell you how glad that makes me. It's about time that one settled down."

"He is," George says.

"I'm not," I say simultaneously.

"You two need to get your stories straight." Mary says, flicking her cigarette ash into an intricate ashtray—the only adornment on the end table next to her chair. The table is the one item in this room that looks as if it was made in this century.

"Hillary is dating a friend of mine," I say pointedly. I promised to keep my Reader nature hidden, but I did not agree to pretend to be dating my aunt in the process.

"Is your friend a Guide?" Mary asks worriedly. I think she's picking up on George's tension.

I ignore George's glare. "No."

"My, my." She shakes her head. "I bet Ronnie boy will have a fit about that." She scrunches her face in displeasure when she says the name.

"Ronald doesn't know about his daughter's choice," George says. "At least not yet."

"Insufferable bore, that young man," Mary says. "I warned Anne about marrying him, I did."

I suppress a smile. Despite her dislike for Readers, Mary seems less close-minded than Hillary's parents.

"I'm sure it's a phase," she says after taking another drag from her cigarette. "I'm sure she'll tire of her Unencumbered plaything sooner rather than later."

And there goes that open-mindedness. I change the subject. "Why was Frederick talking about me?"

"He was just giving me an update," she says, "since he was the one to pull me in today. Such nice young lads, those brothers, don't you think, George? One of them would make a much better mate for Hillary, since Darren here isn't interested, and the two of you didn't work out."

I blink. Wait a second, if what she says is true—

"It wouldn't be right for me to try to set up the twins with members of my family," George says diplomatically. "But as a peer Elder, you could certainly—"

"That's rich. Me, an Elder?" She chuckles. "You're such a flatterer, just like my dear Henry was."

"I'm simply speaking the truth." George's face shows zero hesitation. "Once an Elder, always an Elder."

"Not after your brain gives up on you." Mary takes a deep puff of her cigarette and lets it out noisily. "After that, you're nothing but a curiosity around here."

I'm barely listening to George and Mary. Instead, a little proverbial lightbulb is slowly gathering electricity above my head. Crossing my fingers and hoping I'm right, I ask as casually as possible, "How does it work, Mary, this current lucidity of yours?"

"I thought Georgie would have explained it to you." She puts out what's left of her cigarette. "When they start a Session, they start with me, you see."

My heart rate picks up. "What do you mean, they start with you?"

"I mean, whoever's Session it is, they try to pull me in a few times until they catch me during a functional moment. It seems to help me keep my wits better while in the Mind Dimension. Still, even with this trick, sometimes things get fuzzy. And on some days, the Session starter gives up after a dozen attempts. I fear it will only get worse with time."

Jackpot. My first and only success as a detective.

Before I get a chance to ruminate on my epiphany, George says, "At least you get to enjoy a century this time around. That's more experiences than an Unencumbered has in a lifetime."

Mary nods. "You're right to criticize me for the ungrateful wretch that I am. Now, let's get back to more important things. Darren, tell me what else my granddaughter has been up to."

She resumes smoking, and I proceed to tell her as much as I can about Hillary without elaborating on her role in my recent adventures. I also try not to talk too much about Bert. The story comes out very vegan-agenda oriented.

"Such a shame," Mary says, putting out her third cigarette. "This is all rebellion, I tell you. Ronnie's family were meat farmers—"

"She's doing what she thinks is right," I say, feeling the need to defend my aunt. "I don't think she gives a rat's ass about her father's family business."

She sighs. "If it weren't for Ronald's heavy-handed approach with my granddaughters, I would have gotten a chance to see them from time to time. As is, the younger one is following in the footsteps of the older—"

"Why don't we let Darren go, Mary?" George suggests. "It's his first time on the Island, after all."

"Why do you call me that?" Mary asks, pursing her lips almost petulantly. "Mary this, Mary that?"

"I'm sorry, *Mom*," George says. "I didn't want to confuse our young friend here."

"What's there to be confused about?" She digs through her pockets and pulls out a pack of cigarettes. "When my mind was my own, I looked after George," she explains to me.

"It was more than that," George says. "You know that."

"I had no choice, you see." She looks at me while putting another cigarette into the holder. Taking out a pack of matches, she says, "His parents were killed, just like my dear—"

"If Darren wanted a history lesson, he'd hang out with Alfred," George says. "Also, *Mom,* should you really be smoking so much?"

"It's the Mind Dimension, silly." She gives him that dimpled smile. "I can stand on my head here as far as my poor health is concerned."

"But smoking like this will condition you to want to smoke in the real world. And when the Alzheimer's hits, you won't be able to stop yourself."

She snorts. "If I lose my mind, having a smoke will be the least of my worries."

Despite saying that, she doesn't light up and returns the matches to her pocket. Then she turns her gaze to me. "Darren, Georgie is right. Since it's your first time on the Island, you should go off and play some more. If you don't mind, I'll keep Georgie here a bit longer."

Do I look like a five-year-old to these people? It sure seems so with all these dismissals, not to mention the 'go and play' comment.

Trying not to let my irritation show, I say, "Sure. Great meeting you."

I almost add 'Grammy' at the end, but stop myself in time. For now, I'll have to call her that mentally.

With our goodbyes over, I quickly leave her room and gratefully suck in a lungful of fresh air. As I walk through the Castle halls, I allow myself to focus on my earlier realization.

Mary let slip that Frederick had pulled her in today, and then I was able to get her to admit that she's always the first one to get pulled in. Put this together, and it means I'm currently in Frederick's Mind Dimension. Add in the whole 'you can only go to Nirvana from your own Mind Dimension' rumor, and I come to the following conclusion.

It was Frederick who pulled me into Level 2/Nirvana during my first encounter with the Elders.

I'm nearly at the Castle's entrance when I see the Elders entering. The twins are with them, but I'm not sure who is who. I decide on a brute-force approach and say loudly, "Frederick, may I have a word?"

One of the twins separates from the crowd and walks in my direction. The others track him with curious glances.

"Darren," Frederick says. "I'm surprised you singled me out like that. Surely, if you have more questions, Gustav would be—"

"I know," I whisper, keeping my voice low so that no one else will hear. "And I want to discuss it."

Frederick's expression is more amused than shocked. "I'm curious to know what you think you know."

"You know what it is I'm saying I know. But I'll give you a hint." I switch to an even softer voice. "Nirvana."

He gives his peers a paranoid glance. "Let's get away from prying eyes. This way." He starts walking.

I follow him. We don't talk during the few minutes it takes him to bring me to a room on the opposite side of the first floor. It looks very Spartan, except for two super-comfortable, plush chairs in the middle of it, with a large glass coffee table between them. On the table are board games, puzzles, and a couple of different card decks. Frederick gestures for me to sit in one of the chairs while he plops into another.

"We will have privacy in this room," he says, and looks at me expectantly.

I take a deep breath. Here we go. "I know you pulled me into Nirvana. And it seems like you don't want the others to know about it."

Frederick gives me a sardonic look. "Oh, don't think you have any leverage over me." He reaches over the table and picks up a Rubik's cube. "It's just that I promised the others I wouldn't do it."

"Yet you did." I steal a gaze at his hands. Is he trying to keep them busy with the cube because he's lying? "Pull me in, that is."

"I merely wanted to give you a little nudge." He turns the cube idly in his hands. The gesture is casual; he's messing up the colors on it rather than trying to disguise his nervousness. "I knew you were hiding something, and I knew it wouldn't take much to Guide you to tell us why you came here. The last thing I expected was to discover you have enough Reach for Nirvana, let alone that you've traveled there before."

They did indeed ask me why I came to this Island right before he pulled me in, but I don't let my recollection show as I skeptically reply, "So you say."

His eyebrows snap together. "Listen, Darren. You have as little reason to trust me as I have to trust you, but I bet you have more to gain from my trust than the other way around."

I think about this. It's feasible he really did want to nudge me into telling them why I came here. I had already decided that the person who pulled me into Level 2 is unlikely to be the Super Pusher, as my enemy knows about my Level 2 capabilities. Still, that doesn't mean I should trust Frederick blindly. It would be best for us to find some way to collaborate, but if finding common ground were as easy as making a simple, rational decision, human history would be a lot more peaceful.

"How do I earn your trust then?" I ask. "Outside the whole six-day business?"

"You can start by telling me your agenda." Frederick leans forward. "Tell me why you can't wait the six days. Tell me where you really stand when it comes to the issue of peace with the Readers. Tell me everything."

I proceed to tell him a carefully censored version of the truth, which includes the fact that I'm the grandson of two of the Enlightened. I explain that they want something from me and outline the lengths they've gone to get it. I don't talk about the Super Pusher, however, since there's still a small chance it could be Frederick. And even if it isn't him, it could be someone he's close to.

"So I hope you see why I couldn't tell this to the others," I say in conclusion. "Given the status the Enlightened have with the rest of the Readers, what I want isn't exactly compatible with the task you people want to give me."

"So what did you think we could do for you?" he asks, then peers at the Rubik's cube in his hand. It's randomized, the colors all misaligned. Apparently satisfied, he offers it to me on the palm of his hand.

I cautiously reach for the puzzle. "As you know, I found out that I can reach Nirvana, as you call it. But I only did it once under severe duress and haven't repeated the feat since. If I could do it at will, I could make my grandparents release everyone without having to resort to violence. So, in a way, if you teach me—"

"No," Frederick says as I take the cube. "I will not arm you with such knowledge. It's a power too great for someone as young and inexperienced as you. It would be criminally negligent of me."

"So earning your trust wasn't very helpful after all." I don't bother hiding my disappointment this time. I had been really hoping talking to Frederick would get me closer to my goal. As I consider what to do next, I glance at the cube, then back at him, wondering what he wants me to do with it.

"You didn't earn my trust." He mimes a twisting gesture in the air, universal for 'mix it up' when it comes to this particular toy. "You told me a story that clearly has a lot of information missing. In any case, even if I did believe you, I would not help you by teaching you how to reach Nirvana."

"Well, since I'm not sure how I can make you trust me"—I twist the cube a few times—"it's all moot anyway."

"Actually, it's not," Frederick says, not looking at my hands. "If you are truly committed, there is a way that I can be sure you are telling me the truth. A way that you might not fancy, however."

"What is this mysterious way? Are we going to do trust falls like at executive getaways?" I give the cube a couple of angry twists.

"Trust falls do not work," he says, smiling. "But this would. Let's just say it's a situation where we would be compelled to tell the truth."

"Both of us?" I offer him the now-randomized puzzle. "Or just me?"

"It would allow for mutual trust." He carefully takes the toy. "We would each know the truthfulness of the other."

"Okay, suppose I do want to learn more about whatever it is you're hinting at. Can you tell me what your help would entail?"

"That part is simple." After a quick glance at the cube, his hands begin manipulating it swiftly and without looking. "If I trusted you, I would order a few well-trained people to go with you and extract your friends and family so stealthily that the Enlightened wouldn't know what happened, and thus peace wouldn't be jeopardized."

"That's it? I could've Guided a group of Navy Seals to achieve the same result." In fact, Bert mentioned this very idea in New York.

"I would not trust Navy Seals with a mission this delicate, but I would trust our team." Frederick gives me a steady look. "If they are told 'no casualties,' there will be none. If they are told 'no one is to see you,' they will not be seen. It's just that simple."

"Will you be joining them?" I ask hopefully, remembering his fighting skills against Kate.

"No," he says with apparent regret. "I—or more correctly, we, the Elders—never leave the Island. That would put too much stress on our real-world bodies."

I really miss being able to phase into the Quiet to think during conversations like this. Something about his last statement has implications, but I don't have time to think it through since he's waiting for my response. "If not you, then who will join me?"

"We have many teams." His hands stop rotating the Rubik's cube. "In your case, I think the most logical choice would be Kate's group, since you already know her. George can go as the Ambassador to supervise the mission."

"And they're Guides?" I look at his hands in disbelief. He's solved the cube in seconds without looking, and it doesn't seem as if he did it to show off either.

"Indeed. Guides are much more effective than the Unencumbered can ever hope to be."

I give him an evaluating look. "Are the rest of the team as badass as Kate?"

"It really depends on the task at hand." He puts the solved cube back on the table. "She's an outstanding fighter, and if a situation calls for a sword fight, no one else can match her."

"Do many situations call for a sword fight?"

He chuckles. "Those are my sentiments exactly, but we digress. What do you think of such help?"

I shrug. "It's not like I have that many choices."

"So you want to proceed with proving your trustworthiness?"

I'm not sure if it's just me, but he looks a little too eager. "You have to tell me exactly what's involved, and then I'll think about it."

"I shall do my best." I see a hint of a wry smile; he knows he has me on the hook. "Though it's not an easy task."

"Not a good start." I catch myself shaking my head.

He pauses for a millisecond before saying, "Fine, here goes. It's called Assimilation. It's a process, for lack of a better word, that can only happen in Nirvana."

"That already sounds pretty sinister," I say, my eyes narrowing.

"I won't try to fool you. Assimilation requires a level of trust to begin with, from both parties."

"But why do I have a feeling your risk is negligible," I say sarcastically.

"Because you're smart." He gives me a wide grin. "Indeed, the risk is mostly yours in this case."

"Why is that?"

"Because you still have people with guns pointed at you outside my Mind Dimension." He mimes holding a gun in each hand. "If you harm me in any way, and that includes during Assimilation, you're as good as dead."

"Nice." I cross my arms. "But what about the little problem of me not trusting you?"

He shrugs. "It's up to you if you want to gamble. Bear in mind, though, in a way, I would be teaching you something about Nirvana as a result. And though you would have to take my word for it, you could get me to tell you the truth."

"Sounds like a Catch-22," I say with frustration. "Tell me more about this Assimilation."

"It's hard to explain."

"Of course it is," I say, trying not to roll my eyes.

"Fine, let me try." He sighs. "It allows for a state of being where we would be physically incapable of lying to each other. During this process, you would have no doubts regarding my intentions."

I consider it. Thus far, this whole trip has been a giant waste of time as far as learning anything about Level 2 or the Super Pusher, but this could be my chance.

"You saw me fight Kate," Frederick reminds me. "If I wanted to harm you, I would've done so already."

"Great." I glare at him. "The good old 'since I can kill you, you should trust me' argument. We haven't learned that one in debate class."

"I am just trying to make a case for me having no ulterior motive." He follows these words with a couple of slow blinks.

"Oh, you have one." I try to recall whether blinking means a person is lying. "But it's probably not to make me Inert."

One corner of his mouth twitches, as though he's amused. "And is that good enough for you to give it a shot?"

"I don't have too many choices," I say and exhale audibly. "But I have one condition."

He lifts his eyebrows. "Like you just admitted, your choices are limited. You're in no position to negotiate, but I'll hear the condition as a gesture of goodwill."

"I don't want to wait until the end of the Session to get started on the rescue," I say. "I'm too worried about them, and I'd like to leave right away, as soon as we're done with this Assimilation business. Would it be a problem if I just walk up to my frozen self and get out of the Mind Dimension? I don't want those people to shoot me."

"They won't shoot you, but Gustav will be upset," Frederick says. "You promised him you'll stay until the end of the Session. He's a stickler for promises."

I blow out a frustrated breath, but then a sneaky idea comes to me. "You initiated this Session," I say, "so perhaps you can end it? I would then, strictly speaking, be keeping my word."

"You want me to end the Session?" For the first time, he looks genuinely distraught. "It will be extremely inconvenient for the other Elders. What if they have done some work already? They would lose it."

"Oh, come on." I lean forward in my chair. "They just came back from the Celebration. What could they have accomplished?"

"I guess that's true." Frederick studies me for a few moments before saying, "All right. As a token of my cooperation, I'll do it."

I give him a satisfied smile. Score one for me. "So, how do we do this Assimilation?"

"It's easier to show than to explain," Frederick says. "I will pull you into Nirvana again, where I will let my mind assimilate with yours, and vice versa. That's the best word I can use, hence the term."

My smile fades. "I really don't like the sound of that."

"Do not fret." Now it's Frederick's turn to smile. "In Nirvana, the minds exist in a purer form. Communication there is different from here. It requires the minds to be interconnected, but that is all we are talking about: communication."

"So you just want to have a conversation in Nirvana? Face to face, mind to mind, so to speak?"

"That's a very good way of describing it. I couldn't have put it better myself."

"And when you 'talk' that way, you can't lie?"

"Pretty much."

"Why do I have a feeling that the devil's in the details?" I consider pulling out of this whole exercise.

He must've noticed my hesitation, because he says, "How about this?" He gets up, walks up to the wall, and opens what appears to be a safe. Out of the safe, he pulls out a small revolver and turns to face me. "You can shoot me if something goes awry. You know I wouldn't take being Inert lightly, as it would cost me many millenniums of exile from the other Elders."

"Right, but if you made *me* Inert in Nirvana, I'd end up back in my real-world body next to George's plane. Not to mention I'll still have those people in the real world who would shoot me for making you Inert."

"We already established that if making you Inert were the goal, I could have done it a million times over. As for the people outside, well, I wouldn't want you to decide to use this gun lightly. Still, I have so much to lose that giving you this gun is not an empty gesture."

"Fine," I say and walk over to take the gun. "Let's get on with it."

As soon as I aim the gun at Frederick, my senses go away.

CHAPTER FOURTEEN

Before I fully register anything, a thought intrudes—a thought I recognize as Mimir's.

"Darren, don't trust the Elders with the secret of my existence." As soon as the words reach me, I sense Mimir's presence disappearing.

"Wait," I think back frantically. "Is this what you tried to tell me before? You realize you got cut off at an important point, don't you? You ended up making me think I wasn't supposed to trust someone, and it drove me crazy. In any case, why don't you want them to know about you?"

No reply comes, so after what feels like a few minutes of angry waiting, I turn my attention to Level 2 itself.

You'd think experiencing this sensory deprivation would be easier the third time, but it's just as frightening now as it was on my two prior visits.

The difference lies in how quickly I become aware of that special sense that lets me 'see' neural networks. It's almost instant this time. I see three networks: two frozen networks that are me and Frederick outside Nirvana, and a dynamic one that's the Level 2 version of Frederick.

Though I don't have much experience with these patterns, especially activated ones like his, I can't help but think that Frederick's form is unique. His 'neurons,' if that's what they are, don't remind me of stars—the mistake I made during my first time in this realm. No, the spots of 'color' are more 'orange' than the whiteness of starlight. The synapses remind me of the sun's rays trapped in a piece of crystal.

Suddenly, all that colorful stuff surrounds me.

A wave of anxiety hits me, or at least that's the best way to describe the emotion. It's not fear so much as a sense of being invaded and having my privacy violated. There's a hint of shame too. I felt this way during a dream where I was in the middle of Times Square naked, only this is much stronger.

A weird sensation overtakes me. On one hand, I'm definitely incorporeal, but on the other, I feel as though I'm being erased from existence. How can something that's not physical be erased? I don't know, but I fight the force that's trying to erase me with all my will.

And then the strange feeling subsides, and a new one appears that's just as unpleasant. I feel as if I'm destroying something. As I endure this feeling, I realize that the pattern that is me has the pattern that is Frederick at a standstill.

It's a little bit like when I encompassed Thomas, Kyle, and my own pattern on my first visit to Level 2; my pattern surrounded the others in order to Read, Guide, and phase out. This time differs in that I'm only halfway surrounding Frederick. It's also a more dynamic process. I think these two results are related. Frederick is 'alive' and clearly fighting my pattern as it's trying to absorb his, and vice versa. It's a strange mental tug of war that reminds me of the day I tried to meditate before a tooth extraction, with my adrenaline making it impossible for me to calm my mind.

Then I feel fear, and what makes this fear odd is that I know, without a shadow of doubt, that it's not mine. Well, it's mine now, but it didn't originate within me. A flood of other foreign emotions hits me like a wave. Surfing on this wave is a single thought: "Darren, it's me, Frederick."

The thought is different from Mimir's telepathic voice. I can almost 'hear' it.

"Try your best to speak," another thought says. "You should be able to project your thoughts to me."

A slew of emotions accompanies this advice, and somehow I know he's telling the truth.

So I try to talk, ignoring the fact that I don't have a mouth and that there's no air in this place to carry sound waves. The message I try to get across is: "So, this is Assimilation?"

"That's it," Frederick's projection responds. "You did it. And indeed it is."

Again I know his words are truthful, and this time, I attempt to figure out why I'm so certain of that. Then it hits me: it's the emotions. Our emotions seep through with every word. In this strange state, we've become empaths. When you can feel someone's true emotions, figuring out whether they're telling the truth is easy. It follows the same principles as a lie detector. If Frederick lies, his emotions will betray it. Unlike real lie-detecting machines, which can be duped, this doesn't have any loopholes that I can think of.

"So you're going to ask me stuff?" I project. "And based on my emotions, you'll know if I'm telling the truth?"

"You're a quick study," he projects, his emotions validating his sincerity. "Indeed, that's the plan."

"Okay then, but I also want to ask you a few things."

"I would expect nothing less," he responds.

"Did you make my friends attack me?"

"What?" His response is associated with genuine befuddlement.

"Mira, my girlfriend, and Thomas, my adoptive brother," I clarify. "Did you Guide them to attack me at Kyle Grant's funeral?"

"I did not," he projects, and I know he's telling the truth, but there's also deep confusion in his reply, as I would expect from someone who knows nothing about the attack. "Can I ask my follow-up question now?"

"Go."

"Did you ever intend to harm us, the Elders?" This is accompanied by hope.

"No."

"You're lying." Fear and anger permeate the thought. The weird sensation of being gobbled up begins anew, giving me a very bad feeling.

"Let me explain," I quickly project. "I didn't intend to harm the Elders per se. As a group, I like you guys. I simply expected to discover that one of you tried to hurt me by using those close to me. I would harm that person if I could."

"That is the truth," he replies, and the pressure of the mental violence subsides. "I accept this."

What the hell did he just do to me? I could ask him, but I'd be wasting a question, and I have something more important I need to ask, something that, if he confirms it, will remove a huge number of people from my list of suspects. Besides, I instinctively know what he did. He tried to 'envelop' me—what I'd do if I wanted to Read someone.

"Do the Elders really never leave the Island?" I ask.

"Never."

"But—"

"It's my turn," his projection intrudes.

"You're right. Go."

"Will you unite our people once you're done with your short-term trivia? Do you want Guides and Readers to have peace?"

Ignoring the insult of calling the kidnapping of my friends and family 'short-term trivia,' I think about his question. This is the first time I've genuinely considered it. Hillary once said that as a hybrid, I embody a shift in the age-long hostilities and could make a difference. She thinks someone like me could change the usual tribal thinking that's so prevalent in the Pusher versus Leacher strife, since within me, the tribes are united. I never gave her words much thought because I didn't have to, but I consider them now, and I don't see anything but good things coming from such a peace.

"In theory, I would like to see the problems between Guides and Readers go away," I project. "I want peace, but I don't want to be killed in the process."

"Thank you for telling me the truth," he says. "Now we can—"

"How do I get back into Nirvana?" I project. "That's my next question."

"Just because I have to tell the truth doesn't mean I will answer every question you ask." His projected thought is mixed with feelings of amusement and slight annoyance.

"I will pick and choose which of your questions to answer then," I reply.

"It's not necessary. I was saying that we don't need to continue with this Assimilation. Let's slowly disengage."

As his words register, so does a shift in the arrangement of our patterns. The foreign tension of the Assimilation eases slightly, but doesn't go away.

He seems to be waiting for me to do something. I try to let go of his pattern, to get away.

The tension eases further.

After repeating the same process a few times, we disengage and I can once again 'see' his pattern 'in the distance.' He's absorbing his static pattern, and soon after, I'm back in the Quiet, in my physical body.

* * *

For a few moments, all the sensory input disorients me.

"That was something else," I say to Frederick, and it feels great to be saying things out loud, with my voice echoing off the room's walls.

He nods. "It's something few people ever get to experience."

"How did you manage to have us come back here?" I ask, realizing this is the second time his Nirvana-phasing worked differently from mine. "How come we didn't end up in the real world?"

"It's part of those Nirvana arts you'll learn if you come back and accept the offer we've made." He gives me a smug wink.

I frown at him. "Why didn't you try Assimilating the very first time you pulled me in? Wouldn't it have been just as helpful as Guiding me in terms of uncovering my agenda?"

He shakes his head. "No, that would've been a bad idea, as it would've put us at risk."

"Why?"

"Because if I had ambushed you, you might have tried to fight me, or absorb me, so to speak." His expression is now serious. "If you had succeeded, you would've made me Inert, and you know how I feel about that. Anyway, the more likely outcome would have been me making *you* Inert in self-defense—another outcome I didn't desire."

"It's interesting how you omitted that going Inert was a possibility when doing this Assimilation thing," I say, narrowing my eyes.

"Because it wasn't, not when I didn't have any intention of doing such a thing to you. If anything, I was putting myself at risk, given that for me, going Inert carries greater consequences."

"You know what I mean." I hand him back his gun. "But no point in splitting hairs anymore. I fulfilled my end of the bargain."

"I am ready to do as I promised," he says, taking the gun. "I shall take you to the library so you can wait while I speak with George, Kate, and the rest of the team. After that, I will end the Session early, as promised."

* * *

I pace back and forth in the library as I wait for Frederick to terminate the Session.

To kill time, I look through the shelves for something to read and settle on *How There Can Never Be a Theory of Everything*, written by Victoria. I leaf through it for a number of minutes, skimming its contents. To my huge surprise, this book doesn't mention sex. It's more of a scientific philosophy treatise about the futility of trying to reduce complex phenomena, such as life, to a simple, all-knowing formula. After what feels like an hour of this, but before I can form a real opinion on the matter, I get bored and decide to find something else to read.

An older-looking volume catches my gaze, and I grab it. *The Atrocities,* the title states, and the author is none other than Mary, my newfound Reader-hating grammy. As I leaf through the book, I see why she feels so negatively toward Readers. This book catalogues what I learned before—how Readers tried to exterminate Guides. According to Mary, their favorite tactic was piggybacking on an existing conflict. During World War I and World War II, they were able to get rid of thousands of Guides in Western Europe. And afterwards, during Stalin's Purges, Readers managed to all but wipe out what was left of the Guides in Russia. So yeah, it's no wonder Mary hates them, as all of these things happened during her lifetime.

I put the book back on the shelf and look for something more cheerful to read, which is probably any other book.

Rows and rows of fascinating subjects line the shelves, but one really catches my attention. It has Eugene written all over it. If I don't look inside, he'd never forgive me. The book is called *Making Machines Work in the Mind Dimension*, authored by Alfred. I pull it off the shelf and open the book at a random page. "Steam power is another viable, if primitive solution—"

I don't get to finish the sentence because I'm no longer standing in the library, holding the book.

I'm back in my real body, next to the airplane, with guns pointed at me.

Except the people lower their guns, and after a few insincere-sounding apologies, they turn around and head for the Castle.

"Frederick told me about his agreement with you," George says. "I think his idea to utilize Kate's team is genius."

"And it will be good for their morale," Kate says with uncharacteristic cheerfulness. "Despite it being a simple extraction, the team will be happy to get off the Island. They've been stuck here for months."

"Now, Darren," George says. "Where do we set the course to?"

"Back to where we came from," I say. "We're going to pick up Hillary and—"

"We don't need her," George says. "In fact, I think we should go directly to where your family is and help—"

I hold up my hand, interrupting him. "First, I'm not forming any plans without Hillary," I say firmly. "And second, it wouldn't help us to get anywhere yet. The vans are probably still en route. Even without rest stops, the drive from New York to Florida takes twenty hours."

"So be it," George says. "But I still don't see the need to involve your aunt."

"I won't put her in danger if that's what you're concerned about. You're not the only one who cares about this family."

"Are we interrupting something?" a voice booms from a few feet away.

"No, we just settled on our destination," George says. Then he turns to face the muscle-bound guy who spoke. "Stephen, this is Darren."

"Nice to meet you, Darren," the man says. His handshake reminds me of the time I got my finger caught in a lobster's claw as a kid. Those things do not make good playmates, and neither would Stephen, I'm guessing.

"Where are the others?" Kate asks.

"Eleanor was right behind me," Stephen says. "John and Richard were in the training room at the Castle, so I'm not sure when they'll arrive."

"I'll go ready the plane," George says. "Kate, please go through the safety procedures as you wait for the others." Without waiting for her reply, he walks off toward Pandora.

Kate clears her throat and fishes a pill bottle out of her pocket.

"Are you kidding me?" I stare at her. "I have to take an Ambien again?"

"It's standard procedure for now," she says. "Once the Elders say you don't need it, I won't do it."

"But Frederick trusts me. He wouldn't have authorized all this if he didn't."

"He didn't say anything about safety to me, which means I have to stick to the standard protocol," Kate says.

"Fine. At least let me meet the rest of the team," I say.

We wait in tense silence until the others arrive.

"Is this everyone?" I ask, looking over the four new arrivals—three dudes and one woman. They look vaguely familiar. I think I saw each one of them in the Victoria Sutra room as statues.

"Darren, this is James, John, Eleanor, and Richard," Kate says. "Now take your pill."

"What?" I ask, trying to keep my incredulity out of my voice. "You're telling me this mighty team consists of just the seven of you?" As I say this, I study them.

James looks like a hard man, his fierce expression heightened by a cleft lip scar.

John is just as big as James and Stephen, only he somehow looks less healthy, probably due to the bags under his eyes.

Richard is the scariest of them all, though he's the least muscular. I think it's his bearing, coupled with leathery skin and an intense stare, that creates this effect.

Eleanor has more in common with the guys than with Kate. She's more muscular than me, and I'm not exactly a wimp, even if I currently feel like one in comparison.

If this team were a circus troupe, John would be the sick lion, Stephen and James would be a polar bear and a grizzly bear, Eleanor an elephant, Kate a panther, and Richard a scorpion.

"Who's the seventh?" Richard asks with a sneer. "You wouldn't be talking about George, by chance?"

"Well, yeah. I thought he was the leader," I say.

"He's a politician, a glorified bureaucrat," Richard says. "We don't work for him."

"Sorry, I stand corrected," I say. "I'm sure you guys are awesome and all that."

"If by 'all that' you mean that the *six* of us have never failed a mission," Richard says, "then yeah, we're awesome."

"Enough chatter." Kate demonstratively takes a pill out of the bottle. "Can you *now* take the fucking pill? Or should I make you?"

"I'd listen to her," James says, smiling. "You wouldn't enjoy it if she made you swallow."

Ignoring the merriment James's comment created, I take the pill, trying my best not to choke on it. Before Kate can ask, I open my mouth to show that I did as I was supposed to.

"Such a good boy." Eleanor's voice is deep, matching her physique to a T. "You've trained him well, Kate."

I just walk onto the plane and take the seat I slept in earlier.

I hear the others come in but pay no attention to them.

This time around, I'm determined to fight off the effects of the Ambien by exercising mind over matter. I have free will, don't I? I should decide whether I sleep.

"You really part Leacher, kid?" asks one of the dudes. James, I think.

"Part Reader, yes," I say.

"What's it like to Leach—I mean Read—someone's thoughts?" maybe-James asks.

I yawn and say, "It's like living as them for the duration of the Read. You're your target, like in a super-realistic virtual reality that on top of sight and sound also has taste, smell, and touch."

"Must be trippy," the guy says.

"It's pretty awesome." I yawn again.

I don't hear his next question because my mind goes blank—again.

CHAPTER FIFTEEN

I wake up with a jolt and attempt to move, but find myself restrained for some reason. Did someone tie me up again?

As my eyes adjust to the light, I realize my vision is somewhat restricted too. However, I *can* see, which means I'm not wearing a bag over my head. How crazy would it be if my second trip to see my Enlightened grandparents once again had all the comforts terrorists enjoy on their way to a secret prison?

The world whooshes past me so fast that, for a moment, I wonder whether the plane is plummeting toward earth. In that case, the fact that I'm tied up doesn't matter.

A shot of adrenaline clears the remaining sleepiness from my brain.

The good news is that I'm not plummeting from the sky while inside a metal coffin.

The bad news is that I'm inside a metal (with too much plastic) coffin that's rocketing forward.

The restraints binding me are actually seat belts crisscrossed around my chest. Some kind of visor with tinted glass is restricting my vision. Judging by the person sitting next to me in the driver's seat, I'm wearing a helmet.

All this adds up to me sitting in a car, or a car-like rocket, that's moving faster than my still-groggy brain believes a car can go.

"What the hell is going on?" I try asking, but a grunt-mumble hybrid comes out instead. My voice is hoarse, post-Ambien. I think my mouth was dry like this last time too. As a side note, if you start noticing little patterns like this, it means you've been drugged too many times.

"Rise and shine, sleepyhead." The high-pitched, friendly voice can only belong to Hillary—same with the small, gloved hands on the steering wheel.

"Is the Super Pusher controlling you?" I ask. "And if so, why is he trying to kill us in such an unconventional way?"

I feel the urge to rub my eyes, but the visor and my limited range of motion leave that desire unfulfilled.

"No one is controlling me," Hillary says. "We just needed to get to Apalachicola quickly, and I had this idea, you see."

Palm trees and parked cars zoom past our windows so fast they look like two solid blurry walls of interconnected wood and colorful metal.

"What's your idea, besides killing us in a glorious car explosion?" I ask, my sarcasm missing the bite that comes with not being scared shitless. Also, I'm probably still under the drug's influence; at least I think that's why I feel this intense nausea coming on. "And what's up with all the cars parked on the side of the highway?"

"I had them all pull to the side so we don't, as you say, die gloriously. I'm not crazy."

"You're not? The speedometer reads one hundred and fifty. Even with all the cars out of the way, that's way too fast."

Though I've done similar Guiding in the past, the scale of what she's accomplished—clearing an entire highway for miles and miles—is truly staggering. Now that I'm paying closer attention, I notice that the parked cars are facing us and not away, which means we're speeding down the wrong lane.

"I have two and a half hours to get us to our target," Hillary says. "Given the slightly over three hundred miles we have to cover—well, you can do the math. Your beauty sleep put us behind schedule, so I'm trying to make up the time."

"Why do we need to get to this place so quickly?" I ask.

We swoop through a more deserted area with only a handful of parked cars and no trees. This allows me a view of the other side of the highway, the one moving in the correct direction. I can see a cavalcade of cars, but given our insane speed compared to their law-abiding one, it's clear we'll be leaving them far behind.

"It's so that I can execute my plan," Hillary says. "And your chatter isn't helping me focus, you know."

"Is this a car chase?" I ask despite her very reasonable point about breaking her concentration. Looks as though my curiosity is stronger than my sense of self-preservation, similar to that of some now-deceased cats.

"It's not a chase, per se," she says.

"Are those police on the other side? In those Crown Vics?"

"Yep, that's the law," Hillary says. "And there's more where that came from. More cars will be joining them in a few miles. Also, before you ask,

George and the rest of your new friends are in that Humvee behind us."

I turn and see that, indeed, a Humvee just turned the bend behind us.

Then I hear a motor revving, and something passes us on our right, causing a cloud of dust to billow around us.

Given how fast we're going, I have to assume a ballistic missile just passed us. Upon closer examination, I realize I was only slightly off.

It's a black motorcycle.

"That's Kate," Hillary explains.

She must be right. Though I couldn't see the face under the black helmet, the BDSM-inspired outfit is telling, as is the sword sheathed on her back.

"What are you doing?" I ask when I see her foot press on the gas and feel the vibrations of the car's engine working overtime.

"I'm catching up to Kate," Hillary says. "I want to make sure there's no bloodshed."

"Wouldn't splattering us all over the pavement be considered bloodshed?" I ask. "Can you explain what you're doing? Wait—only answer if you can do so without killing us."

"After you and George left, and after I caught up with my folks, I had this idea," Hillary says, pressing harder on the gas. "Once Mom and Dad started getting on my nerves, I left and went to a local police department."

"I thought you were going to say you cooked up the most elaborate suicide plan."

She continues, ignoring my interjection. "I Guided the local sheriff to aid in my plan. He got in touch with his brother, a Florida State trooper, and they sent out an APB to all the states from New York to Florida.

"Oh," I say, beginning to catch on. "You wanted the cops to catch the minivans? That's a great idea. Why didn't I think of it?"

"The effort turned out to be futile, though," Hillary says. "The cops were out of their depth when it came to your friend Caleb and the monks."

"Shit," I say. "I was hoping—"

"If my original plan had worked, we wouldn't be driving like maniacs right now," she says. "But a version of it may still work. You said the Temple is near Apalachicola, in a forest. That limits the number of ways the vans can get there. So I had the cops create a bottleneck on the roads they're bound to pass."

"And we're trying to get there in time to catch the vans?" I ask.

"Exactly," she says. "Or else Caleb and the monks might repeat their shenanigans."

A strange noise catches my attention. It sounds like an alarm going off during a bank robbery. I tense, wondering if the car makes this sound when some part of it is failing, but realize the culprit is a phone attached by a pink mount to the windshield.

"Can you get that? I don't want to risk reaching for it," Hillary says.

Deciding not to mention the annoyingness of her ringtone, I steady my hand and press the 'speak' button. With a southern drawl, a voice says, "The two Honda Odyssey vehicles are fifteen minutes apart."

"Thank you, Sheriff Jackson," Hillary says. "Which blockade are they heading toward?"

"Just program Telogia, Florida, into your GPS," the voice says, "and it'll take you there. But you don't have much time."

"Thank you," Hillary says. "We'll try to make it."

I take this as my cue to end the call and enter new GPS coordinates into the phone.

"The GPS thinks we'll get there in half an hour," I tell her.

"It assumes we're following the speed limit," Hillary says. "I hope to be there in fifteen." She accelerates.

"Have you spoken with Eugene or Bert?" I ask to keep my mind off our speed.

"Hold on," she says. "And press the voice command button on my phone."

I press and hold the button. Had she reached for the phone herself, I would've mutinied.

"Call George," Hillary says in a clear voice.

The device rings through the car's speakers a few times before someone picks up.

"Hello," George says.

"Put Telogia into your GPS," Hillary says. "And tell the same to Kate."

"No problem," George says, "but we're falling behind."

"Whoever gets there, gets there," Hillary says. "Remind her to only use the tranquilizer guns, okay?"

"Affirmative," George says. "We all understand Darren's friends and family are in those Odysseys."

He sounds annoyed with her implication that he or one of Kate's people would need such a reminder.

The line goes dead.

"Sorry about that, Darren," Hillary says. "Yes, I did talk to Eugene and Bertie. They're a couple of hours behind the vans. They told me not to bother them so they could concentrate on their research, so I haven't."

In the distance, I see Kate veer her bike onto an exit ramp.

"Brace yourself," Hillary says and turns the wheel.

I bet those are some of the most famous last words, right after 'Oops' and, if coming from a doctor, 'This will be uncomfortable.' As we turn, I feel as if I might throw up. Had I eaten anything today, I definitely would have. As is, the world around me goes silent.

Looking at our car from the side of the road, I realize her turn made me spontaneously phase into the Quiet. While my heartbeat calms down, I note how peculiar it is that I'm actually outside the car rather than in the back seat. I must've spontaneously Teleported thanks to George's recent training.

As I study the car, I discover there isn't a back seat to speak of. The car is a full-fledged race car, right down to a large Dish sponsor ad on its hood. In hindsight, I should've figured out that this was a race car by how crammed it is on the inside, not to mention the helmets and the two-sided seat belts.

My frozen self's eyes look as if they might pop out and break through the visor. Since I'm already in the Quiet, I walk over to Kate. She's driving a monster motorcycle that Batman would've been proud to own. I don't dare pull her in; making this turn unscathed must be taking every ounce of her concentration—at least it would be for me. Which reminds me . . . Hillary mentioned clearing the road for us in the Quiet. That means she's been driving like a maniac while phasing in and out. Having done this myself before, I know I ought to be extra thankful we're still alive.

Returning to the race car, I fatalistically phase out—and instantly wish I didn't.

The centrifugal (or is it the G?) forces only *begin* once I phase in. It feels as if I'm getting squished into my seat.

When I can speak again, I say, "Aunt, if you need to clear more of the road, please let me. I want you focused on driving."

"Sure," she says. "But it's likely unnecessary. I cleared quite a long stretch in one go a few miles back. Plus, I'm working with law enforcement—"

"Then whatever else I can do to help," I say as a means of self-preservation.

"Sure, if I think of anything," my aunt says and accelerates some more. "We're getting closer."

We're now on the other side of the highway, leaving the Humvee and the police cavalcade far behind us.

"Where did you get this car?" I ask, more as a way to distract myself from my terror than out of any real curiosity.

"Daytona," she says. "They have NASCAR. If you don't mind, I want to focus on the road. I'm about to push this car to its limits."

The next five minutes are probably the scariest moments of my life, and that includes the last couple of weeks with people trying to kill me.

The annoying ringtone is back. I accept the call, and a voice says, "We couldn't stop them at the merge point."

"It's okay, Sheriff," Hillary says. "We didn't think you could. At least we're now on their tails."

Her gloved hands grip the wheel tighter, and the engine sounds as if it's possessed by a poltergeist.

You know when I said the previous five minutes of my life were the scariest? I'm changing that. These next five put them to shame.

Another bank-robbery alarm interrupts my hyperventilation, and I distract myself by accepting the call.

"Fuck," a voice says loudly. Screams and shots can be heard in the background. "A Honda minivan just went around our blockade. This driver is a maniac. I have deputies on the dirt road waiting for the second Honda."

"Sheriff Wilkin," Hillary says disapprovingly. "Why did I hear shots? You are not permitted to use deadly force. There are hostages in those cars."

"We tried shooting the tires, ma'am," the guy says, "but missed."

"Be ready," she says. "They're a few minutes apart."

"We are," he says.

"Let's hope we catch them first," she says and looks at her GPS.

According to its tracker, we're already there.

A few seconds later, Hilary whispers, "Do you see that?"

I see Kate's figure in the distance but nothing else. I squint and see she's nearing a van.

Hillary squeezes more speed out of our car, the motor revving maniacally. With trepidation, I glance at the speedometer and wish I hadn't. It reads 210 mph.

We get closer to Kate, the sides of the road blurring. I suspect we might be going 'back to the future' at any moment.

Kate parallels the van. The van swerves in her direction, apparently trying to force Kate off the road.

We move closer to Kate and her adversary.

Kate speeds up, pulls a wheelie, and races ahead of the van. I think the stunt was just her showing off, though I'm not sure.

We're nearing the van; our front bumper is almost ready to kiss the circled H logo on the Honda's rear. In the distance is a police blockade; it's also where the road ends and the tree line begins.

"Hillary, you see that, right?" The words come out in a hushed whisper. "Are you sure we'll have time to slow—"

I don't finish that thought, as Hillary tries to pass the van on the right.

At the same time, Kate lets her bike drift, its tires smoking. The bike is angled so low to the ground that her right handlebar is touching the asphalt.

Then Kate jumps off the bike, letting the poor machine fly under the van.

The van swerves into us, the driver clearly not wanting to drive over the motorcycle while moving at this speed, then veers in Kate's direction. We almost collide with its back. Hillary turns the wheel sharply to avoid crashing into the van.

Our car skids toward the side of the road—and toward a big palm tree. If we don't slow down, the emergency workers will have a hard time scraping us out of what will be left of this car.

Hillary slams on the brakes, and I smell burning rubber.

Though we're decelerating, we're still going fast enough that the impact might turn us into burnt toast.

Hillary turns the wheel, gentler this time.

Everything goes silent.

Shit.

Looks like I scare-phased into the Quiet again.

I'm standing next to the palm tree we're about to hit.

Luckily, Hillary's last maneuver pointed the car slightly to the side of the tree; we might not hit it head-on, though I'm no expert when it comes to car physics.

I walk over to where Kate jumped/fell.

I can't believe what I'm seeing.

Kate sliced through the Honda's front tire. She's holding the blade steady, ready to give the back tire the same treatment.

She's insane. If the car veers her way, it'll run her over.

Reluctantly, I make my way back.

I phase out and instantly learn I was wrong about the car's trajectory; Hillary's last maneuver didn't help us.

With the sound of worlds colliding, our race car crashes into the tree.

CHAPTER SIXTEEN

Even with the six-point straps and the neck support of my helmet, the jolt is so violent that I feel as if my whiplash is getting whiplash.

I'm still conscious, however. Hillary managed to change the angle of our impact to lessen its severity, and we skirted the tree instead of hitting it dead-on. We'll live.

My heart, which is currently up my throat, clearly hasn't gotten the memo.

"We have to go," I croak, fumbling to unbuckle my multiple straps.

Hillary beats me to it, unclipping my lap and my right and left shoulder restraints. I take care of the one by my crotch on my own.

Fleetingly, I note the lack of any airbags. Race cars must not have them.

As soon as I'm free, I remove my helmet, stumble out of the car, and look at the road.

The Honda Odyssey is out of control, but driving away from Kate, who's plastered against the road. The van's rims are raining sparks as they scrape against the ground, and the smell of burning rubber mixes with a strange metallic odor.

Please don't flip, I think desperately as I run toward the van.

The vehicle makes it halfway into a ditch and stops, without flipping.

Kate is near the right side of the car. I didn't even see her get up.

The door opens. A monk—who must've attempted to exit the van—is on the floor convulsing from Kate's strike.

"Kate, the passenger door," I scream when I see another monk exit.

In the next moment, Kate is holding two strange, elongated guns.

She shoots one inside the van and aims the other one at where the driver shows up.

Panting, I sprint toward the van, with Hillary on my heels.

The driver monk dodges Kate's shot. Belatedly, it hits me that she's using a tranquilizer gun.

I recognize the monk she missed. He was assisting the Master monk during the attack at the Miami airport.

Kate switches her attention from the door to the assistant monk, which turns out to be a mistake. Another monk's foot strikes her through the open door. If Kate were me, she would've tripped over the unconscious body of the first monk she neutralized. Kate, however, isn't me, so instead of falling, she lets the momentum of the kick carry her body into the assistant monk. I watch her with envy, my martial arts knowledge once again drawing a blank when it comes to Kate's fighting style.

There's no time to dwell on her technique, though. Springing into action, I kick the leg of the monk who just kicked Kate. I hit a bone near the guy's knee, and my big toe feels like it's on fire. I wonder who's hurt worse—me or my opponent.

"Step aside, Darren," Hillary yells.

I do, and a dart hits the monk's shin, right where I just kicked him. Why does Hillary have one of these nifty tranquilizers and I don't?

In my peripheral vision, I see Kate execute a number of moves, and the assistant monk joins his brothers on the ground.

Kate then turns around, aims her gun, and shoots the next monk as he's exiting the car.

Strangely, the monk doesn't fall. He must be more resistant to whatever drug is in the darts.

The monk faces me, the dart sticking out from his neck. His eyes are slightly glazed over. Without a second's hesitation, I punch him in the stomach. Though the hit wasn't all that powerful, the monk doubles over and hits the ground. The lack of oxygen must've finished the job the tranquilizer started.

I look around and see that while I was distracted, Kate took care of a couple more monks.

I look inside the van. The only two people left are my moms, and they're both unconscious. I check their pulses, and when I find it, I feel like a man who's come across a feast after a long fast. At the same time, I'm more than a little angry that they were kept sedated for so long. I hope the monks drugged them when the chase began and they haven't been kept unconscious for the past twenty hours.

Out of the corner of my eye, I see Kate shoot darts into the monks she forcefully knocked out.

"Wait, Kate," I say, but she shoots the last one anyway. "We might have needed one."

"Too late," she says. "What would we need them for?"

"I only vaguely recall where the Temple is," I explain. "We could've asked them some pointed questions."

"I wouldn't worry about that," Hillary says. "We have so many police officers helping us that we can scout the woods for the Temple. These monks aren't Readable, as you found out, and I won't let them be tortured."

"Shouldn't we go after the other van?" I ask. "The one with Thomas and Mira in it?"

"They have a big start," Kate says. "They'll be halfway to the Temple by now."

"So I guess we'll need your team's help after all," I say, frustrated.

"Yeah, and now our job will be even trickier," Kate says. "When this van doesn't show up, the Temple will be put on high alert."

"So what do we do?" I ask.

"Nothing. We'll manage it," she says. "I'm just thinking out loud."

"Before your team gets here and we start looking for the Temple, I want my moms taken somewhere safe." I glance at the two unconscious bodies inside the van before turning to my aunt. "Hillary, do you think you can do me a huge favor? Can you take them? You could take a bunch of cops with you and drive someplace where no one would think to look for you."

Hillary frowns. "What about the Temple? I want to help rescue the others."

"This is the best way for you to help," I say. What I don't add is that this way, I can ensure *she*'s safe too.

"Are you getting rid of me so you can do something violent at the Temple?" Hillary asks, her eyes narrowing.

"No." I shake my head. "I'll pinky swear to do as little harm as possible. After all, my grandparents are there. What kind of monster do you take me for, Aunt?"

She sighs. "Take my tranquilizer gun. And make sure the others use theirs."

I take the weapon and stick it in the back of my pants as Kate demonstratively waves her guns in the air.

Hillary rolls her eyes and walks toward the police blockade.

Ignoring her, Kate walks over to what's left of Hillary's race car and looks for something inside. Then she waves for me to join her.

By the time I get there, Kate has the object spread out on the roof of the crumpled car.

When I get closer, I see that it's one of those primitive items people used in ancient times—the dark ages before GPS apps. The object is made out of a dumb material called paper, which you can't read in the dark and which lacks a zoom-in feature.

An atlas-style map.

"We're here," Kate points to a spot on the map. "Can you show me, approximately, where the Temple might be?"

I examine the area surrounding our current location. Only a handful of roads traverse the whole forest. The one we're currently on leads to the highway I recall taking after I temporarily kidnapped my grandpa, Paul.

I also remember that when we walked out of the forest, I was looking at the driver's side of the car, which means the Temple is on the left side of this road. Furthermore, I remember how long it took me to get onto that highway, so, backtracking, I draw a circle on the map with my finger and say, "Around there."

"Great," Kate says. "This reduces the search radius by a factor of fifty, at least. With extra help, it shouldn't take more than a few hours."

"We can actually do it in no time at all," I say, "if we're willing to forgo the police help and do it in the Mind Dimension."

"That would be a tedious exercise," she says. "Plus, we actually need to kill a number of hours."

"Why is that?"

"We're going to do our extraction when it's dark, so they're less likely to detect us," she explains.

A car honk prevents me from asking my next question.

Glancing up, I see that the Humvee and its police escort have finally caught up with us, and Hillary is back too.

"Be careful, gentlemen," Hillary says to James and Stephen as they carry Lucy out of the van, their muscles not looking the least bit strained. Carrying my mom is as difficult for them as carrying that map is for Kate.

"Watch her head," Hillary says to Eleanor and John, who have Sara.

They put my moms in the back of a patrol wagon. Hillary makes sure they're strapped in, and a couple of competent-looking police officers take up the rest of the space. Hillary gets into the front passenger seat and rolls her window down.

"Call me as soon as it's all over," she says.

"I will," I promise.

"I told Bert and Eugene what's going on," she says. "They should be passing this way in a little over an hour."

"Have they made a breakthrough in their research?"

"Bert was cagey on that," she says. "So not likely."

"Then I doubt I'll need them. Guess you'll be seeing 'Bertie' very soon."

"What should I tell Lucy and Sara when they wake up?" she asks.

I shrug. "Use your judgment. Just don't make them believe anything too crazy."

"Of course," she says. "You better go. Kate and her crew look anxious."

"Thank you," I say. "I'm losing track of how much I owe you."

She smiles and (I'm guessing) Guides the driver cop to start the car. As they drive away, I follow them with my gaze, relieved that my moms are safe.

Two saved, two to go.

I walk over to the little gathering by the sheriff's car, where Kate is coordinating the effort to locate the Temple.

George suggests that each Guide gets an escort of five or six officers. He also explains how we can work together by spreading out once we're in the forest.

I'm paired with Sheriff Wilkin and the deputies from his office. If these folks are anything to go by, then the cops in Florida are a hundred times friendlier than their New York counterparts. Then again, given how a civilian on the streets of New York is at least fifty times meaner than a random Floridian, the New York cops' frostiness is forgivable.

"If the plan is clear, please spread out, everyone," George says, and one by one, the groups enter the forest.

* * *

We've been walking through the stupid forest for about an hour. That's an hour too long.

I'm a city person to the core, a fact that becomes abundantly clear to me every time I wander through nature.

The last time I was in these woods, the mosquitoes, ants, and giant spiders were frozen in the Quiet, making the trips to and from the Temple more bearable, but the critters aren't frozen now. Also, the branches weren't hitting me in the face as often, though that might've been the result of having a competent guide—my grandpa.

If only I could recall where we came from . . .

When I reach a small clearing, I hear footsteps. Must be time for our search party to gather around me again to compare notes.

"How can a drug lord's mansion not show up on satellite imagery?" one of the deputies asks after our status reports are done.

I chuckle at the explanation George gave them about our target and earn a puzzled look from the deputy.

"Like the chief said, they're very connected people," says the sheriff, his southern accent a lot stronger than the deputy's. He's struggling not to pant as he wipes the sweat from his forehead. He's one of those larger people who seem too active for their bulk.

"It sure happens," another deputy says. "Military bases don't show up, same with Area 51."

"I've gone ahead and had my house removed from Google Earth," another deputy echoes. "You can report your privacy concerns to the good people at Google maps, and they'll blur your house, just like that."

"That's just darn stupid," the sheriff says, and everyone snickers at the privacy-concerned deputy's expense.

"Let's spread out again," I say and turn away from my entourage, ready to head deeper into the forest.

The sheriff's walkie-talkie blares to life behind me.

"We found it," a voice says, the static masking the person's identity.

In the distance, southwest from us, a flare arcs into the sky.

This development is so incongruent with our stealth-oriented plan that I instantly phase into the Quiet to make sense of it.

The stupid Teleportation is still causing me to show up in the Quiet at random locations. This time, I end up on the other side of the sheriff, who was, just a moment ago, a few feet behind me.

I look at the frozen-in-time flare uncomprehendingly. The plan was to surreptitiously circulate the Temple's GPS coordinates. We made a point of instructing everyone that they were *not* to alarm the monks. On top of that, the extraction operation was supposed to start at nightfall (without any flares or even a hint of our presence), but it's still daytime.

What the hell is happening? Did the monks send up the flare as some kind of alarm? I have a hard time picturing that.

Realizing I'm just blankly staring at the sky, I stop and walk toward my frozen body. The best way to figure out what's going on is to approach the flare and see for myself who shot it.

Then something catches my eye.

The sheriff's hand.

Maybe the events at Kyle's funeral have made me paranoid, but I don't like the way the frozen sheriff's hand is positioned. In fact, walking up to the nearest deputy, I note the same disconcerting pattern. It's almost as though they're reaching for their side arms.

I walk up to the sheriff and initiate a Read.

* * *

We're trying to listen, but find it hard to concentrate. The black-latex-and-leather-clad woman in charge is too stunning to allow a red-blooded male to function. She gives us our instructions. The plan isn't too different from what we'd do if we were looking for a lost child in the woods, which is the only reason we can follow what she's saying.

"You're not to enter the clearing that surrounds the place, let alone the large mansion that's in the middle of it," the woman says. "Upon finding it, get in touch with your group, then notify the rest of us."

I, Darren, disassociate because at that very moment, a presence enters the sheriff's mind.

If you find the mansion, kill Darren, the young official accompanying you.

If you get a radio transmission that states, 'We found it,' that is also your signal to kill him.

He's an extremely dangerous fugitive trying to escape custody. Wait until your group has gathered and his back is to you, then shoot him. Don't ask questions, don't read him his Miranda rights, and don't do anything that would give him a chance to react. He is extremely dangerous, and if he knows your intentions, you will die. He is your enemy. You are at war . . .

The sinister instructions continue, but I've heard enough to get the general idea. Plus, I recognize this 'voice.' It belongs to the same person who was controlling the police officers at Kyle's funeral.

The person I've been calling the Super Pusher is the one Pushing the sheriff.

But that makes no sense. How could he be here?

The likeliest explanation is that one of the dudes on Kate's team is the Super Pusher. However, Kate mentioned they hadn't left the Island in months. That means they couldn't have been at Kyle's funeral—unless the Super Pusher Guided Kate to say that to provide her team with an alibi.

Alternatively, maybe my assumption that the Super Pusher isn't a man was right. I thought I was wrong after the masked attacker—who was clearly male—had attacked me in the library, but what if Kate is the Super Pusher? What if she Guided some random guy on the Island to attack me to throw me off her scent? That possibility isn't so different from the way these cops were triggered to attack me. Maybe the condition for the masked guy was putting on the mask? She could've Guided him long before we got pulled into Frederick's Mind Dimension to avoid the limitation of not being able to reach Level 2 from someone else's Session. Come to think of it, she was just returning from a walk when George and I were having breakfast. Had she left to put her plan into motion? Using similar logic, Eleanor could also be the one behind all this.

In any case, it seems the Super Pusher is close to revealing him or herself. The most important clue is that he or she turned the surrounding cops into sleeper agents that have been triggered to kill me.

As I ponder why the Super Pusher delayed killing me and consider the mystery of the flare signal, the only probable answer dawns on me.

I was kept alive to make sure the Temple was found first, because I'm the only person who's been there.

Which means the Temple is the Super Pusher's target for some reason.

Shit. My insides grow cold, but I decide to worry about the consequences of this realization later. Right now, I need to make sure the cops don't shoot me once I phase out.

To that end, I make my Guiding instruction succinct and direct, branding the words, '*You will not gun down Darren,*' into the sheriff's brain.

With that, I exit his head.

I sear the same '*You will not gun down Darren*' instructions into the minds of the rest of the team. I find a few men in the distance and do the same to them—no point in taking chances.

Then I phase out to check how well my instructions worked.

When the sounds of the world return, I turn around. The sheriff isn't reaching for his gun anymore. I breathe a sigh of relief.

And that's when I feel a terrible pain in my chest.

As impossible as it seems, there's only one way I can interpret the situation.

I've been shot.

CHAPTER SEVENTEEN

Time seems to slow.

I can't think, aside from something along the lines of *I'm so fucked*, which repeats over and over in my mind.

I lose control of every muscle, including the ones that help keep my body upright, and start falling toward the ground. The fall also happens in that strange, slow-motion way.

And then I'm standing a few feet away from my body, behind the sheriff. My frozen self is suspended mid-fall. The shock of getting shot must've caused me to phase into the Quiet, possibly for the last time.

I run toward my statue-like self to assess the severity of the damage.

To my surprise and relief, I don't see any blood gushing from a wound on his/my body. However, there are wires attached to my chest. These wires lead back to the youngest deputy, who's standing to my right. He's holding something that looks like a Nerf gun, into which the filaments disappear.

I follow the wires back to my body, and finally, it dawns on me.

The deputy shot me with a Taser—a non-lethal weapon cops carry.

Confused, I enter the deputy's head to figure out what happened.

It doesn't take me long to understand the mix-up. Apparently, I got shot as a result of my imprecise Guiding. Both the Super Pusher and I contributed to this situation.

The Super Pusher Guided the deputy to support his senior colleagues in the event of a scuffle. The Pusher must've been in a hurry and didn't bother giving him the detailed instruction of killing me because I was uber-dangerous. So the deputy interpreted this situation in a more reasonable way than the Pusher had anticipated. Being a good man, he decided against using deadly force, opting instead to incapacitate me with the Taser and then cuff me.

On my part, I wasn't specific enough when I Guided this deputy, or for that manner, everyone else. I merely forbade him from gunning me down. Since a Taser is not a gun in the strictest sense, '*You will not gun down Darren*' did not stop him from tasing me.

I'm more specific with the new set of instructions I etch into the deputy's mind and, for good measure, into the minds of the other cops as well.

I'm your master and commander. You will not harm me in any physical or emotional way. You will listen and obey my orders without question. You will protect me with your life. If there is danger, you will believe you're with the Secret Service and I'm the President.

Some of my guiding is perhaps overkill, but I'd rather not repeat the same mistake.

I instruct a couple of the stronger-looking deputies to help me up. The Taser deputy is instructed to remove his finger from the device out of fear for his life.

Satisfied with my Guiding, I gingerly walk back to my poor body.

Without thinking too much, I phase out by touching his/my wrinkled forehead.

I'm on the ground before I can understand what's what. The tall grass dampens my fall.

Aside from my complaining coccyx bone, the pain where the Taser penetrated my skin is the worst of it. The rest of the experience is as confusing as it is painful. The two electrodes, or whatever they're called, are still attached to me, but the shock is gone, and I'm beginning to regain control of my muscles again.

Strong hands help me up and tear out the electrodes.

Once I've recovered enough to move again, I tell the cops, "We're heading in the direction of that flare. If anyone radios in and asks if it's done, you say 'confirm.'"

"Yes, sir," the sheriff says. The others echo the 'yes, sir' in such perfect unison that they would've made a drill sergeant proud.

I make them repeat my command to make sure they understood, and they do.

With my now-loyal squad behind me, I run through the forest. Running is maybe overstating it a bit, but I move as fast as I can without losing an eye to a low-hanging branch or breaking a leg on a treacherous rock.

My feeling of foreboding intensifies with every step, as does my suspicion that I might be responsible for a disaster.

A shot echoes through the forest.

I look behind me. My little squad looks as surprised as I feel.

Another shot rings out, and I know for sure they're coming from the direction of the flare.

I start running in earnest.

Another shot.

I speed up.

Then I hear a chain of gunfire that could only be coming from an automatic weapon.

Blood wells up from cuts where branches bit into my flesh, but I ignore the sting and increase my pace. My heart feels as if it's sending me an SOS in Morse code through my ribcage.

Then, with the sound of an explosion, the world is muted.

In the Quiet, running is easier due to the lack of any wind. I'm also emboldened by the fact that whatever damage the branches inflict on me here will be undone when I phase out.

It takes me a few minutes at this pace to reach the clearing surrounding the Temple. I've acquired half a dozen scrapes and splinters, but I forget about these minor injuries as soon as I look out toward the Temple.

People—lots of people—are doing something they shouldn't be doing.

I have to get closer before I can let myself believe what's happening. In my frenzied state, I don't even register my sprint across the clearing.

The closer I get, the more my fears turn into stark reality.

A full-fledged battle is underway, with violence and death permeating the most serene of places.

At first, I don't even recognize the area. Gorgeous arbors and intricate giant shrubs used to mark the entrance to the Temple's grounds. Most of them are now in shambles, and one gazebo has been blown to smithereens—possibly in the explosion I heard earlier. Bits of what's left of the gazebo crunch under my feet as I look around.

To my left, five cops are frozen in the process of shooting at the orange-clad monks. Some monks have serene, determined expressions on their faces, though most look uncharacteristically frightened. One monk looks absolutely terrified, as anyone in his situation would. A bullet is frozen in the process of entering his forehead.

To my right, an older monk is choking a deputy in a strange, kung-fu-inspired grip. Another monk is holding another deputy's arm in an unnatural position, leading me to believe that the limb has been broken.

I check the guns on the ground. As I thought, the monks took advantage of the moment when the cops ran out of bullets.

Farther in, a young monk is fighting an older one. Not ready to think about it, I file this away as a mystery. This monk-on-monk violence and the shootouts aren't what give my surroundings a particularly hellish feel.

That honor belongs to Kate.

She's standing there with blood covering her black outfit and soaking into the ground around her. Her sword is embedded in a monk's chest. Heads and limbs of other monks surround Kate in a gory mess, like a scene from a slasher movie.

I look away. Though I've never thrown up in the Quiet, right now, while looking at the disemboweled and dismembered bodies of the monks, I feel like I just might. As a kid, after watching *The Three Musketeers* and *Star Wars*, I had a glamorized view of sword fighting. I thought it was cool. Now, and for the rest of my life, I will think of getting killed by a sword as one of the most barbaric and gruesome ways to die.

Unfortunately, looking away doesn't make the horrors go away—not when my gaze falls on George, who's frozen in the process of reloading a shotgun.

In front of him are piles of shot-up monks. Their wounds have turned their orange robes crimson.

I run again, for no other reason than to get away from the carnage.

But the carnage follows me. Slightly farther in, near the incongruently peaceful rock garden, I find Eleanor holding a bloodied monk above her head, and I do mean *above* her head, with her arms almost straight. She looks like a wrestler who's about to break someone's back.

I can't take any more of this, but short of closing my eyes, I can't escape it.

When I do close my eyes and find a second to think, a terrible anxiety hits me. Somewhere in this Temple are Thomas and Mira. After seeing so much death, it's all too easy to picture the worst.

I open my eyes, my heart beating frantically.

I have to get to the Temple.

As I run toward the building, I see more cops and monks locked in deadly embraces near the bonsai trees.

Passing them, I see frozen James raining death on the monks with an automatic rifle, right next to the serene cherry blossom trees. He looks like a grizzly bear standing in a river during salmon mating season.

The fighting gets sparser as I get closer to the giant Temple doors. I see a bunch of bullet-riddled cops on the ground, as well as some cops with knife wounds, and the reason quickly becomes clear.

Two large men are frozen in the midst of an epic fight. Or more accurately, at this point in the fight, one is murdering the other.

It only takes me a moment to recognize the victim as John, the 'sick lion' part of Kate's deadly circus troop. His features are twisted in fury and fear, and I know all too well the person doing the killing. He's probably the cause behind the shot-up and cut-up cops as well. That he's fighting against John and not under the Super Pusher's influence is actually surprising, but not something I'm ready to think about.

Looking at his stern face, I feel a sense of camaraderie. For what feels like the first time, I'm happy to see Caleb, and I'm cheering for him.

Of course, Caleb doesn't need my moral support. His hands are around John's throat, and his frozen knuckles are marble white from exertion. Caleb's grip must be devastatingly strong. The result is something I didn't even think was possible. The tips of Caleb's fingers are *inside* his opponent's neck. I'm not a doctor, but I think Caleb is in the process of ripping out John's Adam's apple.

John also has a knife wound in his belly. Caleb's signature knife is lying a foot away, covered in blood.

Out of all of Kate's people, Richard–the scorpion—is the only one missing.

Is he missing because he's the puppeteer of this madness?

I push the Temple doors open and walk inside.

The halls are almost empty, but in the far corner, I see a lone monk, barely out of his teens. He looks to be heading toward the big doors at the back.

Deciding to try Reading him for any useful information, I reach out and touch his bald head. Nothing happens, though. The raging emotions brought on by what's happening outside make the focused state of Coherence extremely difficult for me to achieve. I focus on my breath and push the horror I witnessed out of my head. In, out . . . In, out . . . Though not calm, I achieve a robotic sense of relaxation, but only after what feels like an hour. It's enough, though, and I get inside the young monk's head.

* * *

We see our brothers carrying the two strangers into the guesthouse, and we follow them curiously. The sight of a young, pretty, long-haired female is a rare one at the Temple. True, we have sisters, but they don't count. This one is even prettier than the younger of the two women staying in the guesthouse.

I, Darren, disassociate from the young monk's thoughts. If I weren't in a state of utter despair, I'd find it curious how the monk tried to fight against his hormone-inspired thoughts. Instead, I focus on the facts. To my huge relief, the two people he saw were Mira and Thomas. They were alive, and the monks were dragging them to where Julia and her mother are staying, and I know exactly where that is. Before I exit the monk's head, I fast-forward through his memories a little more in search of anything useful, and I'm instantly glad I went through the trouble.

"Take me with you," we say to the Master. "Let me protect the Enlightened ones."

"I want you to hide in the forest," the Master says. "I want all the younglings to do so."

"But where are you taking them?" we ask, our heart heavy. "What will happen to us?"

"We're going to sneak them out. There's a path we can use at the back of the Temple," the Master says. "Then we'll hide in the forest, just as you must."

"But the others will fight—"

"They are old enough to make that choice," the Master says, "and wise enough for me to accept it."

"But I must—"

"Please do as I tell you," the Master says wearily. "Do not make this old man beg."

"Okay, Master," we say, lying for the first time this month. "I will run to the forest."

We watch the Master and a few of the older monks leave.

We watch as our brothers walk out to do battle in front of the Temple's entrance.

We have no intention of running into the woods.

We're going to help our brothers.

We're going to join the fight.

But when the gunfire begins, we find it hard to summon the courage to go.

We take a step toward the entrance, then take two steps back.

I, Darren, can't take any more of the fear and doubt inside my host's head, and get out.

* * *

Looking the young monk over, I recognize the resolve and determination on his face. In this moment, he looks as if he won the fight against his fear. He's going to join the massacre.

I re-enter his head and Guide him to follow the Master's advice to run and hide in the forest.

When I'm done with this task, I realize something—an answer to a puzzle I noticed earlier. I couldn't understand why the younger monks were fighting the older monks outside. Now, however, it occurs to me that the young monks, just like the one I Read, haven't mastered the skill of resisting Reading and Guiding. So the Super Pusher, or for that matter, any member of Kate's team, could—and did—turn the novice monks against their brothers.

I find the idea of Pushing monks to fight each other particularly ghastly. Then again, this, at least, I can undo, but it'll have to wait until I take care of something else—well, until I take care of two things actually.

Which do I focus on first? I'm torn between going to the guesthouse to see whether Mira and Thomas are okay, and heading to the back of the Temple to find my grandparents.

I decide to head for the guesthouse.

I go through the outside dojo, which is now empty, and enter the mansion-sized building. No one is there, at least not on the first floor. As soon as

I get to the second floor, however, I find an obvious sign of activity.

The door to the nearest room has been ripped open and is lying on the floor, hinges bent. Before it was forcefully opened, it had been held in place by a latch with a big lock on it. By the looks of it, the door was padlocked from the outside.

I walk down the corridor and spot the back of a figure standing in a combative pose, fists raised, next to another padlocked door. I think I know who it is, even from this vantage point, but I get closer to make sure.

My suspicion was right.

It's Thomas.

When I get a better look at him, my insides turn cold.

Thomas's hands are covered in blood.

CHAPTER EIGHTEEN

I stare at his bloodied hands in a stupefied daze until I realize the blood is coming from his damaged knuckles.

Was he fighting for his life?

No. As I examine the door he's standing next to, I note the bloody prints on it—prints that match Thomas's knuckles.

He hurt his hands trying to enter this locked room.

I check the door that was torn off its hinges. Thomas's blood is smeared across the back, and there are also boot prints. Thomas was likely locked inside this room and broke out, and now he's trying to get into the other room.

I think I know what's happening, but I want to be sure.

I make my way back to the battlefield, this time running as if a rabid tiger is chasing me.

I use a stick to pry the shotgun out of George's arms; I don't want to accidentally pull him into the Quiet with me. Then I return to the upstairs of the guesthouse and use the butt of the shotgun to push Thomas's frozen body out of my way. I don't want to bring him in either.

I fire the shotgun at the door over and over. My ears beg for mercy, but I ignore them. On the fifth shot, the shotgun makes a clicking noise, indicating it's empty. The door is in shambles, and I kick away what remains of it.

As I suspected, Mira is inside. She's lying on the bed, unconscious.

Given Thomas's crazed approach to opening the doors, I have to assume he's trying to break in so he can hurt her. The ferocity on his face and the deep cuts on his knuckles offer no other alternative.

There's only one probable explanation.

The Super Pusher is also controlling Thomas, the way he was controlling him at the funeral.

Thomas is determined to get to Mira, and her door won't last much longer.

Shit.

I look her over.

Mira's face looks almost angelic. The full intensity of how much I missed her hits me. I can't bear to think there's even a chance she'll get hurt.

No. I refuse to contemplate that possibility. I touch her forehead, determined to pull her in and warn her.

Nothing happens.

I touch her again.

Still no effect.

I shake her as though I could wake her up from the Quiet, and even try kissing her as if she were Sleeping Beauty and I her prince.

Nothing.

She must be Inert on top of being drugged up. Knowing Mira, I suspect she fought them as soon as she woke up from the van ride.

Crap. I'll have to continue facing this war zone alone.

I consider pulling Thomas in, but that wouldn't improve the situation. At best, I could make him Inert, but in the real world, he would still be quite capable of breaking down the door and hurting Mira.

Pulling him into the Quiet to make him Inert would be too dangerous, anyway. If I failed to kill him and he killed me instead, I would be made Inert and left with no chance of untangling this mess—not that I can, at present, see any way to do so.

Actually, there is one way.

If I could reach Level 2, I could reverse whatever the Super Pusher did to Thomas. For that matter, I could reverse what I assume he did to George, Kate, and her crew.

Of course, I can't get to Level 2, so it's pointless to dwell on it. For now, I need to get a better grasp on this fucked-up situation.

With purpose adding stamina to my aching legs, I run out of the guesthouse. I have to find a way to get to the back of the Temple.

I sprint, Reading young monks as I go, and I'm glad that I do. The exit is actually a hidden passageway. I have to go down into the Temple's basement and take a bunch of winding corridors, and I do just that.

When I exit the hidden passage, I find myself in the forest, surrounded by cops and Richard. They're all pointing their guns at a white-robed figure.

Edward.

He's one of the Enlightened and my step-grandfather of sorts—husband to Rose, my father's mom. She had my father with Paul, who's not her husband, for the sake of genetic purity. Of course, none of that Jerry Springer stuff matters right now.

The bullet-riddled bodies of monks are strewn everywhere, confirming what's already obvious: Edward is about to get shot.

But then I notice something strange about Edward. He looks frightened, sure, but he also appears determined. If I didn't know any better, I'd say there's triumph in his frozen eyes.

I touch his forehead, determined to pull him in and find out what he's doing.

Bringing him into the Quiet doesn't work, likely because Richard made him Inert.

Edward's right hand is hidden in the folds of his white robe. Something about the way he's standing makes me suspicious of that hand, so I examine it—and my stomach turns.

He's about to pull the pin out of a grenade that's been secured to his body.

He wants to blow himself up and take his attackers out with him.

No, that's insane. There has to be a better way of dealing with this situation.

I enter the mind of the first cop and watch Richard's sickening, execution-style attack on the monks who are now dead on the ground.

Then I start Guiding him.

I instruct the cops closest to Richard: "*You will not shoot this old man. You will swap your gun for a Taser and point it at Richard; then you will pull the trigger. Richard, the big guy to your left, is the FBI's most wanted criminal, and you're here to take him down. As soon as the Taser neutralizes him, cuff him. After this, do not allow anyone to follow the white-robed people.*"

To the cops closer to Edward, I command: "*Use your Taser on the old man and then carefully secure his hidden grenade. You will tell him that everything is okay and that he can catch up with his people. You will make sure they are not followed.*"

I hope my efforts pay off. It'll be a matter of timing, of the Tasers versus Edward pulling the pin from the grenade. Unsure of how else I can help my grandmother's husband, I run deeper into the forest.

After a few minutes, I see a group of white-robed figures. In addition to the Enlightened, there are some regular people here too. Notably, I spot Julia and her mother. I feel a fleeting anger; they took Julia, but they abandoned Mira, leaving her in danger.

I walk back to the cops and get a handgun—just in case.

When I return, I locate my asshole of a grandfather, Paul. Gun ready, I touch him to pull him in.

Again, nothing.

He must already be Inert, which means someone killed him in the Quiet before I got here. Given Richard's current proximity, he's the likeliest candidate—which means he knows where Paul is located in the real world, and by extension, the rest of the Enlightened.

I touch a few more of the Enlightened and get the same results, which supports my theory that Richard knows they're here, hiding.

When I make my way to Rose, my grandmother, and touch her, I finally get lucky.

A second Rose joins me in the Quiet.

Her usually smiling face is filled with sorrow. When she registers me, though, her expression changes to one of confusion, quickly followed by such unfiltered hatred that she looks almost unrecognizable.

"You bastard." She slaps my face with all her strength. "You brought death to your own flesh and blood."

CHAPTER NINETEEN

Rose's words sting worse than her slap.

Rubbing my cheek, I say, "This—whatever this is—is not something I caused. It's the opposite. I'm here because I'm trying to help you."

"Help us, right," she sneers. "Help put us all into early graves."

"Why would I say I want to help if it wasn't true?"

"I can think of a million treacherous reasons," she says bitterly. "Why should I believe anything you say?"

"Because I don't need to lie to you." My voice takes on a sharper edge. I'm quickly losing what little goodwill I had when I pulled her in. My jaw tightening, I show her my gun, trying my best not to make the gesture seem menacing. "If I wanted to harm you, I would've shot you already."

"I think you want to gloat." Her sharp tone matches mine. "You want to enjoy my suffering before you kill me."

"Why the fuck would I want that?" I glare at her. "Where is this shit coming from? If anyone should be angry, it's me, not you."

"Fine, what *do* you want?" The mask of hatred slips off her face, revealing a scared old woman.

"I want you to help me help you, your husband, and the Enlightened."

As soon as I mention her husband, Rose's face twists with pain.

"He's going to die," she says hoarsely, her eyes brimming with tears. "He insisted on being a hero, and there was nothing I could do to stop him."

"That's what I'm trying to tell you," I say, exasperated. "I Guided the cops not to shoot Edward and to use a stun gun to stop him from blowing himself up. They also won't attack you or Edward. They're going to incapacitate their leader instead."

She stares at me. "Is this a cruel trick to give me hope before you snatch it away?"

I sigh. "If you don't believe me, just go Read them."

She gives a curt nod and does as I suggested. On her way to the cops, she looks much smaller and frailer than I remembered her. Today's ordeal seems to have aged her by at least a decade.

Approaching the first deputy, she grabs the flesh of his face in an angry, claw-like grip. I half expect her to poke the frozen man's eyes out or kick him in the nuts, but she finds enough composure to just Read him. Then she does the same thing to another cop.

Looking a bit calmer, she walks up to Edward and touches him. Nothing happens for her either, but she still hugs the old man, stroking his body from head to toe as though expecting to find a magic spot that might bring him in.

I let her do this for a few minutes before walking up to her and gently saying, "I think he's Inert."

She nods and her face crumples, whatever calm she gained dissipating.

"The cops might not make it," she says, her voice thick with tears. "He still might blow himself up, and now it would be for nothing."

"I can make the cops speak to him if you think it'll help," I offer.

She shakes her head. "I don't think it would. He's not in the right state of mind."

"Maybe you can try screaming at him?"

"I'm too far away for him to hear me," she says, and buries her face in her hands.

"Okay, well, maybe when he sees the cops pull out the Tasers . . ." I'm grasping at straws here.

She lowers her hands and nods, her mouth quivering as if she might start crying. I feel awful.

"I'm sorry I pulled you in, Rose," I say. "I was just looking for someone who wasn't Inert. I didn't think it through, how painful it would be, especially for you."

"So you're really not behind all this?" She still seems to be having difficulties believing that. "I was so sure. We all were."

"No," I say. "I mean, I did bring these people with me, but they were supposed to rescue Thomas and Mira, not attack you. It was supposed to be a stealthy rescue operation, with all of you none the wiser. Turning the Temple into a war zone was never the plan."

"But they are Pushers, aren't they?" she says. "We learned that from the minds of the police after they attacked."

"They are Guides, yes, but that doesn't mean they automatically can't be trusted. I didn't think you were prejudiced that way."

"I wasn't, at least not until Pushers tried to kill everyone I hold dear." Her mouth hardens. "Why do you think you can trust them?"

"They work for the Elders," I say. "Your equivalents among the Guides."

Her eyebrows pull together. "You knew *that* and thought the results would be different?"

"When I spoke to them, the Elders wanted nothing but peace with the Readers," I explain. "I was sure of it."

"That's news to me," she says.

I let out an exasperated breath. "We can sort *that* out once we survive this."

"This is hardly the path to peace." She looks at the fallen monks. "It's a way toward a new war."

"Right," I say. "Which might be the reason this is happening. Someone who's against an alliance between Guides and Readers is causing this. I think someone is controlling the people I brought with me, the same person who was controlling Mira and Thomas when your people came to grab me. Someone—"

She looks so horrified that I wonder whether I have maggots and scorpions crawling on my face.

"Someone can control Mira, a Reader?" Her eyes look wild. "So the rumors are true. They can do that to anyone."

I realize we're now on very shaky territory.

"Only some Guides can influence Readers and other Guides," I say carefully. "Everyone thinks only the Elders can do it, but I'm not so sure. And the weirdest thing is that, in theory at least, I can do it too, but that's a long story."

She swallows. "Tell me everything. Please, don't leave anything out."

I give her a disjointed tale of everything I consider relevant to the situation: why I kidnapped grandpa and ran away from the Temple to save my mom, and how my encounter with Kyle revealed my Level 2 capabilities. I tell her about Level 2 because I want the Enlightened to know that their little breeding project was a success a generation early. Hopefully, if we all get out of this alive, they'll leave me alone.

I explain how I learned that someone else can use a power similar to mine, and that he or she Pushed Kyle, as well as Mira, Thomas, and, more than likely, everyone here at the Temple. I also tell her about my trip to the Elders' Island. This allows me to do what the Elders actually want me to do—start the peace conversation. So, to that end, I tell her what they wanted from me.

When I finish, she wipes her face with the sleeve of her robe and says, "Here's my thinking. If all that peace talk was true, and let's assume, for now, that it was, then at least one of the Elders seems to be working against the others."

"Except no Elder is here," I say. "They never leave the Island."

"Right," she says. "So like you, one of the people you brought here might have this whatever-you-called-it power."

"Nirvana," I say. "Or Level 2."

"Yes, that." She looks as if she wants to cry again. "Our plans were doomed from the start. We were generations too late."

"Too late?"

"To a degree, the reason we've been breeding for Depth has been to protect our people against this type of scenario. We assumed that, given enough Depth, instead of being Guided, a Reader would get pulled into that second tier of the Mind Dimension. Back when our groups were at war, some of the captured Pushers divulged information about such a power. We believed them because it's the only thing that could explain the paradox of the Orthodoxy."

I frown at her. "What paradox?"

"Think about it," she says. "Why would the Purists, the people who hate Pushers more than anything else in the world, work with their equivalents, the Traditionalists?"

"I've heard theories. They might, for example, plan to kill one another as soon as—"

"We've thought about this long and hard, and no other theory stands up to close scrutiny," she says. "Take Jacob. The man killed Pushers in his youth, but then one day, he decides to work with one? The Jacob I knew would never do that, not unless he was compelled."

She may be right.

"You weren't too late," I say, deciding to address her earlier concern. "In a way, thanks to my mother's background, you succeeded. Hell, being part Guide, I can do more from Nirvana than a mere Reader."

"Indeed." She blinks rapidly, as if to contain her tears. "Paul and I underestimated you."

No shit, I want to say, but resist the urge.

"I'll try to undo more of this," I say instead. "I need you and the others to keep fleeing."

"Can you please save the monks?" she asks. "They don't deserve to die."

I nod. "That's what I was going to work on next. What I did with these cops, I'll do with the ones attacking the Temple from the front."

Rose's mouth trembles in an attempt to smile. "Thank you. Is there anything I can do to help?"

I consider it. After a short pause, I say, "There is, actually. It would be very helpful if you could pull Caleb in and tell him to work with me. I have no idea why he's not under the bad guy's control, but since he's not, I could use his help, even if I don't know how yet."

"Consider it done." Rose makes a visible attempt to pull herself together. Taking a breath, she says, "I wonder why this Pusher didn't make us, his targets, commit suicide. Why this attack?"

"Don't know," I say, puzzled. "That *would* have been the simplest solution."

"It seems as if, for some reason, we're not accessible to this person, just as you mentioned Caleb isn't." She looks thoughtful. "I wonder why."

"A mystery." I gesture for us to start walking. "It'll have to take a number."

"Yes, you're right. It doesn't change anything." She falls into step beside me. "Where are we going?"

"Caleb's at the front of the temple," I say. "I have to warn you, it's not pretty out there."

"Let's go." She's clearly struggling to keep a stoic expression on her face.

We don't talk on the way. Instead, I spend the time pondering what Caleb and the Enlightened could possibly have in common. What is protecting them from the Super Pusher? If my mind weren't in such turmoil, I might be able to figure it out, but as is, I have no clue.

When we exit the Temple, Rose takes a look at the scene and silent tears stream down her cheeks. I don't comment on them, not wanting to embarrass her.

Instead, in an effort to distract her, I say, "Don't pull him in yet." I nod toward Caleb. "He might attack me."

"Okay." She sniffles. "How do you want to do this?"

"Let me Guide the cops and the young monks. Then you bring Caleb in as I walk back to my body."

She nods, and in the hour that follows, I enter the mind of every cop on the scene and give them the following instructions: *Do not fight the monks. Take down Kate's people, but do not use your guns. Use Tasers and cuff them.*

"I think you should have them killed," Rose says after Reading one of my police targets. "You're making it that much harder for the officers and without good reason."

"Until I know who's controlling everyone, I want a nonlethal solution," I say. "Some of them are innocent, and George is actually my relative."

She looks unconvinced, so I add, a little unkindly, "Unlike for some people, family means something to me."

Her shoulders sag, and I feel like an ass. Since I can't say anything to salvage the situation, I proceed to override the young monks. I order them to attack Kate's team alongside the cops. Under no circumstances are they to fight their fellow monks.

"Wait until I disappear in the forest before you pull Caleb in," I tell Rose after I'm done.

"Go." Her voice sounds more confident; she must've regained some composure. "If Edward survives—"

"Should I pull you in next time I'm in the Quiet?" I ask and begin walking away.

"Only if you need me," she says.

I take it as a no and proceed to walk toward the forest. My walk soon turns into a jog. Though I know no time is passing outside the Quiet, I'm anxious to see what will happen.

The trip back to my body happens in a fog. When I get there, I touch my frozen self on the forehead, barely registering the expression of fear on his/my face.

The sounds of the forest instantly return, and I keep running as fast as I did before I entered the Quiet, ignoring the pain from all the scratches on my body.

As I run, I listen. There are definitely fewer shots sounding in the distance, which is a good start. I don't hear any explosions either—something else that gives me a modicum of hope.

I run, aware of the fact that, in real time, the situation at the Temple is changing, and hopefully for the better.

Then something I least expected happens.

My phone rings.

CHAPTER TWENTY

I always thought cell phones wouldn't work in the middle of the woods.

I take out my phone and stare at the incoming call uncomprehendingly. According to Caller ID, it's Eugene.

I accept the call, mentally thanking the cellular tower deities of the woods, who are, more than likely, my Enlightened grandparents. They must have a booster or something for the Temple. If they don't, I'll have to buy Verizon stock when I get out of this.

"Eugene, where are you?" I bark into the phone. One of the cops looks at me worriedly. He must've mistaken the excitement in my voice for danger.

Ignoring him, I continue, "Have you made progress?"

"We're about to enter the woods via the road Hillary suggested," Eugene says. "Regarding progress, I'm afraid it's a long and disappointing story—"

I don't hear the rest because I phase into the Quiet. Whatever the long story is, I'll have to wait to hear it from Eugene's lips after I walk over to his car and pull him in—which will be much easier than carrying on a conversation while running through the forest.

Before I talk to Eugene, though, I have to check on the Temple.

* * *

Stunned, I take stock of the frozen battlefield.

I *really* fucked up.

A couple of cops are in pieces in front of Kate, their impotent Tasers clutched in their literal death grips. They were good people—honest cops as far as I could tell. The guilt is overwhelming. Their only fault was being Guided by an idiot—me—who thought Kate could be taken down by a couple of Tasers.

But that isn't even the worst of it.

No, that perverse pleasure is reserved for the fate of a much larger majority of the cops, who fell victim to another force altogether.

To my right, a monk is kung-fu kicking an officer in the chest. To my left, a deputy is flying backward from a monk's punch to his shoulder. And these must be the tougher cops, because their colleagues have long since been thrown to the ground, clearly having been beaten up by the monks.

Reading one of the younger monks confirms what I already suspected. The cops stopped shooting the monks, but the monks didn't catch on. Instead of joining the officers in attacking Kate's team, the monks used the opportunity to take out the cops. They didn't understand that the cops are now their allies.

As a result, only a few cops attacked Kate and her people, and they paid with their lives. And this is why I know I *really* fucked up.

I was the one who instructed the cops not to use lethal force, making them easy targets. I should've listened to Rose. You'd think I would've learned my lesson back at the cemetery, but clearly, I didn't. In my defense, what I truly haven't adopted is the willingness to Guide someone to kill willy-nilly.

James's automatic rifle also made matters worse. A number of cops died from his gunfire. I count at least four. Didn't the monks see this? Don't they know the old adage that the enemy of my enemy is my friend?

I feel sick with guilt. To keep myself together, I remind myself that I'm not really responsible for these deaths. Kate and her people are, and they're acting this way because of the Super Pusher. In the end, this is all on his or her head. At least I succeeded in reducing the number of massacred monks, and a large portion of the cops are knocked out, not dead.

It's too bad that due to the monks' shortsightedness, this reprieve won't last, not with Kate and her team behaving so murderously.

Well, not all of them, I see when I walk to where Caleb and John were fighting. Given John's wounds, he's as good as dead.

Caleb left him to bleed out and is now locked in a deadly confrontation with a new opponent— Eleanor. At least, given the circumstances, I assume they're fighting. Strictly speaking, they might also be fornicating. Their sweaty, writhing bodies are tangled up on the ground, with her trying to wrap her legs around him and him trying to lift her back off the ground by her waist.

I pick up a gun, put it in the back of my pants, and wonder whether I should pull Caleb in. No, I decide, not until I know the full situation and can form a plan. This determined, I make my way to the back of the Temple to find out how Edward has fared.

The good news is that Edward hasn't blown himself up, which I already suspected given that I never heard an explosion. The bad news is that he's on the ground. It's hard to say whether he's dead or unconscious, though the Taser cables in his chest indicate the latter.

The proverbial misfortunes never come solo. Instead of being cuffed on the ground, Richard is missing. The cops who tried to tase him are down, but at least they aren't riddled with bullets. It looks as if Richard somehow resisted the effects of the Taser when they went in to cuff him. My best guess is that he knocked them out when they got within range.

When I locate Richard, I discover I made a mistake with him as well. I should've had the cops shoot him. Though he seems to have lost his gun in the fight with the cops, he doesn't need it for what he's doing.

He's trying to kill a bunch of old people.

He's standing over my grandfather Paul, who's on the ground with a bloody lip. The others look on in horror. The old man must've stood up to Richard. I feel a trace of admiration before dread grips me.

Paul won't last a second in this fight. He might have already broken a hip, or worse. If he gets up—and he looks as if he's planning to—he's as good as dead.

As nasty as he was to me when we met, I don't want to lose him. As they say, you don't get to choose your family.

Eugene better have something useful for me. I don't see how I can save Paul without entering Level 2. Even then, if Richard is the Super Pusher, Paul is a goner, as are the rest of the Enlightened.

With my mind in turmoil, I make my way to the guesthouse.

When I reach the second floor, my heart freezes in my chest.

I underestimated the blind, pain-ignoring determination of a Guided mind.

Thomas is no longer standing in the hallway; he won his fight against Mira's door. He left much of the skin of his fists on the wooden frame, but he got into the room.

And now those bloodied hands are an inch away from Mira's neck.

CHAPTER TWENTY-ONE

"Mira!" I scream, though I know it's futile. Even if she weren't in a comatose state, knocked out by the drugs Caleb gave her, she wouldn't be able to hear me from the Quiet.

I take out the gun I picked up from a cop earlier and fight the urge to shoot Thomas in the chest. My finger spasms, itching to pull the trigger. Shooting Thomas would feel wrong, so I shoot the wall instead, over and over until I'm down to one bullet.

My outburst doesn't make me feel better, so with the butt of the gun, I hit frozen Thomas in the liver, which my weird conscience allows. The strike is as effective as shooting him would've been, resulting in a whole lot of nothing in the real world. Not that I'd want to hit Thomas in the liver or shoot him in the real world—not unless, by some fluke, he's trying to kill Mira out of his own volition. I'm just venting, something my therapist—and ironically, Thomas's girlfriend—suggested I do when in stressful situations.

Deciding to vent some more, I throw the pistol at the wall. That isn't good enough, so I break a chair against the wall.

Still nothing. I'll have to tell Liz that yet another one of her ideas doesn't work.

Drawing in a deep, steadying breath, I look at Mira. Her face is as peaceful as the last time I looked at her, frozen in this strange sleep. With irrational hope, I gently brush my fingers across Mira's cheek, but of course, nothing happens.

Certain that Mira's unreachable, I make my way out of the guesthouse, wreaking havoc on furniture as I go.

Once I make it to the woods, I channel my remaining frustration into a run. After a few miles, I feel calm enough to plan where I'm going.

If Eugene can see the forest from the highway, I have a pretty good idea where he is. That doesn't, however, make his location any closer. Still, running is easy, and if I need a boost, all I have to do is think about Mira's current predicament.

I get a déjà-vu-like feeling when I run like this, pumped full of adrenaline. I flash back to high school, when I would use the Quiet to scope out the much older bullies lurking behind corners. Back then, I would run in the opposite direction. Funny how things change with time. If I ran into any of those assholes now, or even all of them put together, I wouldn't run. Not today. Not with how I feel right now. Hell, I'd welcome the encounter.

As I run, many regrets circle through my head. Things like, *I shouldn't have gone to that fucking Island*, or, *I shouldn't have gone to that fucking funeral*, and even, *I should've treasured our time together more.*

Whenever the thought of losing Mira shows its hideous face, I run faster.

* * *

By the time I reach my destination, I wonder whether I could run a marathon.

The U-Haul truck my friends rented is huge. A strange guy is behind the wheel, and after a quick Read, I learn he's some random dude Eugene and Bert hired to drive them.

I make my way to the back of the truck. Peering inside, I'm faced with all the charm of Eugene's secret laboratory, only this place is impossibly messier than his Brooklyn lair. Oh, and there's a pile of bananas in the corner.

The three occupants of the back of the truck look as if they haven't bathed in weeks, instead of only the twenty hours or so it's been. And by three, I mean Bert, Eugene, and Kiki the chimp, of course.

Out of the bunch, Kiki looks most composed. Bert's frozen eyes are so red I wonder whether he indulged in some drugs; he did say he wanted to get Adderall, something he used to take in Harvard. Then I recall the focus boost my aunt offered to give him. His current state must be the consequence of it. Eugene looks normal—as in, it's normal for him to look as if he hasn't slept all night. He's currently holding a phone, with my frozen self on the other end of the call.

I touch Eugene's hand.

A second Eugene joins me and says, with surprise written all over his face, "Darren? What are you doing here?"

"We didn't have time to speak in the real world," I explain. Fighting a new wave of anxiety, I add, "You have no idea how little time."

"What happened?" he asks, sounding instantly worried.

"It's bad. Please tell me you can send me to Level 2."

His worry gives way to a distinct look of regret. "I wish it were that simple."

"You don't understand. You *have* to do it."

He shakes his head. "I can't. We focused specifically on the part of the brain that I suspect is responsible for Splitting, since we had no time to worry about Depth." He glances at Bert and Kiki. "We made some very preliminary progress."

"Eugene, please tell me everything, and quickly," I say. "I'm not a scientific journal. You can tell me, 'My results are half-assed' or whatever."

"The results are inconclusive," he says. "Not something I'd publish, if I were crazy enough to publish this kind of work."

"Your results were never going to be complete without me," I remind him. "I'm the only one who can Split into Level 2 to begin with."

"Right," he says. "But I mean the stages before that—"

"Just tell me what happened," I implore.

"Fine." He exhales audibly. "We tested the device on Kiki. She was trained to touch me under certain circumstances . . ."

I don't know if my loud chuckle is merry or hysterical given the situation, but he gives me a narrowed-eyed stare and says, "If your mind is in the gutter again—"

"I'm sorry," I say honestly. "The monkey was trained to touch you under very special, non-romantic circumstances. Please go on."

"Indeed, she was trained to pull me whenever we placed a mirror in front of her and covered her ears to make sounds go away—conditions that simulate a Split. The conditioning worked, as did my device, because she pulled me into the Mind Dimension." He says this with a hint of defensiveness in his voice. "So, in part, that was a success."

"A phasing chimpanzee," I mumble wonderingly and walk over to the ape in question.

"Indeed," he says without the enthusiasm I would've expected.

"Okay, give me the *but*," I say and fluff the fur (or is it hair?) on Kiki's head.

"We couldn't replicate the experiment afterward," Eugene says. "And here's what's most worrisome: she's no longer Readable."

I try to Read Kiki, just to see it for myself.

"You're right," I say after a few moments. "She's not."

Eugene nods. "It's almost as though she's gone Inert. An unanticipated outcome."

"Could it be that something about chimpanzees is different from humans when it comes to that region of the brain?" I ask hopefully.

"That's exactly what Bert said. Then he convinced me to test the device on him." Eugene gestures at my disheveled friend.

"By your expression, I'm guessing that version didn't go much better?"

"Bert entered the Mind Dimension, pulled me in, and after merely a moment, we Split, leaving the Mind Dimension behind. Since then, he's been as resistant to Reading as Kiki. Needless to say, the machine didn't work on him again." Eugene wearily runs his fingers through his hair. "Please try to Read him, just to make sure it's not something to do with me."

I touch Bert's forehead and enter the state of Coherence.

Nothing. Not even the white noise I get with the monks. It's as if I'm touching a doorknob.

"Nada," I say. "But maybe it would work better on one of us?"

"I was contemplating testing it," Eugene says, "but I was afraid."

"Well, you're in luck," I say without a hint of hesitation. "You've got yourself another lab rat."

"Darren, you don't understand—"

"Oh, I do." I can no longer keep the urgency out of my voice. "If I don't, a lot of people will die, including Mira."

"What?" His eyes widen. "What happened?"

I tell him everything. When I finish, instead of panicking, Eugene starts moving around the van. He looks as if he's tidying up the place, and I'm so confused that I ask, "What the hell are you doing?"

"I'm setting up the device," he explains curtly and continues.

I watch him prepare, impressed by his cool-under-pressure demeanor.

"Try this on." He throws me what used to be a bicycle helmet. With the many holes drilled through it, it now looks more like a pasta strainer.

I put on the device and adjust it; my head is much bigger than Bert's.

"Good," Eugene says and takes the helmet back.

He then proceeds to thread a bunch of cables through it.

"Help me with this." He points to a big device in the corner—the brains of the TMS machine I bought him.

I help him lift the heavy machine onto a funky cart with big wheels. "Why the cart? Where are we going?"

"From what you've told me, you have to be in the proximity of your target when in Level 2," Eugene says. "So we're taking this to the Temple."

"Oh." Fighting confusion, I watch Eugene place the helmet and a bunch of peripherals onto the cart.

"Let's go," he says and rolls the cart down the ramp attached to the U-Haul.

"Wait," I say. "Something just occurred to me. How am I going to use this thing? Technology doesn't work in the Quiet. Not to mention, we have no idea if it will actually work."

He doesn't reply as he goes back into the van.

"Here, start turning this," he says, handing me a gizmo that looks like a can opener. A cable connects it to a square piece of metal.

I eye the device dubiously. "What the hell is this?"

"A wind-up USB charger with a battery," Eugene explains. "I also rigged one so that the turning wheels of this cart will charge it."

I turn the thingy, but my face must look confused, because Eugene adds, "This has to do with technology in the Mind Dimension."

He starts walking, pushing the cart in front of him, and I follow.

"It's only very delicate technology that has a problem with subparts being frozen," he says. "For example, the liquid crystals in LCD screens, or the electrophoretic technology that's behind the Kindle display. As you know, things like wind-up watches and guns do work, as well as many other gadgets, including the majority of electrical ones. It's just that most screens look dead. Also, worse than the display problem is the fact that the power source of most devices doesn't flow electricity, which includes batteries. They don't retain their charges. Since batteries and screens are so ubiquitous in current technology, and so important—not to mention that nearly everything requires a live current—you and many others have gotten the impression that technology doesn't work in the Mind Dimension."

"Interesting," I say. I recall the book I started to read on the Island. Had I gotten a chance to leaf through it, I wouldn't be feeling so dumb. "You're telling me that this machine has no screen?"

"Well, it does have a screen," Eugene says. "But I know how to work it blind, and I made sure the screen is not integral to critical functions."

I wave the USB-charger thingy. "And this charges it?"

"Exactly," Eugene says. "It should all work."

"It has to work," I say, giving the USB charger a good whirl.

"I did tests," he says reassuringly. "It will power up in the Mind Dimension. The part I'm less sure about is what will happen once you use it."

"You think it won't take me to Level 2?" I ask as we enter the forest.

"It should." Eugene manages to push the cart through the tricky terrain. "But I am more worried about what will happen after."

"You mean I'll be made Inert?"

"No, Darren," he says hesitantly. "I mean you might never regain your abilities at all."

CHAPTER TWENTY-TWO

For a few moments, we walk in silence. I'm speechless. I assumed his machine might make me Inert and hated the idea, but to become completely powerless is another matter entirely. I can't even imagine such a life; it's unthinkable. Yet I don't see any other choice. I can't let people die.

More specifically, I can't let Mira die.

In case Eugene is worried, I say, "I'm still going to do it."

"I know," he says, brushing it off. "And you have no idea how much I appreciate you doing this for my sister."

"Are you sure I'll end up—"

"We did the test on Kiki a day ago. According to my dad's notes on the subject, she should've recovered after an hour. But she's still Inert," he says, shooting me a pitying glance.

"But there's a chance she'll recover, right?" I ask. "Your dad isn't infallible, is he?"

"Listen," Eugene says. "Maybe there's an alternative to you Splitting into this Level 2. Can the situation be resolved in some other way?"

"I can't think how," I say. "There's no one near that room, so I can't Guide someone else to save her. And Thomas is being Guided, which means he won't listen to reason. I tried reasoning with Mira the other day; it's useless. Overriding Thomas is the only viable way to save Mira. Plus, there's Richard, who's about to kill my grandfather, and Kate and her friends, who'll kill the rest of the monks and Caleb."

"I'm sorry I couldn't work out a safer solution for you."

"Enough of this," I say, giving the USB charger increasingly vigorous spins. "Let's just work out a plan."

"Well, we'll need to pull in every player," Eugene says. "Everyone you plan on overriding, that is."

I stop spinning the charger and look at him. "What? Are you crazy? They're trained warriors. If we pull them in, they'll make us Inert in seconds, and then I can't use your device to save anyone."

"I understand, but I don't see any other choice."

"Why?"

"From what you told me, you couldn't see any patterns on Level 2 that were not already in the regular Mind Dimension. Am I mistaken?"

"No," I say thoughtfully, realizing I never gave it much thought.

"Well then," he says, "since we only get one chance at this, we must recreate these conditions as best as we can."

"But you haven't seen Kate fight." I gingerly resume turning the wheel in my hands. "Our survival rate—and our chances of keeping our powers—just plummeted."

"Didn't you say Caleb is on our side?" Eugene glances at me. "Surely that should help."

"I'm not sure even *he* can take her," I say. "And she's not alone. There are three of them in front of the Temple—Kate, James, and Eleanor—and they're probably each more capable than our prickly friend. That's not counting John, if he hasn't been killed yet, or Richard, who's on the other side of the Temple. And let's not forget Thomas—our key target—who's also not a pushover."

"Maybe we focus on Thomas and save Mira," Eugene says.

A part of me is tempted to agree with him, but I can't let my grandparents die, no matter how big of an asshole Paul is. The monks also don't deserve to be slaughtered. Besides, when I think about it more, I realize we don't even have the cowardly option.

"No," I say. "Even if I stop Thomas, Kate or the others could replace him in minutes, after they finish off all the monks, which shouldn't take them long. Even if I make it to the Temple in time, I can't stop someone like Kate from using force."

"Blya—I mean, *bitch*," Eugene says, his accent coming through. "What do we fucking do then?"

"Let me think for a bit," I say. "Once we get there, we can consult with Caleb and Rose."

* * *

We arrive at the Temple entrance, and Eugene looks in horror at the chaos surrounding us.

"It's a sacrilege," he whispers.

Even though it's not my first, or even second time taking in this picture, I'm just as disturbed as he is.

"Whoever did this, I hope I get to make them pay," I say.

"Do you have a plan now?" Eugene asks. "Because my brain capitulated."

I turn toward him. "Is that a wind-up watch you're wearing?"

"Yes," he replies. "I use it to make crude time measurements in the Mind Dimension. For more accurate measurements, I have this much better time-keeping device that—"

"Dude." I hold up my hand. "I know we're stuck in this moment and Mira won't get killed any faster if you keep talking, but I still think we should get a move on and not get sidetracked by your science, or anything else for that matter."

"I'm sorry." He looks somber. "You're absolutely right."

"Let's take the machine to Mira's room," I say, feeling a twinge of guilt for chastising him. "You can start assembling it there."

I walk briskly toward the guesthouse, with Eugene following.

Midway to our destination, I pillage a couple of wind-up watches from the frozen cops, ignoring Eugene's confused stare.

As we make our way into the building and nearly break our backs dragging the cart up the stairs, I keep silent (aside from grunts) as I mentally go over my plan.

We're about to enter Mira's room, so I tell Eugene, "It'll be painful for you to see this. Brace yourself."

I take my advice and brace myself as well.

Once inside, Eugene's face fills with horror, which might well match my own expression.

"I'll give you some time with her." I can't help looking at Thomas, who's looming over Mira. Predictably, my heartbeat speeds up. "I'll go pull in my grandmother."

I run all the way to where a horrified Rose is standing. Her frozen gaze is on Paul. Richard is looming over him.

I gently touch her forehead.

"Darren," the animated version of Rose exclaims. "Please tell me you have a plan that can save him."

I nod. "I do have something. Please follow me."

We make our way back to the guesthouse.

"Eugene, this is my grandmother," I say when we enter. "The one responsible for the kidnapping."

Eugene barely looks at her, his gaze glued to his sister. Rose's eyes follow his stare, and she says softly, "I didn't want this."

Her small, wrinkled face looks so remorseful that I believe her.

"Your words are not going to help my sister." Eugene turns to her. His normally kind face takes on a cold, almost savage expression.

"Let's get Caleb." I put my hand on Eugene's shoulder to comfort him. "You can give her a piece of your mind later, if she's alive to hear it."

With that, I lead the group to the front of the Temple.

"We'll stand off to the side," I say, grabbing a shotgun from a fallen officer and giving it to Eugene before getting myself a handgun. "Needless to say, if he hurts us, this plan is out the window."

"He'll do as he's told," Rose says. "However, you're free to aim those guns in our direction if you're worried."

"Like we need your permission for that," Eugene says under his breath.

I take the officers' watches from my pocket and hand them to Rose. "Take one for yourself and give one to Caleb. I don't plan on getting close enough to Caleb to give him this myself."

She takes the watches and walks over to where Caleb is still stuck in his embrace with Eleanor. She carefully locates a piece of flesh that is definitely Caleb's and touches it.

A moment later, an animated version of the big guy shows up. His momentary confusion is quickly replaced by that pouncing readiness only Caleb is capable of.

I take the safety off my gun, and Eugene racks his shotgun.

"You are not to harm these boys," Rose says to Caleb as a greeting. She then proceeds to explain to him the situation with Paul and what she saw happening to Mira.

"Darren has a plan that could save us all," she says in conclusion.

"Not everyone," I say, thinking of the Super Pusher. "But Paul and Mira for sure, and many of the monks too."

"What's the plan, kid?" Caleb asks.

"For you and Rose, it's simple—"

"I can't hear you," Caleb says. "Can you get closer?"

I sigh and walk toward him. Eugene follows. I stop a few feet away and say, "As I was saying, your part is to—"

In a whirl, Caleb closes the distance between us. I'm too stunned to fire my gun, and in the next moment, Eugene's shotgun is in Caleb's hands, pointed at us.

"Caleb, I gave you an order," Rose says, glaring at him.

"You said not to harm them, and I haven't, *yet*," Caleb says, keeping his eyes on us. "Now, kid, throw your gun away."

I throw the gun behind me, though for a moment, I was tempted to throw it at his head.

"Good boy." Caleb smirks. "You were saying?"

"If you kill me, Paul and the others are—"

"Dead, I get it," he says. "That's the only reason you don't have a hole in you already."

I decide to proceed as though nothing's changed. "As I was saying, I want Rose to bring her attacker, Richard, into the Quiet with us, and at the same time, you, Caleb, will bring in Kate"—I point to her, then gesture to the rest of her crew as I name them— "Eleanor, George, James, and John—if he's alive."

Rose looks at me as though I sprouted horns.

Caleb sarcastically asks, "Anything else?"

"Yes," I say, ignoring his tone. "I need you to do it at exactly the same time."

Rose's voice quivers as she asks, "How are we supposed to—"

"Easy," I say. "We synchronize our watches."

"That's not what I was about to ask," she says, her composure improving. "But you knew that."

"Look, the worst they can do is make you Inert," I say. "And you, Rose, don't have anything to lose."

"I do," Caleb says. "Without the Mind Dimension, I'll be at a huge disadvantage."

"I'm sorry," I say, "but that's the best plan I can come up with."

"That's not a plan," Caleb says. "That's just something for us to do. I want to know what the hell you need this suicide mission for *before* I agree to it."

I look at Rose, and she gives me a nod. I gather she doesn't mind Caleb knowing that Readers can be Guided, so I tell him what I, and the Elders, can do. I also tell him my plan—which is to bring Thomas in at the exact same time as Caleb and Rose bring in the others, and use Eugene's machine to go to Level 2 and gain control of the situation.

"It won't work," Caleb says. "At least not for John."

"Why?" Eugene asks.

"Because I made him Inert," Caleb explains. "I tried it with all of them but that one." He points at George. "John was the only one I could beat in the Mind Dimension."

"You mean everyone but John kicked your ass?" I say unkindly.

He gives me a look that says, 'I'm about to kick *your* ass,' so I don't push the point.

"Why didn't you try making George Inert?" I ask instead. "There's no way he could've come close to beating you. He isn't part of Kate's crew. He's a glorified politician for the Elders."

Caleb looks surprised. "I didn't realize that. In fact, I thought it was the opposite. I figured since the guy looks like he's their leader—"

"He's not the leader." I frown. "Kate—the one with the sword—is."

He shrugs. "Not much I can do with that information now."

"But you seem to be doing well there." I look over at frozen Caleb and Eleanor.

"If you used your brain, you'd know that I'm as good as dead," he says. "At least I will be once the others are through with the monks. The cow and I are pretty evenly matched, and I let her get me on the ground. Now she's making sure I'm sprawled like that for a while so her team can finish me off."

"So you might as well try this plan," Rose says. "At least it gives you a chance."

Caleb gives me a cold look. "Fine, but I have one condition. You're going to stay out of my head."

"Sure. Even if I wanted to get into your head, I suspect I wouldn't be able to. Something about your head is special." I chuckle. "At least when it comes to Level 2."

"You mean the fact that he hasn't been Guided by the Super Pusher?" Eugene looks at Caleb as though seeing the man for the first time.

"Yes," I confirm. "Rose hasn't been Guided either. The two of them must be resistant somehow."

"Curious," Eugene says before turning to me. "There's a big flaw with the whole idea."

He looks worried, and I know he's no longer talking about Caleb's strange head.

"What flaw?" I ask.

"If Caleb can't handle them one by one, won't he have trouble with the whole lot of them all at once?"

"You don't say," Caleb says mockingly. "Thank you for this revelation. Did you need that white coat to come up with it?"

"He doesn't need to fight anyone," I explain to Eugene. Then, looking at Caleb, I say, "You can just tap each one, then run away or something."

"Great idea," Eugene says at the same time as Caleb says, "Run away?"

Caleb's face looks menacingly calm as he mutters something softly. The only word I can make out is *indignity*.

"Can I do the same?" Rose asks, ignoring the big man's gripes.

"Yes," I say. "And you have the advantage of hiding behind the trees."

"But the disadvantage of old age," she says.

"I can take your place," Eugene offers. "I can show you how to turn on the machine."

"No," Rose says. "You're the best person to operate whatever that is. I'll run and hide as Darren suggested."

"Okay then," I say. "Let's go. Unless any of you have objections." I see that Caleb's about to speak, so I add, "Other than bitching about having to run from one's enemies."

"Here," Caleb says and turns the shotgun handle toward Eugene. "Take it."

"No, you keep it," Eugene says. "I'll need my hands free to start the device."

"Keep it, but please, don't shoot anyone," I say to Caleb. "No matter how tempting it is."

"I'm not an idiot," Caleb retorts.

"That's arguable," I mutter. Then I say louder, "Let's set our watches for seven-thirty, unless . . .

Caleb, is half an hour enough time for you to pull in the last person at eight sharp?"

"Again—not an idiot, kid," Caleb says, crossing his arms over his chest. "And don't test your luck with a comeback. Kicking your ass wouldn't undermine the plan, so . . ."

I swallow my witty response and say, "Rose, I assume you're okay?"

She nods.

"Eugene, is that enough time for us to get back to the guesthouse and start the doomsday device?" I ask.

"Ample, but I'll go set up." Eugene turns around and heads for the Temple doors.

"Good luck to you too, Eugene," Caleb says to Eugene's back.

"If this works, you'll need to tell Kate and her crew that you're not their enemy," I say to Caleb. "I bet they'll be very confused about what happened."

"And as soon as you confirm they're not aggressive, you're not to kill them," Rose says. "I like this idea of peace with the Pusher—I mean *Guide*—Elders. I'm sure the rest of the Enlightened will want it too. Needless to say, unnecessary killing will not be very helpful in meeting that goal."

Caleb's jaw tenses and he says, "But that'll make things more difficult—"

"It's an order." The imperiousness in Rose's tone is as sudden as it is startling.

"Fine," Caleb concedes. This is the second time I've seen him act almost deferential toward my grandparents. "If the stupid walrus eases her grip, I will too. Same goes for the others. If they leave me be, I'll let them live."

"Thank you," Rose says, her voice sounding more pleasant. "Good luck then."

"Seriously, good luck," I echo. "Let's go, Rose."

"Hey, kid," Caleb says. "If you save the day, remind me to apologize."

"For taking my moms and friends hostage?" I ask, my hackles rising. "Or for kidnapping me prior to that?"

Without waiting for an answer, I turn and walk toward the doors of the Temple. I hear Rose shuffling behind me. Once she catches up, I walk in silence, and she doesn't bother me until we reach the center of the first floor—the place where we're supposed to part.

"Thank you." Rose sounds a bit awkward as she says it. "If your father were alive, he would be proud."

"Umm, thank you?" I say, unsure how else to respond. "Let's hope we live long enough for me to have made him proud by doing something *not* crazy."

"Can I give you a kiss?" she asks unexpectedly.

My first instinct is to refuse, but she *is* my grandmother. So I give her a careful hug and lower my head, putting the right side of my face within her reach. She gives my cheek a small, hesitant peck. Almost as if on autopilot, I touch my lips to her wrinkled cheek in turn. I taste a salty moisture on my lips; I might've kissed one of Rose's tears.

Without another word, she walks away, and I watch her go for a moment. Then, shaking my head at her bizarre behavior, I continue walking to my destination.

I wonder whether women get more mysterious as they grow older.

* * *

"Are you almost set?" I ask Eugene when I enter the room.

"Yep," he says. "Put this on."

He hands me the helmet, which now looks like Medusa's decapitated head.

I put it on and look at my watch. "We have some time to kill."

"Let me check the equipment," Eugene says. "Some of the cables might've gotten loose with all those roots and rocks the cart had to go over."

The cable tethering me to the machine has a couple of feet of slack, so I pace back and forth as Eugene fiddles with his equipment.

"Okay, it's almost time," Eugene says after the longest fifteen minutes of my life. "Which of us will pull Thomas in?"

"Let me," I say. "You start this thing as soon as I do."

"Sure," he says. "Do it when you're ready."

After a minute of tense silence, I quietly ask, "Eugene, what do we do if it doesn't work?"

Eugene gives me an unreadable look, then says confidently, "It's going to work. It has to."

I stop myself from saying anything stupid for the next few minutes. When I next look at my watch, I see that it's exactly 7:58.

"Shit. It's almost time."

I stare at the second hand of my watch in a trance. My index finger hovers next to Thomas's forehead until the last moment, when the watch hand finishes its journey.

When it hits eight o'clock, I press my fingers to Thomas's skin.

With a guttural sound, a second Thomas shows up in the room.

In my peripheral vision, I see Eugene press something on the device. He presses it with a flourish and the kind of finality that tells me it's on.

Only the welcome emptiness of Level 2 never comes, and the newly animated version of Thomas rushes toward me.

CHAPTER TWENTY-THREE

I expect him to attack, but instead, Thomas pushes me aside with an urgency that almost sends me sprawling to the floor. I bump hard into his frozen self, and the statue-like Thomas falls down. This clears the way for the animated Thomas, who proceeds to get into the position his frozen self was in and grabs Mira by the throat.

"Eugene," I whisper. "Why am I still here?"

Mumbling something in Russian, my friend frantically examines his machine.

In stunned fascination, I watch Thomas choke Mira with such force that the veins on his hands strain from the exertion.

My best guess for Thomas's strange behavior is that, in his Guided state, he must not understand that she's frozen. He must not realize that whatever he does to her here won't stick.

The Super Pusher must've been too specific in his Guiding, commanding Thomas to break the door down and put his hands around the girl's neck, while forgetting to specify that the goal was to kill her and not just give her neck a strong squeeze.

I chance a look at Eugene. He's unplugging cables, then firmly plugging them back in. He must think a loose connection is responsible for our delay.

A dreadful thought occurs to me. What if the machine *did* activate, but it can't send me to Level 2?

No. No point dwelling on what-ifs.

I need to act, because at any moment, Thomas may turn his attention to Eugene and me. I have no idea what else the Super Pusher planted in his head, but I don't want to find out.

Taking advantage of Thomas's laser focus on Mira, I give him the karate-style neck chop I never got the chance to execute on the Island.

To my shock, when my hand connects with Thomas's neck, he doesn't react in the way I expected him to.

That is, he doesn't fall to the ground in agonizing pain.

Trying to make sense of his lack of reaction, I hypothesize that, while in this Guided state, Thomas doesn't feel pain in the usual way.

But he does feel *something*—because he turns around, and without much ado, reaches for my neck.

I counter his attack by clasping my fingers around his wrists, stopping him from locking down the deadly move. At the same time, I give his shin a good kick.

Thomas stumbles. Seeing that he's about to fall, I let go of his wrists, but he instantly reacts by parroting my earlier move, and my wrists end up in his vise-like grip. As Thomas falls, he brings me along for the ride.

I manage to land on top of him, making sure my knee hits his side. Though he doesn't react, the move allows me to free my hands. I try to restrain him using an Aikido move, but he doesn't let me get the grip I need. As I struggle to gain the upper hand, I find myself in a position that might look embarrassingly like the one Caleb and Eleanor are in back in the real world. Oddly, instead of wrestling me back, Thomas goes for my neck again.

The command to strangle must really be bouncing around in his head.

I vaguely recall how the black-masked attacker tried to strangle me; it must be the Super Pusher's signature move.

In Thomas's effort to wrap his hands around my throat, his fingers unhook my helmet's strap. I crane my head out of the way, but to my horror, all I accomplish is dislodging my cable-adorned hat. It clanks as it rolls across the floor.

Shit.

Even if Eugene manages to restart the machine, I'm not hooked up to it anymore.

"Dude," I yell. "My helmet."

A shot rings out. My ears feel as if someone smacked each eardrum with a baseball bat.

My stunned brain comes up with an explanation: Eugene found the gun I'd thrown at the wall. He's insane to have used it, though.

There's blood everywhere.

Thomas keeps attempting to choke me. I don't know whether I should feel relieved or panicked that he's alive.

"I shot him," Eugene says, sounding panicked himself. "Why is he still fighting?"

"Eugene, focus on the machine," I manage to croak, and then hit Thomas with an elbow. "If you kill him, you'll make him Inert and that will ruin everything."

My move with the elbow does nothing other than position me in a way that allows Thomas to twist his body. He uses his momentum to execute a head-spinning maneuver—a Hapkido-style throw that, from my vantage point, feels like I just executed a perfect somersault. In the next moment, I'm on my back, with Thomas's knees on my biceps and his full weight pinning me down. The nasty gun wound on his thigh might as well be a mosquito bite for all the attention he's giving it. His calloused hands wrap around my throat again.

I try to move, to buck him off me—to do something, anything—but he has me thoroughly trapped.

I keep twisting every which way, but all it accomplishes is creating a wave of tiredness that spreads through my body like the aftereffects of twenty shots of tequila. The lack of oxygen must already be taking its toll.

Apparently emboldened by my weakening struggles, Thomas tightens his grip.

I begin to see a matrix of white afterglow and try to tell Eugene, "Now would be a good time to help me," but what comes out is a hiss that sounds like a broken vacuum cleaner.

Fleetingly, I wonder why the world isn't slowing down.

The last time I was on the brink of death, I phased into Level 2 on my own—no machine required. Am I really not as scared right now as I was back then? Am I not as desperate? If I survive today, I'll need to rethink my newfound bravery, if that's what's behind my Level 2 dysfunction.

I struggle to stop my body from convulsing, as every movement saps more energy from me.

My mind is slipping. Almost as if I'm in a dream, I feel a pressure around my skull. It takes me a few moments to understand what it means. Eugene must've fastened the helmet back onto my head.

Eugene's voice is right next to my ear. "I'm pressing it again."

A strange noise follows his words—a noise that sounds like humming.

The external humming is followed by the strangest feeling—a series of uncomfortable taps against the front of my head. I vaguely recall reading about this effect of TMS therapy.

Then I'm out.

* * *

I never thought I'd be this glad to have all my senses go away. I never thought I'd welcome the blackness and the lack of everything that is Level 2. If I had a heart in this state, joy would be welling up there right about now. As is, joy wells up in a part of my mind instead.

Hell, I'm so relieved that I'll call this place Nirvana for the time being. As unpleasant as it is being a naked mind afloat in this ether, it sure beats the alternative. If Thomas had beaten Eugene to it, if he had killed me, I'd be back in the forest, Inert and powerless to stop Thomas from choking Mira to death.

Some of my enthusiasm ebbs when I look around.

'Looking' is what I call the foreign sense that allows me to 'see' the starry entities—the representations of other minds. It's not truly vision, but I don't have a better word for it.

After I intently focus on seeing, I make out three patterns that appear 'nearby'—another verbal nicety.

I assume those patterns are myself, Thomas, and Eugene. Mira wouldn't be there, as she's not in the Quiet.

I look around some more.

Nothing.

What about the patterns representing Kate's team, Rose, and Caleb? Maybe they're too far for me to be aware of them in this state, but what does distance even mean in this place?

In any case, the most important thing for me to do is save Mira, and for that, all I need is Thomas's pattern.

I examine the three patterns. Though they're as different from each other as constellations, the hundred-dollar question is: which one is Thomas?

They're pretty close to each other, so I can't orient myself based on their positions. Worst-case scenario is that I accidentally interact with my own pattern, because I would then phase out.

That I can't recognize myself is frustrating, to say the least.

Reminding myself that I have no clue how much time I can spend in this realm, I decide to simply go with my intuition. Maybe intuition is what serves as recognition in this place.

I let my intuition settle on the pattern I think is Thomas.

At first, nothing happens, but then, after a little bit of concentration, I'm halfway to it, without having traversed the intermediate distance.

When in Nirvana, even *I* can teleport like the Elders. Hey, maybe that's how they got so good at teleporting? Maybe practicing it here will allow me to master it in the simpler world of the Quiet? I decide to focus on these teleporting movements as I make them. Unbidden, a dark thought comes: *if there is a later*. After all, there is a chance Eugene's machine will take my powers away.

Anxiety overwhelms me. The emptiness of Level 2 amplifies it to the point that I don't know whether I can take it. If I had eyes, tears would be running down my cheeks. If I had a mouth, I might've yelled in frustration. Because all of this suffering doesn't have an outlet, it's made that much more painful.

Then I recall why I'm here. Thomas is about to kill Mira. I can't fall apart.

Getting my turbulent thoughts under control, I will myself closer to the pattern that is, hopefully, Thomas. And then I'm there and ready to surround it.

As soon as I make contact, I'm in.

* * *

"I shot him," we say. "Why is he still fighting?"

"Eugene, focus on the machine," Darren says, his half-choked voice full of terror. "If you kill him, he'll be Inert, and that will ruin everything."

Self-loathing over our stupidity overwhelms us. We throw the gun we found back on the floor. We almost killed our sister by aiding the Pusher in control of Thomas's mind. There's no way Darren can override Thomas if Thomas is Inert.

That is, if Darren gets to override anyone, we think, but swiftly dispel that treacherous thought. Of course Darren will succeed—even if this is the last time he ever uses his powers. We didn't have the guts to tell him how precise Dad's math is.

We decide to follow our friend's advice and focus on getting him to Level 2. We rush back to the machine and act quickly. Like a juggler, we push the device toward our fighting friends and, at the same time, begin reconnecting the wires we hope are causing the delay.

First the red one, then the blue one. Our heart is pounding painfully fast. This is what those guys who disarm bombs must feel like.

We finish with a couple of cables that only instinct tells us might be loose.

It has to work, we half hope and half pray.

We're about to turn on the machine when we notice something terribly wrong: the helmet fell off

Darren's head, and what's worse, Thomas is choking the life out of him.

We reach for the helmet.

Darren's face is purple. He has seconds, if that.

We grab the helmet and push it on his head.

Thomas is so focused on his murderous task that he ignores us as we adjust the helmet's strap under Darren's chin.

Glad the machine is close by, we press the *on* button.

* * *

Okay, that was Eugene's mind, not Thomas's, which means trusting my intuition was as good as choosing at random. And that means I just took a one-in-three chance on Mira's life. Damn. It also means my next choice has a fifty-fifty chance of being right (or wrong), unless I can think of a way to distinguish the patterns. What makes it worse is that I need to choose quickly, since my Depth is running out at an unknown rate; not choosing will also result in Mira's death.

I waver between choosing at random and strategizing. I spend what feels like an hour flip-flopping, with only a headache as my reward, proving that even a head can suffer from phantom limb syndrome.

Fine, I'll chose one at random then, I think into the ether and choose the rightmost pattern as my next target.

"Please, Darren, not that one," a familiar-sounding 'voice' states from inside my head. "That one is your slowed-down self."

"Mimir," I reply, relieved. "Nice of you to show up. You're getting a knack for doing so when I least expect it."

"You seemed on the cusp of learning how to identify the patterns on your own"—Mimir's thought arrives with a hint of caring and innocence that I suspect he's faking—"until you almost exited *Nirvana.*"

Mimir's thought manages to convey a sense of relish for the new term for Level 2. He clearly likes it.

"So you let me agonize over this choice for my own education, is that it?" I send my thought angrily. "Is watching me squirm something you enjoy?"

"I did not have any evil intentions. You should be able to recognize patterns you've Read before," Mimir replies. "And since you Read Thomas the last time, I thought you'd know him."

"In that case, how do *you* know which one Thomas is?" I send. "You've never Read him, have you? Can you even do that? Read anyone, I mean?"

"I didn't need to know which pattern was his, not when there were two choices left and I knew which one was *yours*," Mimir thinks. "Yours I know as well as I know myself, you see."

"Is that why you didn't stop me when I Read Eugene by mistake?" I notice he never answered my question about him being able to Read. I don't bother pointing it out since I know he knows (by reading my mind right now) that I know he dodged the question.

"Exactly," Mimir replies. "Until you Read Eugene, I didn't know which pattern was his. Unlike the last time we met, the location of the patterns couldn't help me, due to the three of you being very near each other in the Quiet."

I ignore him continuing to pretend as if we're just talking about Eugene's pattern and reply, "Fine, whatever. We can chat about this and the cryptic message you gave me on the Island later. Now that I know which one of these patterns is Thomas, I need to focus on preventing Mira's death."

"I wholeheartedly agree." Mimir's response feels pleased. "You've learned a lot about patience, time management, and priorities since we last communicated."

Allowing him to have the last word, I focus on Thomas's pattern and teleport to him in two jumps, as I did with the others.

When I'm there, right before I enter into the Coherence state, I decide to spare a fraction of a second to see whether I can tell this is Thomas.

I focus. Though my pattern is not enveloping his yet, it's on the verge of doing so.

Sometimes knowing something can be done goes a long way toward actually accomplishing it. That's the only way I can explain it, because now that I try it, I *can* tell that this is Thomas, although explaining *how* I can tell is tricky. If 'seeing' is the approximation for the sense that lets me experience the starry neural networks, then 'smelling' is the best way to explain this new sense that tells me, unequivocally, that this is Thomas. Of course, I'm stretching the definition of the word 'smell' here, even more so than the word 'see.'

Thomas smells of honor, integrity, and patriotism. How can those abstractions have a smell? I don't know, but those are the ideas that spring to mind when I register it all. The closest mundane approximations would probably be the musky scent of sweat from hard work, with a hint of mountain air, and a whiff of that new-paint smell from a newly unpacked flag.

Without any further hesitation, I evoke the state of Coherence. I must say, I'm extra glad I was able to confirm that this is Thomas before I took the plunge. Not that I didn't trust Mimir, but my new motto is quickly becoming 'trust but verify.'

The familiar state overcomes me, and Thomas's experiences come flooding in.

CHAPTER TWENTY-FOUR

We look over all the people who showed up at Kyle's funeral, our thoughts a jumbled mess. To a very large degree, most of these people knew Kyle as little as we did, and maybe less so. We know enough about him to not mourn his passing. If we're mourning anything, it's our chance to learn a little more about him, good or bad; he *was* our biological father, and only a single person in the whole world will ever get that honor. Not that this title is all that special. What really matters is the person you call 'Dad,' and for us, that person lives in Queens. That person may not be our flesh and blood, but he's a million times more of a real father than Kyle could have ever been. He and Mom, our adoptive mom, are the best parents we could've wished for. Our longing for knowledge about our biological parents didn't stem from any sort of dissatisfaction with Mom and Dad.

Thinking of Mom pulls our gaze toward someone else—a woman who, if it weren't for Kyle, would've gladly taken her place. How different would our life have been, growing up under Lucy and Sara's roof? Growing up alongside Darren? Would we have been more like him? Or are we the product of our genes, as Liz insists? That's a frightening thought, given how much of a bastard our father was. Are we capable of the same evil as Kyle?

There it is—the crux of our turmoil. That and regret. We really wish we hadn't made such a big deal of Kyle's passing when Darren was telling us about the whole conference debacle. He probably thinks we harbor him ill will for killing our biological father. Truth be told, at the moment when we realized why Kyle got himself killed, we experienced some instinctual negativity. Shortly after, though, during our drive back to the hospital, we understood that Darren had done the right thing. But since we said, "I don't want to hear more," we've felt a wedge come between us—a wedge that will hopefully dissipate soon. The good news is that Darren doesn't seem like the type to hold grudges, so with time, things between us should return to normal, as if Kyle never existed. This funeral is a good start, and we're here in support of Darren and Lucy as much as for ourselves—possibly more for them.

We can't wait until Lucy is ready to learn about us. Liz thinks Lucy will be ready very soon. If she knew who we are, we wouldn't have to be standing off to the side like a stranger. If only—

All of a sudden, all the sounds of the graveyard go away. Someone pulled us into the Mind Dimension. And then, before we can see who pulled us, a foreign presence enters our mind.

You will kill Darren . . .

I, Darren, disassociate as the sinister instructions begin. I must've instinctively jumped into Thomas's mind during Kyle's funeral, and it paid off. If I had any doubts as to Thomas's motives, they're now gone. He doesn't harbor any resentment toward me. Unfortunately, he didn't get a look at the Super Pusher before the bastard entered his mind.

Oh well. I won't waste any more time. I have to resolve the situation with Mira, so I give Thomas my instructions:

You will halt. You will not harm Mira. She is your adoptive brother's girlfriend and your close friend. You will defend her with your life. Try to wake her up from whatever state she's in. If she wakes up, tell her

Darren is close by. Tell her to stay here, and no matter what happens, keep her and yourself safe.

* * *

Exiting Thomas's mind, I feel like a man who's taken his first breath after swimming underwater for several long minutes.

Mira will not die.

"She will not die by Thomas's hand," Mimir's thought corrects me. "But you haven't secured the Temple for Mira, your grandparents, or the monks."

"You're right," I reply. "I have a few more people to Guide. The question is: how do I find them?"

"I can lead you," Mimir says. "Follow me."

The huge mini-universe of synapses that is Mimir appears in the distance. He then retreats. I teleport after him, and he retreats again. After a few jumps, I see faint entities in the distance. Another couple of jumps, and they become more apparent. Only there are three of them, whereas I was expecting two.

"The one on the right is Julia," Mimir explains, "which would make the other one the attacker, Richard. The one farther in the distance is Rose."

"Julia wasn't Inert?" I wonder if my excitement was transmitted with my thought.

"She was not, and your grandmother wisely delegated the task of pulling in Stephen to a younger woman." His thought sounds reproachful.

"I didn't know Julia was an option," I think, suppressing my defensiveness. "I didn't try bringing her in after I succeeded with Rose. I assumed everyone else was Inert."

"You know what they say about assumptions, but I will not use up valuable time listing the numerous plans that would've been much safer than yours." Mimir's reply is curt.

"I appreciate your restraint," I think back. "I need to know something else, and I know we're pressed for time, but—"

"It was I who prevented the Super Pusher from Guiding your grandmother and, for that matter, all the other Enlightened," Mimir says, answering the question I was thinking of.

"How?"

"He tried to pull her in, and not just her. He tried to pull in every one of them. When he did, he brought a part of them here, to *Nirvana*." He projects the last word again with relish. "Once a part of them was in Nirvana, I was able to be there, in that session, just as I can be in your sessions. Then I prevented the connection, which to the Super Pusher must've felt as if they were Inert."

"But how?" I think. "And what about Caleb? He also seemed immune to the Super Pusher."

"Caleb was protected by another being similar to me—the one the two of you created during the Joining you did when you learned how to fight," Mimir explains.

My head is spinning from his explanation, but more so from the reminder that there are more creatures like Mimir out there.

"Don't call us creatures," his thought tells me.

"Fine. What should I call you?"

"Call us something with more gravitas. How about Transcendental Minds?"

"That's a mouthful," I think back. "How about I call you Trannies for short?"

A mental snort arrives in my mind. "In that case, please call us Omni Minds, or Omnis if you must make everything short. Now, we still don't know how much time you have left, so you must save the Enlightened—now."

"Wait, what about Julia? Was she immune to the Super Pusher too?"

His reply is rushed. "Yes. Another Omni, one that was formed when the Enlightened Joined with Julia. Now focus. I refuse to communicate with you until this threat is neutralized."

I rein in my million questions about the Omnis and focus on the constellation of neurons that is Richard. This time, I teleport without needing an intermediate jump. I think I'm beginning to get the hang of teleporting in Level 2.

Richard's mind has no scent, which makes sense since I've never Read him before, but I do so now.

* * *

Our mind is as focused on our task as a self-navigating missile. *Find the Enlightened. Kill the Enlightened.* The Instructions repeat in our mind as we stalk our targets through the forest.

I, Darren, take a quick mental note of what's going on. This is Richard's mind. He just finished dealing with the cops I turned on him, and he's running to catch up with the Enlightened in the forest. Reluctantly, I let the memory unfold.

We run like a berserker without sparing a thought for the branches and roots in our way. When the white figures appear, every muscle in our body prepares to carry out their execution.

An old man steps away from the group.

"What do you want, Pusher?" he asks, his voice firm. Over his shoulder, he orders, "Go. Now."

On some level, we know he's afraid, but on another very distant level, we marvel that an elderly, weak-looking man like him would even confront us this way.

The instructions take over.

We silently walk up to the man, expecting a chase. He doesn't run; in fact, he tries to stare us down.

We respond by executing a punch. Our fist drowns in the old man's soft midsection. As we watch him double over in pain, we push him.

The old man falls to the ground in a flutter of white robes.

We draw our leg back to kick him, so we can finish the job and deal with the others.

I, Darren, disassociate with a shudder. There's something abominable about turning a man into a living, breathing killing machine the way the Super Pusher has done. Anyone short of a true psychopath would feel *some* empathy when hitting an elderly man like that—at least I would hope so. I'm also touched by Paul's bravery. His treatment of me aside, I'm glad I'll be able to save the old son of a bitch.

I instruct Richard: *You will not kick the man in front of you. Furthermore, you will not harm a single Enlightened or their entourage. In fact, you are their protector, and your primary goal is to get them to the safety of the forest. To show them you aren't a threat, you will kneel with your hands behind your head and tell them, "I am henceforth your protector. Command me. Oh, and hi, Paul. I'm being commanded by Darren, your grandson, who says, 'Hello, asshole. Sorry you're in pain. Rose will fill you in on what's going down.'"*

With that, I exit Richard's mind.

* * *

"Well done." Mimir's thought is the first thing I experience when the blackness of Level 2 overtakes me again. "Now follow me."

He teleports and I follow.

I eventually see them—the bundles of light. I count five, which means Caleb succeeded in his task of bringing in George, Kate, Eleanor, and James without getting killed.

Of the five minds I see in the distance, most are clustered in a group that looks like a small constellation that's roughly a third of Mimir's size. Slightly to the side of them is a single pattern.

"Okay," I think, half to myself, half to my guide. "How do we figure out which is which, or who is who?"

"That is a very good question, with far-reaching consequences," Mimir replies, his neurons flickering brighter than usual.

"Were you about to suggest something?" I think, this time directing it toward Mimir.

"Well, to start, I know someone who can identify Caleb," Mimir explains. "Once he does, we'll have to improvise as we go."

A new collection of neurons suddenly appears in front of me.

The being is alive, with its synapses firing frantically, same as Mimir's. This being is noticeably smaller than Mimir, though—about six times smaller to be precise.

"Yet I'm twice as big as you, kid," a new voice in my head says. "Besides, it's not the size of the mind that matters, but how you use it."

"You're another Omni." I'm overcome with awe at this realization. "The one that's me and Caleb combined, right?"

"No, you're actually schizophrenic, with two voices speaking in your head, not to mention delusions of grandeur." This thought comes with a smirk. "Obviously that's what I am. Call me Daleb."

Ignoring the spike of anxiety his joke provoked, I reply, "You just combined our names together and put the 'D' of my name first. Does that mean mine is the dominant personality that makes you 'you'? Your tone sure sounds more like Caleb's."

"It doesn't work like that," Daleb responds, seriously this time. "I'm both, but neither one. There is no predominant anything. I'm me, not one of you." Then, with another mental smirk, he adds, "I'm Daleb because I didn't want to be Carren, which sounds like a female."

"So you think of yourself as male?"

"Gentlemen," Mimir's thought intrudes. "We're trying to save Caleb. I would think of all of us, you, Daleb, would not want to put his life in jeopardy."

"The mighty Mimir is right," Daleb replies. "The one that's slightly farther from the cluster is Caleb. Easy to spot. Please save him, Darren. I'll owe you big time if you do."

"How did he herd them all into one spot like that?" I wonder. "I wish he hadn't."

"Read him to find out," Daleb suggests. "Maybe he has a visual of where they're each standing."

I teleport to the big cluster and single out Caleb. I intend to do what Daleb suggested: Read Caleb to find out how his mission went.

Coherence comes quickly this time, and with it, I enter Caleb's mind.

* * *

We run toward the Temple doors, ignoring our pursuers' bullets. We focus on those doors as though they're the gates to heaven.

Then we half jump, half slide—a culmination of all those times we stole base as a kid. We're inside. We jackknife to our feet and turn to close the doors. We're going to make it. The heavy doors are almost shut; there's only a sliver left.

The cursed sword manages to slide in through the crack.

Our environment slows down a little, as it often does while we're in battle mode.

The sword jabs toward our torso. We dodge, but don't let go of the doors. Then the sword slices to the left and excruciating pain follows. Stupefied, we see the surreal image of our left hand falling to the ground. Realizing what just happened intensifies the pain in our arm.

We keep fighting, forcing our body to stay alert to prevent it from going into shock, which would undo everything.

All wounds heal once we exit the Mind Dimension, we remind our freaked-out lizard brain.

With our bulletproof vest, we lean on the sword.

The weapon doesn't break, though it should have, but the bitch wielding it decides to pull it back, probably planning to thrust it right back in.

Capitalizing on the temporary reprieve, we shut the doors and then stick what's left of our left arm into the door handles, the way one would with a stick. With our right hand, we also hold the handles shut. We know our forearm can only take a few seconds of pounding.

We wish we could look at the watch, but it's on the floor, attached to our severed hand.

It's way past eight, kid, we think. *What the fuck are you doing to me?*

A kick on the door generates a bone-breaking surge of agony—

* * *

I'm back in Level 2, welcoming its pain-free emptiness.

Those were the last moments of Caleb's mission. He clearly did as we asked by pulling Kate and the others in, but the delay Eugene and I experienced caused him a lot of hassle and pain. The reason Kate and her team are clustered so closely together is because they're standing next to each other in the Quiet, by the door of the Temple.

Remembering the pain Caleb suffered to get this plan to work makes me mentally shudder again. At least his pain will be temporary. Once I'm done in Level 2, he'll be back on the battlefield, wrestling with Eleanor, with all his limbs still attached to his body.

"He's a tough mofo," Daleb's thought reassures me. "And he's been through worse pain."

"We have a big problem." The tone of Mimir's thought is full of concern. "We still don't know who is who."

"Why *is* that such a big issue?" I wonder, shaking off the terror.

"Because, obviously, if you start with the Super Pusher, he will join us in Nirvana." Daleb's thought is snide in that irritating, Caleb-like manner.

"Do we know for certain that he's even among them?" I reply as calmly as I can. As with real Caleb, I can't let him get to me, but the dilemma I face is that if Daleb is anything like Mimir, he can read my mind, annoyance and all.

"Nothing is certain," Mimir interjects. "But I'm fairly sure the Super Pusher is one of these four."

"Oh, come on, kid," Daleb adds. "You already know who he is. On some level, you've known since all this shit went down."

He's right, but I haven't wanted to admit it, because admitting it would mean I've been taken for a fool.

Since I can't hide my thoughts from the two Omnis anyway, I allow the thought to surface in my mind.

"It's George, isn't it?"

CHAPTER TWENTY-FIVE

"Don't be so hard on yourself, kid," Daleb thinks at me. "It could've been anyone."

"It only became apparent after his double cross." Though Mimir's thoughts are attempting to soothe me, I'm getting more and more livid.

"It was George who suggested that each of us walk with five or six cops," I think, as much for my own benefit as the Omnis'. "The fucker did it so he could kill me once he got the one thing he needed from me: the Temple's location."

"Right." Daleb's synapses shine a little brighter as I perceive his thought in my mind. "The Enlightened must've been his target all along."

"But why?" I let my Level 2 vision move from the giant network that is Mimir to the smaller one that is Daleb. "He works for the Elders. He's an Ambassador. He should want what they want. I'm pretty sure they weren't lying to me about wanting peace. Frederick especially."

"You're right." Daleb's thoughts are surprisingly serious now. "I don't think the Elders ordered this. George is clearly acting on his own. As to why, that's something I'm wondering too. Maybe my brainier brother has a clue?"

"I don't have a lot." Mimir's mini-universe is on fire now. I'm not used to seeing him so bright in front of me. "If I did, I would've known George was our man, and I would've warned Darren when he was in Frederick's Nirvana. However, I can venture a guess as to his motivations. Mary, a woman who hates Guides, raised him. He's a fairly traditional man, someone who places emphasis on family values. That and his close association with Hillary's parents link him to the Traditionalists."

"Family values, my foot," I think and wonder whether my neurons are also red with anger. "He's a hypocrite. I'm his family, and he wants to kill me."

"He probably sees it as a necessary evil," Mimir replies.

"There's another clue." Daleb's thought feels almost excited. "Caleb thought George was acting like the leader of Kate's team. He's insightful when he wants to be, that Caleb, and in this case, he was right. George *is* in charge. He's using his fellow Guides as puppets."

"Now that I think about it, other little things are also falling into place," I think, again half for me, half for them. "Like the way his eyes lit up when I mentioned the Enlightened."

"Mentioning them probably saved your life," Mimir adds. "Otherwise, he might've had Hillary stab you in the back or would've done it himself in her parents' house."

"My life was saved at the cost of so many others." I finally figure out what's really been bothering me and think, "He *used* me."

"He did use you, but now it's backfiring." Daleb's thought is not as soothing as Mimir's, but he's clearly trying. "Him using you made sure he brought you here, and now you're undoing the damage he's created. All the death that's happened is on his head, not yours."

"I should've seen it, somehow." I mentally lash myself. "He had a black kimono on, before he took me to see Mary."

"So did the majority of the guests on the Island," Mimir points out.

"He was surprised when he saw me for the first time," I counter.

"It could've just as easily been Hillary who surprised him," Daleb retorts.

"My boss, Bill, mentioned that George was the Ambassador from New Jersey," I think more calmly this time. "That puts him near enough to New York, near enough to have been pulling Kyle's strings. And speaking of Kyle, George was probably at the fucker's funeral—that would explain why Anne was upset he was leaving so soon. He must've arrived just before us with his private plane."

"He did something that threw you off— something that threw us all off," Mimir thinks with a hint of something like shame. "He taught you how to Teleport."

"Yes," I realize. "The bastard even openly admitted that he was teaching me so I would trust him."

"It was pretty clever," Daleb thinks. "He thought you wouldn't survive long enough to master the skill, but teaching it to you made you trust him."

"Except, ironically, it's thanks to that skill that I'm alive," I think. "When I saw the flare, I phased in and randomly ended up a few feet away from the cops with a good view of what they'd been Guided to do. There was a very good chance they would've shot me in the back had George not taught me how to Teleport."

"And he underestimated you in general," Mimir adds. "It's a mistake many have lived to regret."

"Yeah, he shouldn't have attacked you personally on the Island," Daleb agrees. "He was overconfident, where someone wiser would've Guided Kate to assassinate you."

"Maybe he was afraid to do something like that in front of the Elders?" I counter. "Also, once he was pulled in by Fred, he wouldn't have been able to Guide anyone. Can't get to Level 2 from someone else's Quiet. What I really want to know is: why did he attack me at all?"

"It's not like his attack would've killed you. It would've just made you Inert. When Martin and his people forbade you to make anyone on the Island Inert, they wouldn't have cared if you yourself became Inert. George probably only brought you to the Island to earn your trust, so that you in turn would bring him to the Temple," Mimir suggests. "He didn't actually want you to talk to the Elders. If anything, he was probably worried you'd tell the Elders about the Super Pusher. They might've taken that information very seriously."

"I thought one of the Elders *was* the Super Pusher," I think defensively.

"And that was reasonable," Mimir responds, "but George didn't know that was your theory, or maybe he thought you might blab regardless."

"So he brought me to the Island and then tried to make me Inert, but to what end?"

"Probably so he could offer you help," Daleb projects. "Being Inert would've made you more open to accepting his help. He would've suggested a rescue team of his own, with people already loyal to him. When making you Inert didn't work, his plan needed only a slight readjustment, given that it was Frederick who provided you with a team. Since George was able to Guide them, he still almost got what he was after."

I process all that for a moment, and then think, "Something else just occurred to me. Hillary suspected that George might become an Elder. She all but told me he was as powerful as one of them. I just didn't fully—"

"I hate to interrupt this dialogue, especially given how cathartic it is for you, Darren," Mimir interjects, "but you might run out of Depth at any moment, and we still have an important task for you to do. As Daleb pointed out, George almost got what he was after, and you need to make sure he doesn't."

"Okay, so how do I avoid pulling George in?" I think, refocusing my attention on the present.

"No idea," Daleb replies.

"Me neither," Mimir echoes.

"And if I do pull him in?"

"He'll attack, and you'll likely end up Inert." Mimir's thought is tinged with sorrow. "And I know you're about to ask if we can help, but we can't."

"And let's not forget that you going Inert will lead to the monks dying, and Mira and Thomas remaining in danger," Daleb adds.

"Why can't you help?" I wonder.

"We do not want the Elders to know of our existence," Mimir explains. "And we have a moral code that strictly forbids us from interfering with a mind, even George's. You wouldn't understand."

"Or approve," I think, projecting my grudge as best as I can through my thoughts. "Fine, you don't want to mess with minds. I can sort of understand that. But what about this secrecy? You mentioned it on the Island, which, I may add, caused me a lot of confusion. What you never explained is why? Why can't the Elders know about you?"

"Why don't Readers and Guides let Unencumbered know about their existence?" Mimir asks. "Why did you hide your true Depth from your friends?"

"Fine," I reply. I'm convinced there's more to it than he's suggesting, but I'm confident he'll remind me that time is running out if I press.

"Time *is* running out, though." Mimir's mental voice sounds mischievous.

"Any last-minute suggestions?"

"Use your instincts," Daleb thinks at the same time as Mimir projects, "Pick at random."

I pick the brightest constellation of the bunch—the one closest to me—and teleport there effortlessly.

Both Mimir's and Daleb's lights disappear.

"Guys, wait," I think, but no response comes.

They're gone.

Fine, I think pointedly. *I'll manage without you.*

With that, I reach for my intuitively, or randomly, chosen victim.

* * *

The Leacher we're tangled with is strong—strong enough to provide us with a rare challenge. Cutting through the battle rage is an unwelcome thrill of feminine awareness.

I, Darren, disassociate with disgust. I'm in the mind of Eleanor, who, despite the Super Pusher's command to kill him, is lusting after Caleb. Without further ado, I start Guiding her:

The man you're fighting is not your enemy. You will say the words, "Caleb, Darren did it. I'm now on your side. Help me take down the man responsible for all this shit." Then you will get up and apprehend George. That's your primary goal. If you see James or Kate trying to hurt the monks, try and stop them. That's your secondary goal.

And with that, I exit Eleanor's head.

* * *

As the floating sensation of Nirvana returns, I decide that perhaps my choice was more intuitive than lucky. Perhaps I have some idea, on a subconscious level, of who's who. A more skeptical part of me reminds me that my chances of choosing correctly were three in four.

I pick the next pattern carefully, letting my intuition do its job, in case it's actually working. I teleport to my choice and envelop it, ready to start Reading, but nothing happens.

Then I notice a new pattern has shown up near me.

It's a moving version of the pattern I just engaged.

If I had eyes, I would be blinking them to make sure he's here for real, but I have to settle for the mental version of this, which consists of becoming more certain that there's a live mind in front of me.

There's only one reason for this happenstance.

My intuition isn't worth a damn.

I just pulled George in.

Before these thoughts finish running through my head, the collection of neurons that is my enemy gets uncomfortably close to me.

I'm not sure whether my perception of his pattern is colored by my anger and disgust with George, or by his own intentions, but for the first time, a mind in Level 2 looks positively repulsive to me.

Gone are the outer-space visuals. Instead, there's something about him that reminds me of creatures from the deep sea. His synapses, in particular, look slimy and unwholesome, like the stingers of some giant jellyfish that luminesces to lure in its prey. His neurons similarly remind me of the lights on tips of dorsal spines of monstrous anglerfishes; I can't help but imagine rows of sharp teeth and ugly faces hiding behind each speck of light.

And then, to my sheer mental horror, this abomination envelops me.

CHAPTER TWENTY-SIX

I instantly realize that George initiated Assimilation—the strange, empathetic mind meld that Frederick and I engaged in on the Island.

An avalanche of anxiety hits me, quickly evolving into a tornado of debilitating fear. It's as if I received a shot of adrenaline directly into the fear center of my brain. Rationally, I know this is due to my fear combining with any trepidation George is feeling, but that doesn't make it better. Fear is never rational.

I try fighting it, but as soon as I regain some semblance of sanity, I feel a wave of emotion that I can best describe as rejection. It's my negation of what George is trying to do to me, and his version of the same emotion. We both feel as if the sanctity of our minds is being violated. Describing the feeling is difficult. All I can compare it to is pain, only it's much worse. It makes the pain Caleb endured when he lost his hand feel like a scrape in comparison.

The usual sense of nonbeing I associate with Nirvana is gone. Instead, I again feel a strange sense of corporealness. As soon as it appears, it slips away, almost as if it's being erased. This happened during my Assimilation with Frederick, only this is a hundred times worse.

George has only one goal: he wants to complete this process of erasing me, the success of which would make me Inert.

I have to do something about it, I realize, and mentally push back.

An extremely unsavory sensation overcomes me. It feels as if I'm killing an innocent or vandalizing something beautiful.

I remind myself that George isn't a unique and beautiful snowflake. He's the fucker who tried to choke me on the Island. With that mental reassurance, I push again.

The turbulent feeling intensifies. A fresh wave of fear arises from George, its intensity mixing with my own. I feel echoes of that 'being erased' feeling emanating from him, or maybe they're my own; it's hard to tell.

"Stop, Darren," his vile thought tells me. "Please."

Due to the Assimilation, I know he really means it; he really wants me to stop.

Well, no shit. That just means that whatever I'm doing is working. Good. I push hard, capitalizing on my success.

The feeling of being erased increases, but I can tell it's him who's being affected and not me.

My discomfort from feeling as though I'm doing something horrible increases too. I fight it, trying to make my mind ruthless. I remind myself how close Mira came to death before I reversed Thomas's instructions. This revitalizes my resolve, and I try to crush the mind responsible for nearly killing her.

"Let's make a deal, Darren," George tries again. "I can't lie right now. Can't you tell that?"

I feel myself disappear, just a little, but getting erased even a little is worse than getting kicked in the face—and I'm speaking from experience.

He's distracting me with his words, trying to wiggle his way out. And the worst part is that, for a moment, it worked.

Well, two can play this game, I decide, and try to speak the way I did when I was dealing with Frederick. "Why are you doing this, George? Why are you trying to kill the Enlightened?"

As I await his reply, I gather my energy for my next mental attack.

"The Elders are fools to want to foster this peace," he responds, but I sense he's not actually being truthful with me.

"You're lying," I challenge, mostly to keep him off-balance. I don't care that much about his explanation.

"I just didn't say the whole truth," he responds. "I have other, more personal reasons that I don't think are as relevant." This time, his response is more truthful. "A Leacher killed my parents."

I gather more energy and say, "That's still not the complete truth."

"What do you want, a full list of my grievances against the Leachers? You probably don't have enough Reach for me to enumerate them all. The Leachers started this war, not us. Why should their atrocities be forgotten?"

His reply is truthful, if not very informative. He must realize this, because he explains, "I'm not doing this solely for me. I'm here on Mary's behalf. Markus Robinson killed Henry, her husband. She never recovered from that, as you yourself witnessed."

The feeling of being erased gets a little stronger as I ruminate on what he just said. That would make Henry, Mary's husband, my great-grandfather.

"Who the hell is Markus?" I ask. Robinson was my dad's last name . . .

"He was the father of one of these so-called Enlightened," George answers truthfully. "Now his son, Paul, will pay with his life, as will the rest of them, putting any notion of peace to rest once and for all."

As I lose a little more of myself, I process what he's saying. If Markus is Paul's father, it means one of my great-grandfathers killed the other. I'm not sure how that's supposed to make me feel. Did my parents know?

Suddenly, I feel a chunk of me disappear. George used my confusion to his advantage. With a sense of vertigo, I feel as if I'm shrinking. If this continues, he'll win, and soon.

"Stop fighting me, and I will let you live," George's thought arrives, and to my surprise, he's telling the truth. "I will even let your Leacher girlfriend live if you give up now."

The offer comes with another mental assault.

Instead of replying, I unleash all the mental energy I've been saving during this back-and-forth. When I feel it take effect, I give him my counteroffer. "Stop killing everyone, and *I* will let *you* live. Stop fighting me now, and I'll take it as you accepting my offer."

He responds with a renewed mental onslaught, but it's less forceful now.

I need to use his strategy against him.

"Why did you try to have Kyle kill all those scientists?" I ask.

I'm fully prepared to ignore his answer, reminding myself why I need to erase this man.

"If I die, you will never know," he replies, but his answer is way more fearful than truthful. "Without my work, the Unencumbered will use transformative technology to become uncontrollable—"

I only partially register his words. My goal is to distract him. Instead of listening, I apply pressure again.

I feel *something* that makes me think my plan is working. George's mind noticeably gives. I'm assaulted by his emotions—fear, disappointment, and something else, something that might be his belated realization that I duped him.

It's frightening how intertwined our emotions are. As I destroy him, I almost feel as if I'm losing myself, or more accurately, making him part of me. I feel overwhelming pity, so much so that I'm not sure I can go on.

I need to hold on to myself if I'm to win. I need to push through my doubts. Thus determined, I focus on erasing him some more, all the while reminding myself that if I succeed, I'm merely making him Inert.

The anguish coming from George is maddening. I need to find a way to become unwavering. I need to center myself so I can finish this grisly task.

I turn George's crimes into a mantra that I repeat in my mind as I attack him. I remember how I felt when Thomas and Mira attacked me at the funeral, when the cops almost shot me, and when I was standing next to Mira and my moms. I channel all that anger and frustration into mentally squashing him.

A wave of mental terror hits me, but I ignore it. I focus on the memory of the time he attacked me in the library. I take the recollection of his hands around my throat and use it to push. I can feel his growing fear and dismay, but I replay the memory of seeing those bloodied monks for the first time and push harder.

"No, please, no," he begs, and with a tsunami of horror, he gives in a little more.

I replay the scene of Paul getting punched in the stomach and push harder. George's hold on me shrinks.

Ignoring his desperate pleas and squishing that bothersome feeling of doing something sacrilegious,

I remind myself how Thomas was ready to choke Mira to death.

This memory is what does it.

As I channel the threat of losing Mira, I feel George growing smaller and smaller.

I feel frighteningly powerful. Something tells me no mortal should do what I'm about to do, but I ignore the feeling, focusing instead on George's atrocities for my last mental assault.

After a moment of anguish that seems to last an eternity, I feel the release of crossing that final threshold.

Suddenly, I regain the insubstantiality of Level 2, and George's mind is gone—and I don't just mean his neural network that I've been fighting. Even the frozen-in-time version of him is gone, which makes sense since he's now Inert.

Instead of elation, I feel as though I've been trapped in a sensory deprivation chamber for a year. I no longer have the sense that I'm floating in Nirvana; instead, it's as if I'm drowning and falling from a great height at the same time. It's so disconcerting that if my frozen self were in front of me, I'd be tempted to phase out, the rest of Kate's team be damned.

"I'm sorry you had to go through that." Mimir's tone of thought is sad. "But you have to deal with them."

I gather whatever mental reserves I have left, and without responding to Mimir, I choose one of the two remaining minds and fall into its memories like a brick into a lake.

* * *

Our stepbrother's fist looks enormous as it slams into our nose.

The pain is jarring and we stand there, momentarily stunned by it. The world seems to slow down, as it often does when we're in trouble.

"Is the little Puddy Tat going to cry?" he says in his ever-changing, squeaky thirteen-year-old voice.

His taunts are worse than the pain of his assaults, and they snap us back to attention.

"My name is Kate," we want to scream but suppress the urge. Instead, we cup our nose with our small hands in the hope that he perceives it as a submissive gesture. We make heaving motions to make him think we're crying, but in reality, we're distracting him so we can scan the room for something to use against him. With a side glance, we notice he's rubbing his fist.

Of course, we think scornfully. He's never been in a fight against someone his size, or likely any size. All he's good at is bullying an eight-year-old girl. Well, we intend to make this go very differently from how he imagined.

We spot what we're looking for: a toy sword a few feet away. It's made out of wood, and in our opinion, it's something a boy his age should've outgrown.

We grab the glorified stick and swing it at his head.

He's stunned when the stick connects with his face, but we don't use the moment to gloat. This time, we aim the sword at his crotch.

I, Darren, disassociate. This is Kate, but Kate from a very, very long time ago. In my post-Assimilation fugue, I must've jumped back much further than I intended. That she was already frightening at such a young age is something I file under 'deal with later.' For now, I can't waste even a second more, so I begin Guiding her:

You will stop killing monks and cops. You will instead focus on protecting Darren and assisting Eleanor . . .

* * *

I'm back in Level 2. The sensation of drowning has intensified. I don't even recall exiting Kate's mind, but I'm confident I gave her enough instructions that she won't be a problem anymore.

One more person to go, and then I can get out of here.

And possibly lose my powers forever, a part of me thinks. The feeling of drowning grows even stronger.

James's mind should provide some relief, I hope as I initiate the connection. Again, I enter the mind violently, like a bungee jumper whose rope has snapped.

* * *

Warm. Comforting. Safe.

I, Darren, am confused. I'm supposed to be in James's mind, but James isn't in his own mind. Only the faintest sensory perceptions exist. Did I jump to a time when James was comatose? Is that why his awareness is lacking conscious thought?

No, that theory wouldn't explain all the weirdness. For starters, this darkness isn't what I'd expect from a dream. This darkness is different, as though James has his eyes open while sitting in a dark cave, with only vague hints of starlight coming in from the outside.

Stranger still is the floating sensation. At first, it makes me wonder whether I've finally lost it and am currently back in Nirvana, where I feel like I'm floating in the dark. But no, Nirvana-floating is an illusion caused by not having a body. Here, James is truly floating; it's just happening in a tight, dark place.

I allow his memory to overtake me.

Unlike the silence of Level 2, there are sounds here. Specifically, some kind of a steady thumping sound that comes in at regular intervals, and the tiny part of us that is James finds it very comforting.

Then I discover another parallel to Level 2: we're not breathing.

After a few moments of trying to piece all of this together, it finally hits me.

When I thought I'd jumped too far into Kate's mind, it was nothing compared to this.

James isn't comatose.

He hasn't been born yet.

I'm James so early in his life that he's still in his mother's womb.

This realization comes with little details I didn't comprehend before, like the distant sound we really like, which must be his mother's voice. Some more primitive senses are available to us, allowing us to taste the subtle flavor of curry in the amniotic fluid we just swallowed. His mom must've eaten Indian food. The comfortingly squishy feeling of pushing against the boundaries of our little world is what makes me realize how creepy this is. In fact, I'm not sure whether I should be in awe or creeped out, but I experience both in equal measures.

Suddenly, the Reading is interrupted.

* * *

I hear the sounds of the forest and the footsteps of my police entourage, and I smell greenery.

I'm back in the forest.

I must've finally run out of Depth and phased out. I'm running with my hand still clutching the phone, and my muscles are aching.

All this lasts for only a moment before the tip of my shoe catches on a root and I fall, my head slamming into a nearby tree.

CHAPTER TWENTY-SEVEN

"Sir," a voice with a southern accent says. "Are you all right?"

I lie there, considering the answer to that question. A cowardly thought enters my mind. I wonder whether everything that happened today—the attack on the Temple, the Assimilation, the too-deep jumps into memories, and most importantly, Eugene's machine that took away my abilities, maybe forever—were delusions brought on by falling and hitting my head. There's only one way to test the realness of the situation.

I try to phase into the Quiet as I usually would.

I can tell it didn't work, because I hear, "Sir, do you want me to radio in for medical help?"

"Yes." I open my eyes. "Have them helicopter in a lot of medical help, but not for me."

As the man says something into his radio, I touch the side of my head. I have the mother of all bumps there, but otherwise, I feel well enough. My right hand hurts—I'm still clutching my phone in a death-like grip—so I pocket the object.

"How long was I out?" I ask the sheriff.

"You were out?" He looks at me, confused. "You fell down a second ago."

And before I can respond, a gunshot rings out through the woods.

The sudden sound makes me realize that there's been relative silence coming from the direction of the Temple, which is good news. However, since I didn't succeed in reversing James and because George is simply Inert and not neutralized, I know I need to get back there to see what's happening.

"Help me up," I say as I try to stand on my own. The sheriff and a young deputy help me to my feet. Once I make sure I'm not too dizzy to stand, I tell them, "Follow me. We're not far now."

I run as fast as I can without repeating the falling fiasco. I think I'm getting the hang of running while hurt, hungry, and exhausted. If they make this into an Olympic sport, I might try for the gold.

Surprisingly, running clears my mind when it comes to dealing with the things that transpired in Level 2. It even dampens my gnawing fear about the possibility of being Inert forever, though I might just be exercising my favorite coping mechanism— which, according to Liz, is denial.

Finally, I see the clearing through the trees that surround the Temple.

A couple of officers, including the sheriff and the young guy who tased me, step out of the forest first. I quickly follow them. This is when I see them staring at a figure in the distance.

George.

He's about twenty feet away, and as soon as he sees the cops, he yells, "Protect me as per your orders—"

Then his eyes focus on me, and even from this distance, I can see powerful emotions contorting his face—a little bit of horror, mixed with fear and hatred. He must've instinctively tried to phase into the Quiet and failed.

With substantially less confidence in his voice, George continues. "Twenty-three. Order twenty-three. Attack that man."

He points at me at the same time as he takes out a shell from his pocket and loads it into his shotgun.

Though I can't phase into the Quiet, the world does seem to slow down—the effect of an adrenaline rush.

In this slow-motion state, I realize I don't need my powers to know what's going on in George's mind. He thought he could use these cops against me; he must've implanted some kind of code word in their minds that would allow him to take control of them, but that was before I overrode his orders.

In my most commanding tone, I say, "Don't listen to him. He's an escaped convict, apprehend him using—"

I don't finish my sentence.

George must've caught on to my reprogramming. He stops reloading his gun and takes a few steps backwards. As he does, he retrieves something from his pocket.

My entourage reaches for their guns, their movements so eerily synchronized they seem rehearsed.

I take out the long-barreled tranquilizer gun Hillary gave me—a reminder of how this mission was supposed to be surreptitious and casualty-free—from the back of my pants.

Meanwhile, George is holding a round and familiar-looking object. I recently saw its cousin in the folds of Edward's robe.

"Grenade!" I shout in case the cops missed it.

I'm about to say more, but the words die in my throat when George frantically pulls the pin and throws the grenade in my direction.

Conditioned by having seen this type of scenario play out a thousand times in movies, I do what the about-to-get-blown-up people always do: I fall to the ground. More specifically, I drop as though I'm about to do a push up.

I look up and see that George has done the same thing, only he isn't peeking; he's holding his head in both hands.

Instantly, I realize dropping to the ground won't save me.

The grenade landed a few feet away from me. If falling on the ground saved people from grenades at this distance, they'd be pretty useless.

Paradoxically, for someone about to die, I'm more upset about my lack of powers. If I hadn't lost them, I'd phase out, walk to the Temple, make sure everyone was okay, and then, eventually, when my Depth ran out, I'd go out with a bang. In fact, given my Depth, I could've pulled Mira in and spent a lifetime with her in the Quiet, similar to what the Elders do. No, wait, Mira is either Inert or unconscious right now, so that wouldn't have worked . . .

Why hasn't the grenade exploded? I wonder, the thought interrupting my glum reflection. *Must be a time-delay rather than an impact one,* I realize in the next moment.

Then I wonder how many people have had this exact, final thought.

Another long millisecond of my life follows. I realize that being in danger while Inert has another disadvantage: you can't Guide someone to save you. Were I callous enough, I could have—

In a blur of motion, the sheriff's body lands on top of the grenade. It's as though he knew what I was thinking. A deputy falls on top of the sheriff; then another cop jumps on top of them both. The rest of the cops fall on top of me. I can only imagine what Thomas felt like at the cemetery, though his cop pile was worse than mine. My kindergarten experience is definitely dated; being at the bottom of a human pile really sucks.

But what the hell is going on?

Then it clicks. I Guided them to protect me with their lives. I explicitly stated they were the Secret Service to my President.

Though that command will save me, it will cost them their lives.

Guilt doesn't have the chance to hit me because the grenade finally explodes.

The boom sounds just like the cherry bombs Bert and I set off in the Harvard cafeteria during our freshman year, only multiplied by a factor of ten.

Through a small opening between the tangles of limbs in front of me, I see that George is already on his feet.

"Get off me," I order, but I'm not sure my defenders heard me. "Don't just lie there."

The smell of burned flesh enters my nostrils, and I instantly feel like throwing up. I can't—the one perk of not having eaten in the last twenty hours—but I do dry-heave.

Another bang makes me think that another grenade went off, but it's actually George firing his shotgun. I think he just shot at what was left of the three men piled on top of the grenade, but now he's aiming the barrel right at my pile of people.

I try to roll to my side, but the weight of the bodies keeps me pinned.

I cover my face as George fires another shot. I smell gunpowder and the metallic scent of blood.

Another shotgun blast follows.

I feel a trickle of blood run down the back of my neck, but since I feel no pain, I assume it isn't my blood.

I feel under me for the tranquilizer gun. No luck.

This next bang sounds louder.

Giving up on the gun idea, I frantically grab for anything from the cop on top of me. His gun is under someone else's body, but I can reach his Taser and his set of handcuffs.

I try to push myself off the ground by essentially executing a push up. I pray to my surge of adrenaline and years of bench-pressing at the gym for strength. I only manage to straighten my arms halfway, but it's enough for me to get my knees to my chest.

After the fifth bang, I move to get up.

In the gym, my record for squats is four forty-five-pound plates on each side of a forty-five-pound bar. That's a total of 405 pounds, unless my math is off. What I'm doing now is in many ways harder, since I never squat this close to the ground, not to mention that my left knee has been bugging me on rainy days ever since I set that personal record. I'm not sure what the combined weight of the cops on top of me is, but it feels much heavier than those 405 pounds. As the bodies fall aside, my legs and knees scream for mercy.

I ignore everything, making George the center of my universe. He's reloading his damn shotgun.

Purely on instinct, I aim the Taser and pull the trigger. The tiny cables stretch the twenty feet between us and embed into George's chest, but the man is still standing. Then he freezes and begins convulsing, right before he falls backwards onto the grass.

The problem with the way he falls is that the little cables get pulled from his chest.

Having no idea how long he'll be out for, I make a split-second decision and run.

I didn't run after pressing those 405 pounds, and now I see the wisdom in that decision.

Despite the pain and the strain, I cover half the distance between George and me in a second. I probably could've done it faster, had the bodies of my unmoving protectors not slowed me down by a critical half-second.

George stirs.

I pick up my pace, knowing if there's a tree root in my way, I'll be splattered across the ground.

George jackknifes to a standing position.

To my surprise, my legs have enough stamina left for a move I believe is derived from tae kwon do.

I use my momentum to execute a jump kick—a maneuver designed to topple people off a galloping horse.

My foot slams into George's forehead with a satisfying smack. He falls backwards, and unfortunately, I follow his example.

As I fall, I wonder how I'm able to think so much in such a short time. I always have more thoughts than I expect in these about-to-get-hurt situations. Yesterday, I would've said it was a side effect of the Quiet, but now, falling while Inert, I realize it's just some kind of brain mechanism that everyone must have. This is what allows people to relive events while in life or death situations.

I hit the ground. My tailbone violently objects, but the real pain comes from my ankle. I must've twisted it when I landed, or when I executed the kick.

Ignoring the agony, I grab the handcuffs off the ground and create makeshift brass knuckles by holding them through the two loops. I try to jump up into a sitting position but end up performing more of a clumsy seesaw motion. Fighting against my wounds for every inch of movement, I eventually push myself into a sitting stance. From here, it's an easy struggle to my feet.

Once standing, I see George. He's an arm's length away, and he's holding his shotgun. If he loaded a shell in it as I was getting up, I'm done for. But I have to assume he didn't load the gun, because he swings it at me in a wide arc.

I have two choices: dodge or take the hit.

I go for the painful route. I move, allowing the butt of the gun to hit my right side, and plunge my handcuff-armed fist into George's jaw just as pain erupts in my side. I'm only vaguely aware of the pain in my right hand, which I suspect is bleeding from the handcuffs. Since I don't care to cut my palm any deeper, I throw the handcuffs at George's head.

I miss, but on the bright side, it's not because he dodged. He doesn't look in any condition to counter my attacks. His eyes seem dim, and he appears ready to fall over. The shotgun slips out of his hand.

I try to calm my ragged breathing, but it's hard. Something inside me acquired a piece of red-hot iron, and it's poking me when I inhale.

Oxygen or no, I have to capitalize on George's dazedness. I step closer and ready myself to punch him.

I'll never know whether George was faking or if he regained his strength at the last second, but his wooziness doesn't prevent him from doing a strange half-stomp, half-kick on my injured ankle.

I inhale sharply, provoking the red-hot pain in my side. Instantly, I forget about punching George and focus on not crumpling to the ground in a fetal position.

Emboldened, George raises his fists, boxing-style, and swings.

I realize something then: my martial arts training is more defensive than offensive. Seeing a fist flying at me makes my brain ignore the pain and follow the conditioning of my training.

I meet George's fist with my elbow and throw a punch at his solar plexus.

George must do crunches daily, because my hand meets hard muscles.

Instead of doubling over in pain, the fucker counters by grabbing my neck with both hands, proving once and for all that he has a fetish for choking people.

Due to my body's already-low air supply, I weaken quickly and with a sense of déjà vu.

I see white and black lights in front of my eyes, and they remind me of our recent Assimilation battle. I remember how I motivated myself by replaying all the things George has done, and my weakness slowly gives way to an all-consuming anger.

The anger gives me a small burst of energy, but I know that if I don't use it wisely, this is the last burst of energy I'll ever get.

I note that my hands are up and bent at the elbows—a natural reaction to someone choking me from the front. The dumb thing to do would be to try and unclench his hands; his grip is powerful, and in the condition I'm in now, I lack the strength to stop him. So I use my modicum of energy to grab

George's wrists and pull his arms backwards, as though I'm trying to get him to choke someone behind me.

The gambit works, and his grip slips, his arms swooshing by my shoulders.

I accompany the maneuver with a Krav Maga—and Mira's favorite—move: a kick to the groin.

George grunts but doesn't fall over. I need him to fall because I'm about to. So I do something I would've done in a drunken bar brawl.

I head-butt him.

My forehead connects with the bridge of his nose. The sound of bone cracking reverberates, though it could've come from my skull just as easily as from his nose.

As I fall, I see George topple over as well. I hit the ground, and all my body wants to do is lose consciousness, but with a monumental effort of will, I hold on.

With my remaining strength, I pat the ground for the cuffs. The fingers of my right hand meet the soothing coldness of metal. I grab the cuffs, crawl over to George, and fasten them on my knocked-out opponent.

Then I reach into his pocket and remove a shotgun shell. I roll over to the shotgun, which was just out of reach, and load it.

To save my strength, I drag it across the ground and put the barrel parallel to George's head. It's a shotgun, so good aim isn't critical.

I place my finger on the trigger.

George opens his eyes and whispers, "Please. No."

He proceeds to cover his face with his hands as though that could stop a shotgun blast.

Slightly louder, he adds, "You can't. We're family."

I must be in worse shape than I thought, because my finger refuses to pull the trigger. Or more accurately, something within me prevents me from pulling it. Some part of me tells me that I can't kill him, that it wouldn't be right.

I argue against whatever part of me is having these very untimely qualms.

Was it his plea? I wonder. No, I don't really buy his 'we're family' comment for a second.

Is it that he's cuffed and at my mercy? That sounds more like it, but that would make my reluctance irrational. He was trying to kill me just a moment earlier. I could've killed him with a punch and slept soundly, but I still can't pull the trigger.

I reason with myself some more. George is too dangerous to be allowed to live. Also, as far as justice goes, he deserves the ultimate punishment solely based on the number of police casualties on his head. Add in the dead monks, and he deserves double the death penalty.

I raise the gun to shoot him, but find that I still can't.

What's wrong with me? It's not like George would be my first kill.

I killed that Russian mobster, the one who shot at Mira at the warehouse. I shot Jacob on that bridge. I Guided Kyle to get himself killed at the science conference. Sure, the first two times I acted in the heat of the moment, protecting people I care about. But with Kyle, it was colder. I *meant* to kill him from the get-go. Even though it was Victor who pulled the trigger, it could just as easily have been me.

The irrational part of me that's preventing my finger from pulling the trigger is a hypocrite.

Still, I can't do it. I can't shoot someone who deserves it. If these injuries don't kill me, I'll need to visit my shrink. Some wires have clearly gotten crossed inside my head.

Frustrated, I mimic George's earlier maneuver and use the gun as a club. I hit him on the head, knocking him out. Nothing stopped me from doing *that.*

I aim the gun again, hoping that without him staring at me, I'll be able to do what I must, but my finger refuses to budge.

All of a sudden, a shadow crosses us.

"Let go of the gun, kid," Caleb says. He's pointing a pistol at me.

Clubbing George zapped the last of my strength. Actually, I might've borrowed some energy from my future. I can't even imagine raising the gun to aim it at Caleb, so I drop it. Not like I was going to fire it anyway.

Caleb aims and fires. Blood and brain splatter everywhere. Given that I can see the resulting gore, I obviously wasn't Caleb's target.

"He was too dangerous." Caleb sounds almost apologetic. Did Caleb of all people also have reservations about killing George? "No one should be able to Push a Reader."

He steps closer, looming directly over me. He proceeds to aim his pistol straight down, at my forehead. Now I understand the reason for his apologetic tone.

It's killing *me* that's giving him pause.

Apparently, it's possible to be too worn out for self-preservation because I don't do anything other than watch him.

His face looks torn. Did I look that way a minute ago? Is growing a conscience contagious?

"If you pull that trigger, I'll take your head," a female voice says—a voice I recognize as Kate's. A sliver of metal appears alongside Caleb's neck.

I should be worried about getting a bullet to the head, but all I can think is: how did she sneak up on Caleb? Given the man's reflexes, that's no easy task.

Kate gently moves her blade, generating a streak of blood across Caleb's neck. "Let go of the gun. Now."

Caleb smirks and obeys.

The gun falls on my head, and everything finally goes black.

CHAPTER TWENTY-EIGHT

I wake up to numbness.

I try to phase into the Quiet, but it doesn't work.

Of course it doesn't, I recall with a jolt. I'm Inert.

I open my eyes, find the room too bright, and close them again.

"I think he just blinked," a voice says. The voice sounds a lot like Thomas's.

"Darren, are you awake?" asks a soft, pleasant female voice that I instantly recognize as Mira's.

I squint at them. Mira is sitting next to me on the bed. Her hand is on mine, but with all the warm numbness, I didn't feel it until this moment. Her clothes are different. I think she's wearing a man's shirt, but by undoing a few of the top buttons, she's definitely made it her own.

Thomas is sitting in a chair next to a bunch of hospital machines. His hands are bandaged, but he otherwise seems okay.

I open my eyes wider. All the medical equipment next to Thomas is hooked up to me, as is the IV bag hanging next to Mira's head.

I feel the slightly uncomfortable sensation of an oxygen assist in my nose. Even with the assist, I need extra air, so I take in a deep breath and regret it instantly. The numbness gives way to pain in my side.

"Can you get the doctor or a nurse?" Mira asks Thomas. She must've seen me cringe. "They should give him more pain medication."

Thomas walks out. Did he look guilty as he got up?

"I'm in the hospital." This is a mix of a question and a statement, demonstrating the sort of wit that only painkillers can inspire. As I speak, I learn that talking hurts too. Also, my speech sounds slurred, even to my overmedicated ears.

"Yes." Mira brushes the tips of her fingers across my cheek. "Eugene called. He told me how you saved me . . . again."

Bracing against the pain, I ask, "Are he and Bert—"

"They're on their way here," she says.

"How long has it been?" I speak more softly, and it hurts less.

"I'm not sure." She looks at her phone. "A few hours."

"Is George—"

Kate walks into the room, incongruently accompanied by Rose.

"George is dead," Kate says, her face as expressionless as Thomas's usually is. "Didn't you see Caleb shoot him?"

I look from Kate to Rose, who, to my surprise, is looking me over with genuine concern. Do I have to be this beat-up to trigger her grandmotherly instincts?

"Yeah, I saw," I say, realizing Kate is waiting for an answer. "I just needed to be sure. I wasn't exactly in the best shape . . ."

"You're not exactly in great shape now." Kate smiles. "But yes, the only way George could be deader is if I'd gotten to him first."

"And James?" I decide to keep my breaths shallow; the pain in my side is increasing. "I didn't get a chance to override him."

"I figured as much." Kate's smile fades. "He was the reason George managed to escape."

"No, I mean, is he alive?" A sharp stab in my side reminds me that I forgot to speak softly.

"James is alive. Eleanor and Caleb knocked him out. Even John survived, though he's in surgery." As she talks, her eyes become suspiciously moist.

Making sure I don't infuriate my injury, I loudly whisper, "What about the police officers? The ones George—"

"If you're talking about the ones at the Temple, we tried to save as many as we could, but I won't lie—there was collateral damage. Same goes for the monks. If you mean the officers who accompanied you when George was running away, then I'm afraid none of them made it."

A wave of intense guilt washes over me. My Guiding cost the sheriff and his deputies their lives, which wasn't my intent. I was only trying to reverse George's compulsion. As if sensing what I'm feeling, Mira places her other hand on top of my palm, as though to warm me up.

"None of this is your fault," Kate says, shrewdly picking up on my tension. "It's all on George."

"No," Rose interjects. "We bear some of the responsibility."

"Sorry to interrupt." A tall man in a white coat enters. He stops, Kate standing between him and my bed. Though she isn't wearing her sword, her body language speaks clearly, and the guy instantly grows roots.

"ID," she orders.

The guy points at his pocket and then to his face. Kate does her best imitation of a TSA agent, first staring at his badge, then at his face.

Finally, she says, "Okay, speak."

"Umm, I was going to introduce myself. I'm Doctor Churin," he says.

"Hi Doc, I'm Darren." I try to sound friendly. It's always been my policy to keep doctors happy with me, especially while I'm in their hospital. "You can tell me about my condition in front of my friends and family."

He looks at the chart, then around the room. Clearing his throat, he says, "You have a mild concussion, and your x-rays show a cracked rib."

Kate whistles, Mira narrows her eyes, and Rose worriedly exhales.

"You should be fine," the doctor says, half to me and half to the women. "We'll just need to make sure to provide you with proper pain management so you can breathe, cough, and laugh normally. The painkillers will also help your right ankle. It's swollen and might be painful to step on. Now tell me, how do you feel?"

I give the doctor a big list of complaints, which he writes into my chart.

"I'll check back in an hour." He returns his pen into his breast pocket. "Meanwhile, I'll send in our best nurse to give you something for the pain."

"Wait, doctor," Mira says. "Can he sleep? I heard you can't sleep with a concussion."

"Since he can carry on a conversation, I wouldn't worry. If you're extra conservative, you can rouse him every few hours to make sure his condition isn't deteriorating. We do that with children."

"I'll do that then," Mira mumbles, more to herself than to the doc.

Rose looks at her with unabashed curiosity.

The doctor leaves. He was so helpful that I wonder whether Thomas Guided him.

Now that I know my body will recover, I allow myself to worry about my Inert state. What if Eugene was right? What if I never recover my abilities? Imagining myself without my abilities is like imagining being blind.

The nurse comes in next, distracting me from my blues. Before she's allowed to do anything, Kate gives her the same ID treatment she gave the doctor. Thankfully, she clears her, and the nurse administers my feel-good juice.

"I'm going to get something to eat," Kate says when the nurse leaves the room. "But don't worry. Eleanor is just outside this door."

"Are you guys protecting me?" I ask.

"You and her people." Kate waves at Rose. "The Elders want you and the Enlightened safe."

Warmth and contentment spreads through me, though I'm not sure whether it's brought on by the knowledge that Kate's team is protecting me, or by the drug the nurse gave me. Whatever it is, it spreads nicely through my body and makes it very easy to breathe.

"They're a little overbearing," Rose says after Kate leaves the room. "But we're putting up with it, for the sake of peace."

"Speaking of overbearing," I say, feeling giddy at the joke I'm about to make. "How is Paul?"

She chuckles. "He's got some bumps and bruises, but he'll be okay. He's grateful to you, even if you won't hear him admit it. When that woman told him about Caleb trying to kill you, he was livid."

She stops talking because there's some kind of a scuffle coming from the hall.

A few seconds later, Eleanor walks in. Her hands are on her hips, and she has Eugene's head between her body and her right elbow. On her left, she has Bert's head in the same position.

"Do you know these two?" she booms.

"Yes, please let them go," I say at the same time as Mira snaps, "Let my brother go, you bitch."

Eleanor complies, giving Mira a dirty look.

"Thanks, Eleanor," I say. "Please wait outside."

To my shock, the big woman nods and exits. It might be the drugs, but I thought I saw a hint of respect in the gesture.

"Darren, how are you?" Eugene exclaims.

"What happened?" Bert's voice is an octave higher than Eugene's.

"Hi, Eugene," Rose says with a sly smile.

"Do I know you?" Eugene asks, frowning at her.

"No." Rose's smile widens. "But I saw you in Darren's memories. You know, Julia is in the hospital . . ."

And with that, she exits the room, leaving Eugene with a flabbergasted expression on his face.

Not waiting for my friend to recover, I proceed to tell them what happened, including the stuff Eugene already witnessed, even though it's obvious they heard some of the story already.

"So you gave up your Depth, your powers, to save me?" Mira's expression is hard to pinpoint. Maybe it's shock, or maybe it's something else. Something like gratitude.

I feel warm again, and this time, I know it's not from the painkillers. Mira's reaction almost makes the loss worth it.

"Cheer up, dude," Bert says. "I can't do what you do, and I'm okay."

"But you're like a person born without hearing." I know I sound gloomy, but I can't help myself. "Of course you don't miss something you never had."

"I read that people who lose their sight or hearing eventually adjust," Eugene says. "With time, they become just as happy as they were before the tragedy."

"Zhenya, what did I tell you about your ability to make people feel better?" Mira's voice is clipped.

Bert's phone makes an R2-D2 sound, which I recognize as his text message ringtone.

He looks at the phone and says, "Sorry, it's Hillary. She's still not sure what to do."

"How is she? How are my moms?" I ask, belatedly remembering that I had Hillary take them to safety.

"They're all fine," Bert says. "But Hillary is unsure if she should tell Sara about your situation."

"She's got those smart genes," I say. "Tell her to bring them here, leisurely, under any pretext other than 'Darren is hurt.' I'm sure she can make something up. Once they get here, I'll handle them. If Sara learns about my fractured rib and other mishaps the wrong way, she'll end up in this hospital with a panic attack."

"Got it," Bert says, and his fingers dance on the phone's keypad.

I yawn. All this talking is very energy-consuming.

Mira notes my yawn with a frown. She then glances at Bert and Eugene and asks, "Did you two eat anything? Did you sleep?" Sniffing the air, she adds, "For that matter, did either of you shower in the last couple of weeks?"

Bert looks at Eugene as if saying, *She's your sister, dude.*

"We'll go eat now," Eugene says. He clearly knows how to handle Mira. "Thanks for the reminder, sis."

After they exit, Mira gets up, walks over to the door, and demonstratively closes it. She then takes a chair and props it up, blocking the door. After that, she turns off the bright hospital lights, sits on the bed, and leans in to kiss me.

I return the kiss, trying my best not to say something unmanly, like 'ouch,' as I do. I'm enjoying the kiss, but my ribs are less enthusiastic.

She pulls away and says softly, "Why don't you nap? The doctor said it was okay."

"Let me try," I say, unable to stifle another yawn. "It might not work. I set a record when it comes to sleeping today."

She says nothing and takes my hand in her palm again.

I close my eyes to test things out. The warmth of her touch mixes with the effect of the painkiller, and I drift off.

As I sleep, I have a recurring dream.

Someone wakes me up, asking if I'm okay, and afterwards, someone sings me a Russian lullaby.

CHAPTER TWENTY-NINE

"If you try eating something, I'll let you get up," Mira tells me.

I know Mira well enough to recognize an ultimatum when I hear one, so I don't bother arguing.

Besides, she's right. I've been feeling pretty weak since I've woken up, and especially after I tried phasing into the Quiet and failed—again.

My stomach chooses that very moment to growl, and Mira gives me her signature 'I told you so' look.

I examine the hospital food she's brought me, wrinkle my nose, and say, "I'll try these pseudo-mashed potatoes that I suspect are made from powder."

"Good," she says. "The Jell-O is also pretty decent. I had some myself. Even a hospital can't fuck up Jell-O."

As I eat, Mira gives me an update on what happened while I was sleeping. The news sites are already covering what they think happened at the Temple. As she details the elaborate cover-up the Elders—or more likely, some Ambassador—cooked up, I'm glad Bert isn't here. Hearing about a real-life cover-up would only encourage his tendency to make up conspiracy theories.

According to the media, some ex-mercenary turned drug lord started a cult in northern Florida. His followers shaved their heads and wore robes like Buddhist monks, and they trained in martial arts as part of their crazy religion. During an inter-departmental police mission to rescue a missing child, the officers came across the cult and their giant mansion/temple. Things escalated from there, turning into an ugly confrontation.

"It's scary," Mira says once I've finished my food. "If the Elders can make regular people believe such a load of bullshit, it makes you wonder what other world events they twisted."

"You sound like Bert." I push the tray away from my face. "Help me get this crap off me."

"No." Mira glares at me. "Let me get the nurse. Stop trying to be a fucking hero."

The nurse comes over so fast I'm convinced someone Guided the medical staff to be at our beck and call.

The nurse gives me more painkillers, changes the bandages on my head, takes out the IV, and assures Mira I'll be fine without the oxygen. Both women help me get to my feet.

"Crap, my ankle really hurts," I say to the nurse when my foot touches the ground.

"I'll bring you a chair," she says. "This way your girlfriend can—"

"No wheelchair," I say, horrified by the idea. "I'll just walk slowly."

I take a couple of tentative steps. It hurts, but it's bearable—barely. The nurse leaves, and I limp out into the hallway, refusing Mira's assistance.

Kate is standing guard by the door outside. "You're walking." Her smile appears genuine. "That's a very good sign."

"How's John?" I ask.

Her smile falters. "Not as good as you, but he'll pull through. The surgery went without a hitch. Thanks."

"Good." I remember Caleb's fingers digging into John's throat and mentally shudder. Shaking off that image, I tell Kate, "We're going to walk around. Do you know which room my grandfather, Paul, is in?"

Kate nods. "Walk down this hall until you see Eleanor."

Mira and I slowly make our way to the room, and after saying hello to Eleanor, we enter. Turns out that Paul is sharing a room with Edward. Rose and Marsha are here as well. Mira looks at the setup curiously. I already warned her that my grandparents each have significant others, but it must still seem strange to her.

"Darren," Rose says, smiling. "Glad to see you up and about."

"Just wanted to check on Paul," I say. "Rose, Marsha, Edward, Paul, have you met Mira?"

Paul looks me over, his typical 'just ate a lemon' expression warmer than usual.

"Rose told me what you did for me," he says gruffly. "And I'll never forget what that Pusher, Richard, said when he stopped beating me up. Thanks for that."

I recall the little joke message I Guided Richard to deliver to Paul and chuckle. Clearly Paul didn't take offense.

Turning my attention to Edward, I ask, "How are you?"

"I'm just here to keep Paul company," my grandmother's husband says. "I'm not hurt enough to need a hospital."

"Thanks for saving my husband," Marsha says.

"And mine," Rose adds.

I incline my head in acknowledgement of their thanks, and say in a not-so-subtle-warning, "I hope this puts an end to any unfortunate visits from Caleb or the monks."

Paul nods. "Let's forget the past." He sounds as if he's talking about a manufacturing defect his company was responsible for.

"Sure. But first, do you ladies or gentlemen have anything to say to Mira?" I ask, unable to help myself.

Mira gives my arm a painful squeeze.

"We're all sorry about what happened, Mira," Rose says. "Truly, we are." She gives Paul a look.

"You were asleep when we left you in the guestroom," Marsha echoes. "For what it's worth, we thought it was your friends who were shooting everyone, so we didn't think we were leaving you in any danger."

"This whole thing got out of control," Edward adds. "Caleb shouldn't have taken anyone. His orders were to grab Darren as he was leaving the funeral, that's all. Still, even though we didn't order your abduction, Mira, we shouldn't have gone along with it. We should've ordered him to return you to Darren."

Paul doesn't say anything, so I sigh and say, "Okay, I'll go now."

"Darren, wait," Paul says, and I stop. "Come visit us once we've rebuilt the Temple and settled down," he says in a low voice. "Rose and I are your family, and I know she wants you to be part of her life and . . . so do I."

I figure this is as close to an apology as I'm going to get from Paul, so I say, "Sure, Grandpa."

"You too, Mira," Paul adds. "Please come with him."

Mira nods and pulls me out of the room, probably sensing that I'm on the verge of saying something snarky that might ruin the goodwill the Enlightened are trying to create.

We walk silently toward the elevator, with me trying to move without aggravating my ankle and Mira looking thoughtful.

"You *are* going to stay in touch with them, right?" Mira says as we stop in front of the elevator.

"Are you really asking me to be nice to them?" I press the elevator button and turn to look at her. "You, the person they kidnapped?"

"They're your only connection to your dead father." The elevator doors open, and she walks in. "I'm not suggesting you forgive them, or that what they did was right. My point is: what harm could it do to stay in touch with them? See where it leads?"

I give her an amused look. "You know, I sometimes forget you're actually younger than me."

I limp into the elevator and press the button for the first floor.

I expect Mira to say something like, 'In terms of maturity, I'm double your age,' but she just steps up to me, rises on her tiptoes, and kisses me.

I kiss her back. Having her close almost makes me forget about the missing Quiet in my life—a lack that might be everlasting.

We're still kissing when the elevator doors open. Thomas and Liz are standing there, observing us with varying degrees of fascination.

Being caught kissing by my shrink makes me feel surprisingly like a naughty schoolboy. I steal a glance at Mira, who doesn't seem fazed at all. Her manner is so casual, it's as if she was caught wiping dust off her shirt.

Thomas gives me a sly smile, while my shrink studies Mira.

"Liz, you're here, at the hospital?" I ask, realizing the silence lingered too long.

"Liz? What are you talking about? She's not here," Mira teases. "Imagine how ironic it would be if your hallucination took on the shape of your shrink."

Liz smiles and says, "I came as soon as I heard." She protectively loops her arm through Thomas's elbow. "Thanks for rescuing him."

"No problem." I don't know what else to say, so I just exit the elevator, doing my best not to make my ankle worse. I follow the hallway sign to the cafeteria, and the others follow.

"We were actually going up to see you," Thomas says, speeding up to walk beside me. "I just heard from Hillary. She and your mothers are about to arrive."

"Oh." I give Mira a worried look. "How bad do I look?"

"You're walking, you're talking." Mira runs her fingers through her hair and grabs the scrunchy holding it in place. "Sara shouldn't freak out too much." In an elegant gesture, Mira tightens her hair into a much neater ponytail. "What's our story, by the way?"

"About that." I look over at Thomas and Liz. "I was thinking of going for the big-bang approach."

"How big of a bang?" Thomas asks, his eyes gleaming with hope. "The *whole* truth?"

"Yes, like that oath in the court room." I feel a little lightheaded. "Liz, is this a good idea? I mean, is Lucy ready to hear the truth about Kyle?"

As I wait for her to answer, I lean on the sterile white wall to rest for a moment.

"She's as ready as she'll ever be." Liz and everyone else stop walking, waiting for me to recover.

"Can you do your Xanax thing on both of them as I tell them all this stuff, including how I got hurt?" My moment of weakness passes, so I resume walking and my friends follow.

"I think I can do better." Liz looks surprisingly excited. "If Mira would assist me, I think we can do something unprecedented in psychiatry. I can Split, pull her in, and she can monitor Lucy and Sara's thoughts from the Mind Dimension. She'll tell me what needs adjusting, and I'll fine-tune their reactions in real time."

I stop again. "I'm not sure that would work," I say, remembering how I couldn't pull Mira into the Quiet back at the Temple. I look at her. "Aren't you Inert, Mira?"

"No." She shakes her head. "I was, but I've recovered now. I ran out of Depth during the trip, when I woke up from being drugged and tried to figure out where we were, but as of this morning, I have a couple of minutes of my Depth back. It's not a lot, so we might need to use Hillary's Mind Dimension, but I can certainly help Liz."

"Oh, great." I suppress an irrational flare of jealousy as we start walking again. I'd kill for even a couple of minutes of Depth right about now.

"Yeah, it's going to be very interesting," Liz says. "Would make for a great research paper, if only such things were allowed."

"I see. You want to use my moms as Guinea pigs." I nod a silent thanks to Thomas for holding the cafeteria door, and gesture for Mira and Liz to go in ahead of me.

"I think it could be a very effective method of therapy," Liz says, accepting my chivalry with a smile.

"She might be right," Mira says as she follows. "This sounds like a way to minimize their distress while still giving them all the information."

"Wait, Liz," I say when I've caught up. "You don't mind if I tell them about the existence of Guides, right?"

I'm prepared for a negative answer; I've always suspected she was on the conservative side of this issue.

"I don't mind," Liz says without hesitation. "Provided you take full responsibility for them knowing, by which I mean you will Read and Guide them to make sure they don't do something crazy— like go to a newspaper."

"Of course I will, and in any case, they wouldn't," I say, realizing Liz doesn't know that my Inertness might be permanent.

"Then why would I mind?" Liz smiles. "I don't see how else you could explain Thomas's situation without delving into such matters."

"Speaking of that," I say. "Thomas, how about you? Are you ready for this?"

Thomas's voice thickens as he says, "I don't even know what to say . . ."

"He's been dreaming of this, I assure you," Liz says, and Thomas gives her an unreadable look.

Is this why she's being so accommodating? For Thomas's sake?

Instead of voicing any of this, I just say, "Well, good. Hopefully, the shock of the truth will obscure the parts where I was almost killed. Though when it comes to Sara, I'm still worried."

"We'll take care of it." Liz winks at Mira. "Don't you worry."

I can't help but think how amazing it is that Mira and Liz—or Mira and any Guide—are working together. If someone wanted to put the Elders' dream of peace to the test, this would be the way to do it. If they (Mira especially) don't rip each other's hair out, there's hope that our people can come to an understanding.

We select a secluded table in the cafeteria, and Thomas instructs Hilary to find us there. Meanwhile, Liz brings everyone some food. Having worked up an appetite during our walk, I decide to have a doughnut and coffee, which pleases Mira disproportionally.

As we eat our food, Liz explains her proposed Reading/Guiding process to Mira in greater detail while I plan out what I'm going to say to my moms when they get here.

* * *

"Darren, what happened to your face?" My mom Sara's voice is predictably tense and high-pitched. I hope Mira and Liz are on it, as Sara's on the verge of hyperventilating.

Thankfully, Liz and Mira don't disappoint. They look slightly distracted for a second, and then Sara noticeably relaxes—well, relaxes as much as Sara can. She probably now feels the normal amount of anxiety a parent should experience upon seeing her offspring banged up.

In other words, she looks as worried as Lucy.

It seems as though Mira and Liz are successfully working together—so far, at least. I wonder whether they bickered while in the Mind Dimension. Damn it. If I weren't Inert, I could've been there to see for myself.

"I'm okay, Mom," I say to Sara. "Please, sit."

I try to project health and vitality—not an easy feat when you're brimming with as much morphine (or was it oxycodone?) as I am.

"Those stupid bandages probably make me look worse than I actually am." I figure telling them the truth doesn't mean I need to burden Sara with the gory medical details about my ribs, concussion, ankle, et cetera. The truth is, physically, I *am* okay, or will be soon enough.

They sit down, and Lucy asks, "Did someone do this to you, or was it an accident?"

Her voice is calm, but I recognize a dangerous question when I hear one. That is, the answer would be dangerous for whomever I might name as the responsible party. She's in that lioness mode of thinking.

"I fell on the ground and got bruised," I say. Then, much less confidently, I add, "I also got into a little fight, but the person can't bother me anymore, Mom."

I take a nervous sip of my lukewarm coffee and prepare for an avalanche of follow-up questions.

I see Lucy mentally put on her detective hat, but a second later, she looks unnaturally relaxed and doesn't ask me whatever it was she was about to ask. Liz, who's sitting on my left, winks at me, and Mira bumps my knee with hers, signaling that team Mira and Liz scored again.

Hillary is sitting very quietly, which tells me my friends have briefed her in the Quiet and are likely using her prodigious Reach to help with their task. Usually, they would've used me. That thought heightens my feeling of being left out of those secret, outside-of-time conversations. Then again, maybe I should get used to it.

"There's something I've been meaning to tell you guys," I say. I rehearsed this line in my mind a million times over. "It's going to be hard to believe."

I prove how much of an understatement my preamble was by hitting them with factoid number one: the secret existence of Readers and Guides.

Predictably, my suspicious detective mom and her ever-skeptical, scientifically minded partner look unconvinced. So we give them demonstrations that makes the stuff I did for Bert at the airport look like a cheap magic trick. Mira tells them to think of random facts, and then tells them what those facts are. I talk about information I gleaned from them the two times I Read far into their past, such as their trip to Israel, the funeral of the M&Ms (their nickname for my parents), and that time Lucy had drinks in a bar with Kyle and my dad. I mention details that only they would know.

To clinch the deal, we ask Hillary to perform a Guiding demonstration. My aunt makes everyone in the cafeteria, including my moms, dance the Macarena. As my moms watch the others dance, their resolve noticeably waivers. In the end, though, I'm confident that the reason they finally look as if they've accepted this incredulous information is because of Liz and Mira's secret manipulations. Otherwise, this process would've likely taken a few weeks of nonstop demonstrations. My moms are just that skeptical by nature; plus, they long ago adopted the illogical attitude of 'Darren knows stuff he shouldn't because he's *that* smart.'

"Okay." Lucy crosses her arms. "Assuming we believe you, why do I get the feeling that there's a lot more to this than telepathy and hypnosis?"

"Reading and Guiding," I correct her. "And yes, you're right. There is more. It has to do with my parents."

I proceed to tell them how the M&Ms—Mark and Margret—were respectively a Reader and a Guide. I tell them a little bit about the animosity between the two groups, and how things are changing. When I talk about the wars between Readers and Guides, I surprise even my friends when I mention how my Reader great-grandfather killed my Guide great-grandfather. Since it looks as if my moms are taking all this in stride, I move on to trickier information. I tell them how my biological mother used her powers on them, making it so they couldn't speak about me not being Sara's biological son for many years. I include this last tidbit as an extra bonus, since I'm sure they—and Sara especially—harbor guilt over keeping that fact from me for as long as they did. Their eyes widen as I tell them this part of my tale, but at regular intervals, Liz and Mira must do their magic, because Lucy and Sara calm down and accept the information relatively meekly.

"So you can do both? Read minds and make people do things?" Sara asks. "And your time-stopping delusions were actually for real?" She looks at Liz.

"She probably owes you a big refund," I say, thinking of all the therapy to cure me of my 'delusions.' "Anyway, it's probably more accurate to say that I *did* Read and Guide—past tense."

They look surprised, so I do my best to hide my sadness and explain, "The situation has changed. I can't do either at the moment, and there's a chance I'm like you now—well, almost like you, since no one can Read or Guide me in my current state."

Sara looks at me worriedly, as if she actually understands what I've lost. Seeing the pity in her eyes only worsens my ache for the Quiet.

Lucy has been looking troubled throughout all of this. Seems like even Liz's juju hasn't been enough to completely sidetrack Lucy's analytical brain.

"So," she says in that 'about to uncover a secret' voice. "People get amnesia when someone Guides them to do something that's too out of their character, right?"

"Hmm, I think I know where you're going with this, honey," Sara chimes in. "For some reason, I can't recall the last couple of days. Did one of you—"

"I'm sorry," Hillary says. "I made it so the two of you wouldn't worry about your situation, which, given that you were kidnapped and all, probably made you forget certain things in the process."

"We were kidnapped?" Lucy's more shocked by this than by some of my earlier revelations. Or perhaps Liz dropped the ball and didn't stop her from worrying.

Sighing, I proceed to tell them the lengthier tale of how the Enlightened, my biological grandparents, kidnapped the two of them, Mira, and Thomas to use as leverage against me. As I talk, I feel as though either Liz is slipping in her duties or my moms are getting more resistant to her treatment, because the idea of being kidnapped and then forgetting about it seems to be causing them noticeable distress. If I could phase in, I'd have a talk with Liz about it. As is, I just give her a look, and she surreptitiously gives me an okay sign. Whatever distress they're feeling, my guess is she's allowing it on purpose.

Lucy's face darkens as she says, "Are you done beating around the bush?"

"What do you mean, Mom?" I ask with concern, though again, Liz is nodding as if everything is cool.

"There's a big secret. Something very disturbing that I was made to forget." She doesn't ask this; she states it as fact. "That's why I've been going to see her." She points to Liz. "That's why I have this lost time . . . these gaps in my memory."

Sara looks worriedly at Lucy, but then suddenly, her face relaxes. Whatever Liz's strategy is, worrying Sara is not part of it.

"Yes, Mom," I say, deciding to go with it. "There's something so big that I don't know how to tell you."

"Give me the worst of it," Lucy says, staring at me. "And give it to me straight."

"Kyle made you kill my parents," I blurt out, wishing someone would Xanax *me* for this part. "He used you as his weapon. You shot them, and then he made you forget about it. He also tried to have you kill yourself later."

My moms look shellshocked, and that's after whatever Liz did.

As I watch Lucy's face, I see how quickly her shock gives way to quiet contemplation.

"Of course," she whispers to herself. "That's why I couldn't solve the cursed case."

She must feel like medieval people did when they learned the Earth isn't flat.

After murmuring to herself for a few more seconds, she looks at me and says, "As bad as *that* is, I think there's something worse. Something you still haven't told me." She takes in a breath. "Something deeper. Something that also has to do with Kyle." She says his name with trepidation.

Hoping Liz has planted the necessary seeds, I gently say, "There is, and as bad as it is, it might not be *all* bad."

I look at Thomas and feel a treacherous knot in my throat.

"Kyle . . . he—" I swallow. "He forced you to . . . to sleep with him." I try to control my voice to keep it from cracking. "You had a child . . ."

She looks horrified, but there's also a glimmer of recognition in her eyes. Liz prepared her for this, but at the same time, nothing could ever prepare a woman to learn she was raped. Nothing could prepare her to learn she was forced to give up her baby.

I watch her realize how she was wronged, and it pains me to watch the turbulent emotions kaleidoscope across her face. Finally, tears form in her eyes and spill down her cheeks. Covering her face with her hands, Lucy quietly sobs.

Sara hugs her, her own face showing her incomprehension.

"What—what happened to . . ." Lucy's unable to finish her thought as another bout of grief takes hold and wrenches more emotions out of her.

"That's the happy part," I say, tears sliding down my face. "It's Thomas." I gesture at my friend, who's been sitting on her right. Now that I look at him, I see that Thomas's typically emotionless face is tense and twisted with sorrow.

Lucy turns and stares at him intently.

She keeps on looking for what feels like a dozen heartbeats without saying a word. Is she in shock?

Thomas stares back at her, and then suddenly, they hug.

She's sobbing loudly, and he's looking pretty emotional, especially for Thomas.

They speak softly to each other, and I can only hear pieces of what they're saying.

"I knew something was special about you the first time we met," I think I hear her whisper.

"You're exactly how I always imagined you'd be," I hear him say.

I feel as if I'm invading their privacy, listening in like this, so I wipe my face with my sleeve and look away.

Liz, her voice choked-up, says, "Why don't we take a walk and give them a moment?"

Everyone complies in a dazed manner.

"Sara," Liz says when we're far enough away from the mother-son reunion. "Why don't you take a walk with Hillary and me? We can answer any questions you have."

"Thank you," Sara says, her tone zombie-like. I think Liz overdid it with the Xanax therapy.

"Are *you* okay?" Mira asks, wiping the moisture from her cheeks with her index finger.

"I think so," I lie, cognizant that Liz is still here. "I'm glad it's done. I'm glad they know."

"Darren, isn't that Eugene over there with your little friend? And there's a woman with them," Liz says, her voice once again composed.

I look at where she's pointing. I see Eugene running toward us, and I do mean *running*. Bert is accompanying him, and to my huge surprise, Julia— Eugene's ex-girlfriend and the almost-mother of my child—is with him too.

Hands on her hips, Mira stalks toward her excited sibling. I follow as fast as my hurt ankle will allow.

"Zhenya, what the hell?" Mira's voice has that irritated quality it sometimes gets when she's exposed to too many emotions. She points at Julia. "And why bring *her* here?"

Eugene looks from his sister to Julia, then back at his sister. "Julia has nothing to do with my news. I was just showing her the mobile lab, so she was around when I made this discovery."

"Tell him already," Bert says. "Tell him what happened. You know he's probably dying to know."

"Yes, sorry," Eugene says. "Darren, I have good news for you."

"Just tell him." Bert looks as if he's about to start jumping up and down.

"I can Read him now." Eugene jerks his thumb at Bert. "Him and Kiki."

"I tried also," Julia says, "to make sure."

Mira looks thoughtful for a second.

"I just Read Bert also." Narrowing her eyes, she buttons up the top of her shirt and says, "Thank you, Bert. It seems they were indeed showing."

Bert turns beet red, but I ignore him.

Instead, I do my best to process this development.

"You're saying I'll recover my Depth?" I ask, hardly daring to let myself hope. "That I won't be Inert forever?"

"Correct," Eugene says. "My dad's calculations were off. I was always better with math, and I should've triple-checked before worrying you so much." He smiles sheepishly. "It will take twice as long as your regular Inertness, but you will certainly recover."

I don't even say thank you. Tears blur my vision, and I suppress a sniff. This hospital must be atypically dusty, and all this dust is clearly causing my allergies to act up—again. Bert and Eugene look at me as if I sprouted a second head. They don't know how allergic I sometimes get, especially when I'm around my crying moms.

I'm so full of happiness that I get this odd feeling, like if I currently had my powers, I'd jump right into Level 2 from all the emotions running through my system.

I'm overwhelmed with relief—brimming with it. I don't know whether this state is somehow related to the rollercoaster of emotions I just went through with my moms, or if I really feared losing my powers that much, but in this moment, I feel like a disaster survivor.

I grab Mira and give her a deep kiss, like the sailor in the famous *V-J Day in Times Square* photograph.

As I kiss her, I finally feel like everything will be all right.

I feel unstoppable elation.

I feel like myself.

SNEAK PEEKS

Thank you for reading! If you would consider leaving a review, it would be greatly appreciated.

If you'd like to know when the next book comes out, please sign up for my new release email list at www.dimazales.com.

If you like epic fantasy, I also have a series called *The Sorcery Code*. Additionally, if you don't mind erotic material and are in the mood for a sci-fi romance, you can check out *Close Liaisons*, my collaboration with my wife, Anna Zaires.

If you like audiobooks, please check out this series and our other books on Audible.com.

And now, please turn the page for a sneak peek at *The Sorcery Code* and *Close Liaisons*.

EXCERPT FROM *THE SORCERY CODE*

Once a respected member of the Sorcerer Council and now an outcast, Blaise has spent the last year of his life working on a special magical object. The goal is to allow anyone to do magic, not just the sorcerer elite. The outcome of his quest is unlike anything he could've ever imagined—because, instead of an object, he creates Her.

She is Gala, and she is anything but inanimate. Born in the Spell Realm, she is beautiful and highly intelligent—and nobody knows what she's capable of. She will do anything to experience the world . . . even leave the man she is beginning to fall for.

Augusta, a powerful sorceress and Blaise's former fiancée, sees Blaise's deed as the ultimate hubris and Gala as an abomination that must be destroyed. In her quest to save the human race, Augusta will forge new alliances, becoming tangled in a web of intrigue that stretches further than any of them suspect. She may even have to turn to her new lover Barson, a ruthless warrior who might have an agenda of his own . . .

* * *

There was a naked woman on the floor of Blaise's study.

A beautiful naked woman.

Stunned, Blaise stared at the gorgeous creature who just appeared out of thin air. She was looking around with a bewildered expression on her face, apparently as shocked to be there as he was to be seeing her. Her wavy blond hair streamed down her back, partially covering a body that appeared to be perfection itself. Blaise tried not to think about that body and to focus on the situation instead.

A woman. A *She*, not an *It*. Blaise could hardly believe it. Could it be? Could this girl be the object?

She was sitting with her legs folded underneath her, propping herself up with one slim arm. There was something awkward about that pose, as though she didn't know what to do with her own limbs. In general, despite the curves that marked her a fully grown woman, there was a child-like innocence in the way she sat there, completely unselfconscious and totally unaware of her own appeal.

Clearing his throat, Blaise tried to think of what to say. In his wildest dreams, he couldn't have imagined this kind of outcome to the project that had consumed his entire life for the past several months.

Hearing the sound, she turned her head to look at him, and Blaise found himself staring into a pair of unusually clear blue eyes.

She blinked, then cocked her head to the side, studying him with visible curiosity. Blaise wondered what she was seeing. He hadn't seen the light of day in weeks, and he wouldn't be surprised if he looked like a mad sorcerer at this point. There was probably a week's worth of stubble covering his face, and he knew his dark hair was unbrushed and sticking out in every direction. If he'd known he would be facing a beautiful woman today, he would've done a grooming spell in the morning.

"Who am I?" she asked, startling Blaise. Her voice was soft and feminine, as alluring as the rest of her. "What is this place?"

"You don't know?" Blaise was glad he finally managed to string together a semi-coherent sentence. "You don't know who you are or where you are?"

She shook her head. "No."

Blaise swallowed. "I see."

"What am I?" she asked again, staring at him with those incredible eyes.

"Well," Blaise said slowly, "if you're not some cruel prankster or a figment of my imagination, then it's somewhat difficult to explain . . ."

She was watching his mouth as he spoke, and when he stopped, she looked up again, meeting his gaze. "It's strange," she said, "hearing words this way. These are the first real words I've heard."

Blaise felt a chill go down his spine. Getting up from his chair, he began to pace, trying to keep his eyes off her nude body. He had been expecting something to appear. A magical object, a thing. He just hadn't known what form that thing would take. A mirror, perhaps, or a lamp. Maybe even something as unusual as the Life Capture Sphere that sat on his desk like a large round diamond.

But a person? A female person at that?

To be fair, he had been trying to make the object intelligent, to ensure it would have the ability to comprehend human language and convert it into the code. Maybe he shouldn't be so surprised that the intelligence he invoked took on a human shape.

A beautiful, feminine, sensual shape.

Focus, Blaise, focus.

"Why are you walking like that?" She slowly got to her feet, her movements uncertain and strangely clumsy. "Should I be walking too? Is that how people talk to each other?"

Blaise stopped in front of her, doing his best to keep his eyes above her neck. "I'm sorry. I'm not accustomed to naked women in my study."

She ran her hands down her body, as though trying to feel it for the first time. Whatever her intent, Blaise found the gesture extremely erotic.

"Is something wrong with the way I look?" she asked. It was such a typical feminine concern that Blaise had to stifle a smile.

"Quite the opposite," he assured her. "You look unimaginably good." So good, in fact, that he was having trouble concentrating on anything but her delicate curves. She was of medium height, and so perfectly proportioned that she could've been used as a sculptor's template.

"Why do I look this way?" A small frown creased her smooth forehead. "What am I?" That last part seemed to be puzzling her the most.

Blaise took a deep breath, trying to calm his racing pulse. "I think I can try to venture a guess, but before I do, I want to give you some clothing. Please wait here—I'll be right back."

And without waiting for her answer, he hurried out of the room.

* * *

The Sorcery Code is currently available at most retailers. If you'd like to learn more, please visit my website at www.dimazales.com. You can also connect with me on Facebook, Twitter, and Goodreads.

EXCERPT FROM *CLOSE LIAISONS* BY ANNA ZAIRES

Note: *Close Liaisons* is Dima Zales's collaboration with Anna Zaires and is the first book in the internationally bestselling erotic sci-fi romance series, the Krinar Chronicles. It contains explicit sexual content and is not intended for readers under eighteen.

* * *

A dark and edgy romance that will appeal to fans of erotic and turbulent relationships . . .

In the near future, the Krinar rule the Earth. An advanced race from another galaxy, they are still a mystery to us—and we are completely at their mercy.

Shy and innocent, Mia Stalis is a college student in New York City who has led a very normal life. Like most people, she's never had any interactions with the invaders—until one fateful day in the park changes everything. Having caught Korum's eye, she must now contend with a powerful, dangerously seductive Krinar who wants to possess her and will stop at nothing to make her his own.

How far would you go to regain your freedom? How much would you sacrifice to help your people? What choice will you make when you begin to fall for your enemy?

* * *

The air was crisp and clear as Mia walked briskly down a winding path in Central Park. Signs of spring were everywhere, from tiny buds on still-bare trees to the proliferation of nannies out to enjoy the first warm day with their rambunctious charges.

It was strange how much everything had changed in the last few years, and yet how much remained the same. If anyone had asked Mia ten years ago how she thought life might be after an alien invasion, this would have been nowhere near her imaginings. *Independence Day*, *The War of the Worlds*—none of these were even close to the reality of encountering a more advanced civilization. There had been no fight, no resistance of any kind on government level— because *they* had not allowed it. In hindsight, it was clear how silly those movies had been. Nuclear weapons, satellites, fighter jets—these were little more than rocks and sticks to an ancient civilization that could cross the universe faster than the speed of light.

Spotting an empty bench near the lake, Mia gratefully headed for it, her shoulders feeling the strain of the backpack filled with her chunky twelve-year-old laptop and old-fashioned paper books. At twenty-one, she sometimes felt old, out of step with the fast-paced new world of razor-slim tablets and cell phones embedded in wristwatches. The pace of technological progress had not slowed since K-Day; if anything, many of the new gadgets had been influenced by what the Krinar had. Not that the Ks had shared any of their precious technology; as far as they were concerned, their little experiment had to continue uninterrupted.

Unzipping her bag, Mia took out her old Mac. The thing was heavy and slow, but it worked—and as a starving college student, Mia could not afford anything better. Logging on, she opened a blank Word document and prepared to start the torturous process of writing her Sociology paper.

Ten minutes and exactly zero words later, she stopped. Who was she kidding? If she really wanted to write the damn thing, she would've never come to the park. As tempting as it was to pretend that she could enjoy the fresh air and be productive at the same time, those two had never been compatible in her experience. A musty old library was a much better setting for anything requiring that kind of brainpower exertion.

Mentally kicking herself for her own laziness, Mia let out a sigh and started looking around instead. People-watching in New York never failed to amuse her.

The tableau was a familiar one, with the requisite homeless person occupying a nearby bench—thank God it wasn't the closest one to her, since he looked like he might smell very ripe—and two nannies chatting with each other in Spanish as they pushed their Bugaboos at a leisurely pace. A girl jogged on a path a little further ahead, her bright pink Reeboks contrasting nicely with her blue leggings. Mia's gaze followed the jogger as she rounded the corner, envying her athleticism. Her own hectic schedule allowed her little time to exercise, and she doubted she could keep up with the girl for even a mile at this point.

To the right, she could see the Bow Bridge over the lake. A man was leaning on the railing, looking out over the water. His face was turned away from Mia, so she could only see part of his profile. Nevertheless, something about him caught her attention.

She wasn't sure what it was. He was definitely tall and seemed well-built under the expensive-looking trench coat he was wearing, but that was only part of the story. Tall, good-looking men were common in model-infested New York City. No, it was something else. Perhaps it was the way he stood—very still, with no extra movements. His hair was dark and glossy under the bright afternoon sun, just long enough in the front to move slightly in the warm spring breeze.

He also stood alone.

That's it, Mia realized. The normally popular and picturesque bridge was completely deserted, except for the man who was standing on it. Everyone appeared to be giving it a wide berth for some unknown reason. In fact, with the exception of herself and her potentially aromatic homeless neighbor, the entire row of benches in the highly desirable waterfront location was empty.

As though sensing her gaze on him, the object of her attention slowly turned his head and looked directly at Mia. Before her conscious brain could even make the connection, she felt her blood turn to ice, leaving her paralyzed in place and helpless to do anything but stare at the predator who now seemed to be examining her with interest.

* * *

Breathe, Mia, breathe. Somewhere in the back of her mind, a small rational voice kept repeating those words. That same oddly objective part of her noted his symmetric face structure, with golden skin stretched tightly over high cheekbones and a firm jaw. Pictures and videos of Ks that she'd seen had hardly done them justice. Standing no more than thirty feet away, the creature was simply stunning.

As she continued staring at him, still frozen in place, he straightened and began walking toward her. Or rather stalking toward her, she thought stupidly, as his every movement reminded her of a jungle cat sinuously approaching a gazelle. All the while, his eyes never left hers. As he approached, she could make out individual yellow flecks in his light golden eyes and the thick long lashes surrounding them.

She watched in horrified disbelief as he sat down on her bench, less than two feet away from her, and smiled, showing white even teeth. No fangs, she noted with some functioning part of her brain. Not even a hint of them. That used to be another myth about them, like their supposed abhorrence of the sun.

"What's your name?" The creature practically purred the question at her. His voice was low and smooth, completely unaccented. His nostrils flared slightly, as though inhaling her scent.

"Um . . ." Mia swallowed nervously. "M-Mia."

"Mia," he repeated slowly, seemingly savoring her name. "Mia what?"

"Mia Stalis." Oh crap, why did he want to know her name? Why was he here, talking to her? In general, what was he doing in Central Park, so far away from any of the K Centers? *Breathe, Mia, breathe.*

"Relax, Mia Stalis." His smile got wider, exposing a dimple in his left cheek. A dimple? Ks had dimples? "Have you never encountered one of us before?"

"No, I haven't," Mia exhaled sharply, realizing that she was holding her breath. She was proud that her voice didn't sound as shaky as she felt. Should she ask? Did she want to know?

She gathered her courage. "What, um—" Another swallow. "What do you want from me?"

"For now, conversation." He looked like he was about to laugh at her, those gold eyes crinkling slightly at the corners.

Strangely, that pissed her off enough to take the edge off her fear. If there was anything Mia hated, it was being laughed at. With her short, skinny stature and a general lack of social skills that came from an awkward teenage phase involving every girl's nightmare of braces, frizzy hair, and glasses, Mia had more than enough experience being the butt of someone's joke.

She lifted her chin belligerently. "Okay, then, what is *your* name?"

"It's Korum."

"Just Korum?"

"We don't really have last names, not the way you do. My full name is much longer, but you wouldn't be able to pronounce it if I told you."

Okay, that was interesting. She now remembered reading something like that in *The New York Times*. So far, so good. Her legs had nearly stopped shaking, and her breathing was returning to normal. Maybe, just maybe, she would get out of this alive. This conversation business seemed safe enough, although the way he kept staring at her with those unblinking yellowish eyes was unnerving. She decided to keep him talking.

"What are you doing here, Korum?"

"I just told you, making conversation with you, Mia." His voice again held a hint of laughter.

Frustrated, Mia blew out her breath. "I meant, what are you doing here in Central Park? In New York City in general?"

He smiled again, cocking his head slightly to the side. "Maybe I'm hoping to meet a pretty curly-haired girl."

Okay, enough was enough. He was clearly toying with her. Now that she could think a little again, she realized that they were in the middle of Central Park, in full view of about a gazillion spectators. She surreptitiously glanced around to confirm that. Yep, sure enough, although people were obviously steering clear of her bench and its otherworldly occupant, there were a number of brave souls staring their way from further up the path. A couple were even cautiously filming them with their wristwatch cameras. If the K tried anything with her, it would be on YouTube in the blink of an eye, and he had to know it. Of course, he may or may not care about that.

Still, going on the assumption that since she'd never come across any videos of K assaults on college students in the middle of Central Park, she was relatively safe, Mia cautiously reached for her laptop and lifted it to stuff it back into her backpack.

"Let me help you with that, Mia—"

And before she could blink, she felt him take her heavy laptop from her suddenly boneless fingers, gently brushing against her knuckles in the process. A sensation similar to a mild electric shock shot through Mia at his touch, leaving her nerve endings tingling in its wake.

Reaching for her backpack, he carefully put away the laptop in a smooth, sinuous motion. "There you go, all better now."

Oh God, he had touched her. Maybe her theory about the safety of public locations was bogus. She felt her breathing speeding up again, and her heart rate was probably well into the anaerobic zone at this point.

"I have to go now . . . Bye!"

How she managed to squeeze out those words without hyperventilating, she would never know. Grabbing the strap of the backpack he'd just put down, she jumped to her feet, noting somewhere in the back of her mind that her earlier paralysis seemed to be gone.

"Bye, Mia. I will see you later." His softly mocking voice carried in the clear spring air as she took off, nearly running in her haste to get away.

* * *

If you'd like to find out more, please visit Anna's website at www.annazaires.com. *Close Liaisons* is currently available at most retailers.

ABOUT THE AUTHOR

Dima Zales is a *New York Times* and *USA Today* bestselling science fiction and fantasy author. Prior to becoming a writer, he worked in the software development industry in New York as both a programmer and an executive. From high-frequency trading software for big banks to mobile apps for popular magazines, Dima has done it all. In 2013, he left the software industry in order to concentrate on his writing career and moved to Palm Coast, Florida, where he currently resides.

Dima holds a Master's degree in Computer Science from NYU and a dual undergraduate degree in Computer Science / Psychology from Brooklyn College. He also has a number of hobbies and interests, the most unusual of which might be professional-level mentalism. He simulates mind reading on stage and close-up, and has done shows for corporations, wealthy individuals, and friends.

He is also into healthy eating and fitness, so he should live long enough to finish all the book projects he starts. In fact, he very much hopes to catch the technological advancements that might let him live forever (biologically or otherwise). Aside from that, he also enjoys learning about current and future technologies that might enhance our lives, including artificial intelligence, biofeedback, brain-to-computer interfaces, and brain-enhancing implants.

In addition to writing The Sorcery Code series and Mind Dimensions series, Dima has collaborated on a number of romance novels with his wife, Anna Zaires. The Krinar Chronicles, an erotic science fiction series, is an international bestseller and has been recognized by the likes of Marie Claire and Woman's Day. If you like erotic romance with a unique plot, please feel free to check it out. Keep in mind, though, Anna Zaires's books are going to be much more explicit.

Anna Zaires is the love of his life and a huge inspiration in every aspect of his writing. She definitely adds her magic touch to anything Dima creates, and the books would not be the same without her. Dima's fans are strongly encouraged to learn more about Anna and her work at www.annazaires.com.

Lightning Source UK Ltd.
Milton Keynes UK
UKHW02f1820250718

326289UK00021B/682/P

9 781631 420764